BLACK POWDER

Ally Sherrick

2 PALMER STREET, FROME, SOMERSET BA11 1DS

Text © Ally Sherrick 2016
First published in Great Britain in 2016
Chicken House
2 Palmer Street
Frome, Somerset BA11 1DS
United Kingdom
www.chickenhousebooks.com
Ally Sherrick has asserted her right under the Copyright, Designs and
Patents Act 1988 to be identified as the author of this work.

Cover design and interior design by Steve Wells
Illustrations © Alexis Snell
Typeset by Dorchester Typesetting Group Ltd
Printed and bound in Great Britain by CPI Group (UK) Ltd, Croydon CR0 4YY

The paper used in this Chicken House book is made from wood grown in sustainable forests.

1 3 5 7 9 10 8 6 4 2

British Library Cataloguing in Publication data available.

ISBN 978-1-910655-26-9
eISBN 978-1-910655-65-8

A MESSAGE FROM CHICKEN HOUSE

Can one moment change the course of history? That's what this book is all about! Ally Sherrick tells a rollicking tale of conspiracy, treachery and betrayal set at a time when religions were at war. One plucky boy and a brave girl stand up for each other and what is right, against all the odds. Oh, and isn't there something about remember remember the fifth of November, gunpowder, treason and plot?

BARRY CUNNINGHAM
Publisher
Chicken House

*To Stevie who has always had faith
With all my love*

The Year of Our Lord, 1605.
Queen Elizabeth I, daughter of Henry VIII, has
been dead for over two years. A new king, her
cousin James VI of Scotland, sits on the English
throne as James I of England. English Catholics
have suffered years of persecution under the old
Queen. Now in the minority, they are hopeful that
the new King, although also a Protestant, will be
more tolerant. But James and his ministers, led by
spymaster Robert Cecil, reinforce the old harsh
religious laws against them. Most feel there is
little they can do except live quietly and
worship in secret where they can.
But there are some – more desperate and
dangerous – with very different ideas . . .

Chapter One

Friday 25 October 1605

The hangman stood hunched at the top of the wooden scaffold like a hungry black crow. A mob of screaming gulls wheeled above him, but his eyes stayed fixed on the noose as it swayed to and fro in the cold sea breeze.

Tom's heart jolted. He didn't want to watch a man die, but if he ran away now, everyone would know he was a Catholic for sure. He gripped the handle of the pail and steeled himself.

A murmur rippled through the crowd. He craned his neck but his view was blocked by a mass of sweaty bodies.

"Ere. Climb on this, lad.' A pock-faced man next to him seized the pail and turned it upside down. Before Tom could stop him, he'd grabbed him round the middle and heaved him up on to it.

'No, it's all right, really, I . . .' He made to jump down, but the man blocked his way.

'Your first, eh? Well, you'd better get used to it. There's plenty more thieving Catholics around here that deserve a good hanging, and make no mistake.'

'What did he steal?'

'Two of the constable's own pigs. Or so he says . . .' The man gave a sly wink and thumped him on the back.

Tom shuddered. Everyone knew what a bully Constable Skinner was. He bit his lip and forced himself to look out over the swarm of bobbing heads. The mutters around him grew louder and a forest of fingers jabbed the air. He sucked in a breath. A small procession of figures was heading towards the scaffold from the direction of the town gaol. As they neared it, he recognized the sandy hair and red face of Skinner. Trust him to be leading the way.

Stumbling behind him, escorted by two grim-faced men carrying halberds, came the prisoner, head bowed, wrists shackled. Tom's stomach twisted. Was this ragged, tousle-haired wretch really their neighbour, Henry Cresswell? It must be, because there, ten or fifteen paces behind, was Mistress Cresswell, a white kerchief pressed to her face. And, clinging to her skirts, the Cresswells' three children – Nicholas, Peter and little Grace.

As the group reached the scaffold, the crowd fell silent. Even the gulls had flown off.

'Death to the Pope-lover!' the pock-faced man cried. Others roared their support.

Tom tensed. He should get away now, while he still had

the chance. Before anyone recognized him. But try as he might, he couldn't tear his eyes from the scene. Henry Cresswell jerked to a stop at the foot of the ladder and glanced wildly about him. One of the constable's men jabbed him in the back with the point of his halberd. Slowly Cresswell began to climb.

A lump rose in Tom's throat. He swallowed against it, praying it was all a terrible dream. That any moment now, he'd wake up and find himself back at home in his bed. But the cries of 'Papist devil!' and 'Coward!' told him it wasn't.

The hangman stepped forward as the prisoner reached the top rung. He hauled him into position, grabbed the noose and thrust it over his head. He gave the knot a quick check and stood to one side.

Henry Cresswell closed his eyes. He raised his right hand and made the sign of the cross with blood-stained fingers. The sky darkened and a rumble of thunder sounded. A shadow crept across the square, and for a moment Tom saw his own father standing there waiting to die.

A spike of fear shot through him. He leapt down from the pail.

The pock-faced man swiped at him. 'Hey! Come back. You're missing the best bit!'

'Get off me!' Tom tore free and made to run, but a sudden clatter followed by a strangled cry rooted him to the spot. The silence that followed thrummed against his ears. Then a loud cheer went up. People jostled against him, pointing and laughing, but Tom didn't look up at the scaffold. He knew only too well what he would see.

Instead, taking a deep breath, he tucked his head down and shoved his way back through the heaving crowd. He had almost reached the edge of the square when a piercing cry sounded above him. He glanced up. A grey-backed bird arrowed past him. Swooping over the heads of the crowd, it skimmed the top of the scaffold then soared up until it was nothing but a small black speck in the afternoon sky.

He squinted after it. A falcon? He'd never seen one in the centre of town before. A cunning-woman would call it an omen. His parents told him such talk was nonsense. So why was he trembling? He hugged his cloak to him and ran for home.

Chapter Two

Tom stole through the gates and across the courtyard. He was nearly at the back door when footsteps rang out on the cobbles behind him.

'Where have you been?'

His heart sank. Mother!

'Nowhere. I . . .'

'Don't lie to me, Tom Garnett. I sent you to fetch the water nearly two hours ago.' Her blue eyes flashed with anger.

'I did, but . . .'

'So where is it?' She put her hands on her hips and fixed him with a hard stare.

He hung his head. 'I . . . er . . .' He pictured the pail lying on its side in the middle of the market square.

Cries of 'Hang the papists!' and 'Leave him for the crows!' echoed through the gates from the street outside.

He shivered.

Her fingers forced his chin back. 'Tell me you didn't go to that poor man's hanging?'

A twist of guilt curled through him. He tried to look away, but her grip was too tight.

'How could you?'

'I – I didn't mean to, but I had to cross the square to get the water and the crowd was already there and . . .'

She dropped her hand. 'Poor Mister Cresswell. What will his wife do now?' Her eyes filled with tears.

Tom licked his lips. 'A man in the crowd said he'd stolen two of Constable Skinner's pigs.'

His mother frowned. 'There wasn't a thieving bone in Henry Cresswell's body. But the constable hates Catholics. And with the country so whipped up against us, it's easy for him to accuse a man like Mister Cresswell of a crime he didn't commit.' She clutched at the frayed edge of her apron and twisted it between her fingers.

His eyes widened. 'They can't hang you just for *being* Catholic, can they?'

His mother's frown deepened. 'Not yet, no. But there is no doubt it has been harder for us since the new laws were passed by the Parliament in London. You know that your father risks being fined if we refuse to go to the Protestant church. And if they found us celebrating the Mass in secret, it would be prison. As for our priests? If the King's men discover them preaching the faith, then, yes, they will hang.' She shuddered and crossed herself.

'But that's not fair!'

She gave a deep sigh. 'It's how it is. All we can do is bear it and pray that one day the King will look more kindly on us.' She shot him a sharp look. 'But none of this lessens the fact you were there with the rest of them gawping at our poor neighbour's last moments.'

'But I didn't stay long enough to—'

She held up her hand. 'That's enough! I'm disappointed in you, Tom. And your father will be too when he hears.'

He groaned. Facing Mother was bad enough, but Father would be even angrier with him. More than likely he'd cancel the trip round the merchant ship he'd promised him for his thirteenth birthday next Sunday.

'Don't tell him, please. I'll do extra chores. Chop enough wood to last us until Christmas. Fetch a wellful of water. Play with Edward every day . . .'

His mother tilted her head and narrowed her eyes. 'I'll think about it. Now, go to your room. And make sure you remember the Cresswells in your prayers.'

'Yes, Mother.' He slumped his shoulders and trudged towards the door.

When he reached his chamber he flung himself down on the bed and closed his eyes. He'd been looking forward to the trip down to the harbour for ages. If only he'd gone a different way to fetch the water. If only . . .

A rustling sound made him start. Jago! He'd been so quiet, he'd forgotten all about him. He reached under the bed and pulled out a small wooden box. He placed it on the threadbare coverlet and slid back the hole-studded lid.

'Sorry, boy. Were you asleep?'

A pink nose poked through the gap and a pair of red eyes shone up at him. Then, in a flash of white fur, the mouse jumped out of the box. Darting inside Tom's shirtsleeve, he tickled his way up his left arm, across both shoulders and down his right one. It was a trick they'd learnt together, not long after Tom had rescued him from one of the mousetraps in the stable.

He was an odd colour for a mouse, but that was part of what made him special. Mother had got a fright when she discovered him running about Tom's chamber, but it was only a few days after they'd buried William and in the end, she let him keep him.

His brother's pale face flickered up before him. He scrubbed at his eyes with his fists. It was bad enough trying not to think about the hanging, and now William too.

Light paws brushed the side of his leg. He blinked. Jago sat perched on his knee, whiskers twitching, beady eyes gleaming.

'Who's a clever mouse?' Tom ran a fingertip over the shiny patch of fur between his pale pink ears.

Footsteps sounded on the stairs. A few moments later the door swung open and his mother came in carrying a bowl of steaming broth, a hunk of bread and a lighted candle.

'Your father is late.' She chewed her bottom lip. 'He should have been back from the harbour by now.'

She waited for Tom to scoop Jago back into his box, then, handing him the food, she took the candle to the window, pushed it open and stared out into the gathering darkness. Tom's mouth watered at the smell of hot vegetables and herbs. He tore off a piece of bread, dipped it in the broth and wolfed it down. It tasted good.

His mother sighed. 'I pray he has not got himself mixed up in any trouble. It's as bad as it was in the old Queen's day, with spies and soldiers everywhere sniffing for signs of rebellion. And always seeking to make us Catholics the scapegoats.' She touched her right hand to the glass.

Tom wiped his mouth with his sleeve. 'Maybe he met someone off a ship and they got talking?'

'Maybe . . .'

'Are you . . . are you going to tell him?'

'Tell him what?' Her voice was distant, as if she was thinking of other things.

'About earlier? Mister Cresswell and the—'

She spun round. 'No. But if it happens again . . .' Her blue eyes sparked with warning.

'It won't.' Tom clenched his knuckles. He never wanted to go to another hanging as long as he lived.

'Good.'

A thin wail wound up the stairs.

She gave another sigh. 'I must see to your little brother. Now finish your broth, then into bed.' Placing the candle in the holder on the stool by his bed, she looked back through the window one last time then slipped out.

After feeding a few of his leftover crumbs to Jago, Tom slid the lid back over the box. He lay down and waited, listening for the ring of his father's footsteps on the cobbles below. But the warmth from the broth stole through him and it wasn't long before he drifted into sleep.

When he woke, the moon was up and shining through the window, making diamond patterns on the floorboards. Voices rose up from the courtyard. Mother's, soft and worried-sounding, then Father's, low and urgent. Tom's stomach fluttered. So he was back. Clambering out of bed, he tiptoed to the window and peered out.

His mother stood in her nightshift, a woollen shawl wrapped around her shoulders, her plait of blonde hair hanging down her back. The glow from the flickering candle she held lit up the black cloak and broad-brimmed hat of his father. What were they saying? He stuck his head out further and held his breath.

'But why, Richard? You know the risks. The constable already has his eye on us.' She clutched at her husband's arm. 'If he finds him here, it's the gallows for us.'

Tom's knees wobbled. Gallows? What was she talking about?

His father gave a sigh. 'I know, but the journey from France stowed away in a hold full of stinking bilge water has not served him well. And how could I leave a man of God, who has travelled here to preach the true faith, to the mercy of those rats and dogs down at the harbour?'

'Where is he now?'

'Here.' His father turned. 'Step forwards and show yourself. Don't mind my wife's words. She will make you welcome; you can be assured of that.'

A black-hooded figure stumbled out of the shadows. Tom stifled a gasp. As the figure drew closer, the edges of his cloak parted and a flash of gold sparked in the candlelight.

Heart pounding, Tom leant forwards to get a better look. A cross. So the man was a priest. Mother was right. If Constable Skinner and his men came looking and found him here, it would be his parents on the scaffold next. He stifled a groan.

His mother turned and swung the candle up towards him. 'Tom, is that you?'

He pulled back quickly and ducked, but not before he caught a glimpse of the stranger's sunken cheeks and blood-less lips. And his eyes! Jet black and full of fear. The eyes of a man used to looking over his shoulder.

A man on the run.

Chapter Three

Saturday 26 October

Cock-a-doodle-doo! Tom started and blinked himself awake. A cold grey light spilled through the window and across his bed. He shivered and dragged the blanket up under his chin.

Then he remembered the stranger. He jumped out of bed and tiptoed downstairs in the half-light, praying he'd gone. He was about to poke his head round the door of the main room when a clip-clop of hooves sounded outside. He dashed to the front door and yanked it open. His father stood there, dressed in his riding cloak and boots, Old Hector and Sweet Jenny at his side.

'Father! Wait!' Tom jumped down the steps and ran towards him, ignoring the scrape of cold grit on the soles of his feet.

Sweet Jenny snorted. His father steadied her, then glancing quickly over his shoulder, put a finger to his lips and frowned. 'What are you doing out here?' He kept his voice low. 'Go back inside and look to your mother. She will need your help today.'

'But where are you going?'

His father hesitated, then jerked his head at the courtyard gates. 'Getting a friend to safety before our neighbours wake.'

Tom followed his gaze to the dark figure waiting in the shadows. His heart missed a beat. So the priest was still here. 'It's him, isn't it? The man from last night.'

His father grabbed him by the arm and drew him close. 'So you were awake! What did you hear?'

'Ow!' He pulled away.

Hector whinnied and reared up.

'Steady!' His father let Tom's arm drop and reined in the cob. 'Sorry. I didn't mean to hurt you. But you've got to promise me you will never speak of this to anyone.' His grey eyes hardened. 'The King's minister, Robert Cecil, has his spies everywhere. If word were to get out we have been harbouring a—' He checked himself and wiped his hand across his mouth. 'I have said too much. Now go inside and comfort your mother.'

'When will you be back?'

'Before nightfall I hope.'

'Don't go!' Tom flung his arms round him. He pressed his cheek tight against his father's cloak, breathing in the familiar smell of sheep's wool and warm leather.

'I have to.' His father loosened his arms and pushed him away.

'Why?'

'Because the Lord tells us we must help those in need.'

'But it's too dangerous. Look what they did to Mister Cresswell. And he wasn't even hiding a prie—'

'Hush!' His father gripped him by the shoulders. 'Such talk helps none of us. I owe it to my conscience to speed our friend on his way to London and a safe house he knows of there. The sooner I do, the quicker I will be home again.'

Tom bit his lip. How stupid he was! Father didn't want to hear a coward's words at a time like this.

'Let me come with you then!'

His father shook his head. 'No, Tom, I must do this on my own.'

He swallowed and looked away. It was clear Father wasn't going to change his mind. But what if it had been William standing here? It would have been different then, for sure.

'Here.' His father's face softened. He pulled his knife from his belt and handed it to him. 'Something to whittle away the time with while I'm gone. It was going to be a gift for your birthday next Sunday. Still . . . what's a few days?'

Tom's eyes widened. 'Thank you.' He took it and traced a finger over his father's initials etched in the blade's silvered surface.

His father's mouth twisted into something approaching a smile. 'When I get back we'll go down to the harbour and I'll get you a passage round that ship like I promised.'

A lump grew in Tom's throat. He didn't care about the merchant ship. He just wanted Father back with them again. He looked up, blinking back the tears.

His father ruffled his hair. 'Farewell, son. And remember, while I'm gone you are the man of the house. I'm leaving your mother and brother in your care.'

Tom's chest filled with a sudden flush of pride. He stared down at the knife, then back up at his father. 'I won't let you down, Father. I promise.'

Sweet Jenny snorted again, and for a moment they were enveloped in a cloud of her warm, grassy breath.

'Good!' His father beckoned to the priest. 'Come, Father Oliver. We must go.'

The man shuffled forward, his cloak wrapped tightly around him. Tom's father handed him Sweet Jenny's reins. The priest gave a dry, rattling cough as he mounted her.

Sliding his left foot through Old Hector's stirrup, Tom's father hauled himself on to the cob's twitching back. He clicked his tongue against his teeth then dug his heels into the horse's flanks. The priest did the same with Sweet Jenny and the two animals lurched forwards.

Tom ran after them. As they turned on to the London road, he opened his mouth to call goodbye, then clamped it quickly shut again. Fool! What was he thinking of? He glanced at the windows of the houses opposite. If any of the neighbours woke now . . .

When he looked back at the road, the horses had already picked up speed. A few moments later, riders and mounts disappeared, swallowed up by the early morning mist.

Tom closed his eyes and gripped the knife handle tight in his palm.

Please, Lord, let them go safely and let Father be back before nightfall like he said.

Chapter Four

Tom was nearly done with chopping wood in the yard when a commotion started up in the street outside. He darted through the gates to the front of the house, hatchet in hand. His mother stood at the door, Edward straddled over her left hip. Four men crowded in on them from the steps below. He wasn't close enough to hear their questions, but from the look of fear which flashed across his mother's face, he knew they'd come to make trouble.

'Mother?' He elbowed his way between them and ran up the steps to join her.

She bit her lip, then thrust Edward at him. 'Take your brother, Tom, and go inside.'

'Not so fast!'

Tom froze. Constable Skinner! He turned round. Sure enough, there was the constable, hands on his hips, legs apart, his fleshy lips twisted into a sneer. A spark of panic shot through Tom. Had Father and the priest been captured? He searched his mother's face for a sign. A pink flush stained her neck, but her eyes were a steely blue.

'I said, take your brother!' The sharpness in her voice surprised him.

Reluctantly he dropped the hatchet and reached for Edward. But as his fingers closed round his chubby body, one of the constable's gang, a scrawny man with weasel eyes and scabby hands, darted forwards and ripped the baby from him.

'No!' Tom's mother gave a strangled cry.

'Leave him alone!' Tom made a swipe, but Weasel Face was quicker. He swung Edward out of his reach and dangled him by the neck of his gown.

The baby screwed up his face and screamed.

'What a tasty morsel. How about we take him back to our lodgings, stick him on a spit and roast him for our dinner?' Weasel Face slid his tongue over a row of needle-sharp teeth. The other men laughed.

Edward's howls grew louder.

'Please, no!' His mother stumbled down the steps with Tom close on her heels, but Constable Skinner stepped out and blocked their way.

'Why must you papists always make such a spectacle of yourselves?' He jerked his head at the group of men and women who had gathered on the opposite side of the street.

Tom waved at them frantically. 'Help us!'

A few shook their heads and pulled back into their houses. The rest just stood there. Anger spurted up inside him. These people were their neighbours. Why didn't they do something?

Constable Skinner snorted. 'Seems you're not very popular in these parts. Take her inside for questioning.' He signalled to Weasel Face, then grabbed Tom by the collar and shoved him back up the steps.

He squirmed against Skinner's grip. 'If you dare hurt them . . .'

Skinner leered at him. 'You'll do what? Now stop wasting my time. I've got two papist curs to catch, and you and your precious mother are going to help me, like it or not.'

So Father and the priest were still free. Tom closed his eyes. *Thank you, God.*

'Save your prayers, Pope-worshipper,' Skinner snarled. 'You'll need them later. Now inside, before I lose my temper.' He bundled Tom through the door, and called back over his shoulder, 'One of you take the runt upstairs. I can't think straight with all that bleating.' He marched Tom down the passageway and into the kitchen.

Weasel Face joined them a few moments later, dragging Tom's mother by the wrists. He kicked the door shut and pushed her down in the chair by the hearth.

'Tie her up, man. Good. Now, reveal where your husband is, sweet mistress, and I might let you go free.'

She glared up at Skinner and pursed her lips.

'We've got a stubborn one here. Time she was taught a lesson.' Skinner nodded at Weasel Face, who raised his right fist.

She winced and twisted her head away.

'No!' Tom broke free and dashed towards Weasel Face. He was almost upon him when a foot clipped his heels. He sprawled to the floor. Skinner dragged him to his feet and forced his right arm up behind his back.

'Reckon yourself a hero, do you? Well, there are easier ways to save your mother's pretty face. It's simple. All you have to do is tell us where your father and that Jesuit dog have gone.'

'No, Tom, don't!' His mother's chair scraped the flag-stones as she strained against the ropes that bound her.

'Silence!' Skinner pulled a greasy kerchief from his jerkin, yanked back her head and rammed the cloth into her mouth. She gagged against it trying to spit it out, but it was in too far.

Weasel Face's scabby fist quivered inches from her right cheek. A dribble of cold sweat trickled down the side of Tom's face. What should he do? If he told them Father and the priest were bound for London, they'd hunt them down and catch them for certain. But if he kept quiet, they'd beat Mother, maybe even kill her.

What would William have done in his place? He clenched his jaw. It didn't matter. William was dead. He was the man of the family now. He scrunched his eyes shut. *Think, Tom Garnett. Think!*

Skinner shook him. 'Praying again? Well, God won't help you now. So, what's it to be?'

Weasel Face snatched back his fist and took aim.

'Don't hurt her. Please!' Tom made to leap forwards but Skinner hauled him back. He shot his mother a desperate look. 'Father said the man needed help. He was hungry and . . .'

The constable narrowed his eyes. 'So, the hellhound *was* under your roof. Where did they go?' He swung him round and pressed a stubble-covered cheek against his own smooth one. Tom gagged as a wave of ale-soured breath enveloped him.

A muffled cry sounded behind them. He jerked round. His mother shook her head and rolled her eyes.

Skinner dug his fingers into his shoulder. 'Speak, or it will go the worse for her.'

Tom's ears filled with a rushing sound. It was no use. He'd have to tell him. What else could he do? He blinked. Once. Twice, then sucked in a breath.

'They . . . they took the London road at dawn.'

His mother groaned and closed her eyes.

Constable Skinner's lips twisted into a cold smile. 'So, one of the vipers turns on its own. Thank you, Master Garnett. You've been most helpful. I will raise a mug of ale to you when we have them both safely under lock and key and I have collected my reward from Robert Cecil's men.' He turned to Weasel Face. 'Fetch the runt. Give him to his brother and release them.'

Weasel Face nodded, yanked open the door and disappeared.

'Wh-what about my mother?'

'I'm afraid my men will be settling her in some new, less comfortable lodgings in the town gaol.' Skinner gave a brown-toothed grin, then turned and planted himself in front of Tom's mother. 'You are under arrest, mistress, on suspicion of harbouring a priest. And if we find your worm of a husband and not the priest, I am sure a cold knife at your lovely white throat will persuade him to talk.'

She threw back her head and rocked from side to side.

'Let her go, please!' Tom tugged at Skinner's sleeve.

He pushed him off. 'Quiet, or I will throw you and your brother in gaol too and feed you to the rats. We've got some monstrous big ones.' He bared his teeth. 'And they are always hungry.'

Heavy footsteps echoed down the passageway outside and with them the sound of a baby's cries.

Tom's mother jerked her head up. The door banged open and Weasel Face hurried inside, a bundle in his arms. A pair of pink fists pushed up from it and beat against his chest.

Weasel Face shoved the bundle at Tom. Edward wriggled and squirmed, his face scrunched and angry-looking.

'As I'm a reasonable man, I'll give you a few moments to say your farewells.' Skinner gave another mean grin then turned to Weasel Face. 'Once they're done with their weeping and wailing, send him and his brother packing and take the woman to the gaol.' He turned on his heels.

'Where are you going?' Weasel Face called after him.

'To the stables to get the horses. You heard what the boy said.' The constable threw Tom a look of glittering menace. 'There's a pair of wily Catholic foxes on the road. We must go after them in the King's name and hunt them down.' He threw open the door and strode out into the passageway.

'No! Please!' Tom made to dash after him.

Weasel Face blocked him. 'Get back! And don't think of trying anything, or my friend here'll teach you a lesson you won't forget.' He fingered the knife at his belt then slid out after his master, slamming the door behind him.

Tom stared down into Edward's tear-stained face. *What have I done, little Ned? What have I done?*

Chapter Five

A strangled groan jolted Tom to his senses.

'Mother!' He set Edward down on the floor and rushed over to her. Pulling the cloth from her mouth, he fumbled at the rope round her middle.

'Don't worry about that.' She gave a hoarse cough. 'Edward, is he all right?'

He picked him up again and checked him over. 'Yes, just hungry, I think.' He held him out to her.

'Thank God.' She pressed her dry lips to the baby's rosy pink cheek and closed her eyes.

Tom swallowed against the knot in his throat. How long would Father stay safe now he'd betrayed him? He lay his brother down again and sank to his knees in front of her. 'I – I – I didn't want to tell them, but that man. He was going to hit you and . . .' The words dried into shuddering sobs. He hung his head.

'Shhhh, son. It wasn't your fault.'

'But it was. Father told me to look after you and Ned while he was gone. And I tried, but—'

'I know, Tom. But, you are just a boy and they' – she licked her lips – 'they are devils.'

A boy! He jumped up, cheeks burning. But she was right, wasn't she? Only a puny milksop would betray his own father and give in to Skinner like that. His eyes stung. He turned away so she wouldn't see his tears.

'Listen to me. There's still a chance your father will get the priest to safety before those brutes catch up with them.'

'But what if he doesn't? And if they do escape, how can Father ever come home again?' He hugged his arms to his chest and stared at his boots. If only Father had never met the priest in the first place . . .

'Tom.' His mother's voice sounded urgent. 'You want to help your father, don't you?'

He shot his head up. 'Yes, but . . .'

'Then you must listen to me very carefully.'

His heart leapt. Did she really know a way?

'My prayer book. It's inside a small pouch fixed to the underside of my apron. Get it for me please.'

He sighed. So that's what she meant. Well, praying wasn't going to help Father now.

'Quickly!' Her eyes darted to the door. 'That rat of a henchman will be back soon.'

He bent down and flipped up the edge of her apron. A small sleeve of cloth was sewn into it about halfway up. He reached inside and fished out a leather-covered book. He cleared his throat. 'Which page do you want me to read from?'

A sad smile flickered across her lips. 'It's not for that.'

He frowned. 'What then?'

'It's the key to the help we need.'

'What do you mean?' He shook his head. She wasn't making any sense.

'Open it to the first page.'

He did as she told him. Beneath the printed title someone had written a short neat inscription in black ink: *To my dearest sister, Anne, as a token of love on her birthday – Anthony M., Cowdray House, December 1588.*

His frown deepened.

She cleared her throat. 'It was a gift. Your uncle gave it to me on my sixteenth birthday. The day before I left my family home for good. It's him I want you to go to now.'

His eyes widened in amazement. 'I've got an uncle? You never told me! Who is he? What's he like?'

His mother's cheeks flushed pink. 'I know and I'm sorry. When I left Cowdray, I severed all ties with my family. I thought it best to put that part of my life behind me.'

Tom looked down at the inscription again. 'But why? I don't understand.'

She furrowed her brow. 'It's complicated. Now is not the time for explanations.'

'But if you haven't seen him for all these years, how do you know he'll want to help us?'

'I don't. But' – her eyes took on a faraway look – 'I was always his favourite sister. He used to call me his own dear

Nan. I pray God that in spite of the trouble that has passed between us, he will take pity on us now.'

'But even if he agrees, what can he do? Father's broken the law. If they catch him with the priest, they'll hang him for sure.' Tom chewed on his lip, trying desperately to stifle more tears.

His mother sat up straight and jutted out her chin. 'Listen to me, Tom.' Her eyes shone back at him. 'My brother Montague is a rich and powerful man. In spite of the fact he is a Catholic, the King still counts him a friend.'

Tom gasped. 'The King?'

She nodded. 'Your uncle is a nobleman. He moves in the highest circles. If anyone can save your father, he can.'

'But—'

Footsteps echoed down the passageway outside. His mother looked quickly over her shoulder. 'We're running out of time.'

Tom bit his lip. There was so much he wanted to ask her. But she was relying on him. He couldn't let her down. 'What do you want me to do?'

'Go to the Fosters. Jem Foster knows where Cowdray lies and his wife will look after Edward. They are good people and I'm sure when they hear what has befallen us, they will help. You know their house, down near the harbour?'

He nodded.

'Good. Now, quickly.' She jerked her head at the prayer book. 'Hide the book. Only bring it out again when you reach Cowdray and have found your uncle. If he doubts your story, it will help prove to him that what you say is true.'

He slammed it shut and stuffed it inside his jerkin. A few moments later, Weasel Face burst into the room.

'You've had yer chance for sweet farewells.' He grabbed Tom by the arm and pulled him towards the door.

'Wait!' He yanked free and ran over to where Edward lay whimpering in his blanket on the floor. He gathered him up and glanced at his mother. 'What if they hurt you?'

'They won't. Not now that you've told them what they wanted to know . . .' A look of anguish flashed across her face.

Tom hung his head. She didn't need to say any more. In betraying Father, he had betrayed her too.

'I'm sorry.' His mother's voice was gentle. 'Do not blame yourself, Tom.' She fixed him with a burning blue gaze. 'And remember, never give up hope. The path before you will be filled with many tests. But you are your father's son. Put courage in your heart and, with the good Lord's help, you will overcome them.' Her eyes glittered with tears. 'Now' – she nodded at Edward – 'take your brother and go.'

Chapter Six

When Tom reached the Fosters' house and told them his story, they were shocked. Jem offered to take him to Cowdray the next day, but he couldn't afford to wait. Father was in danger *now*. There was only one thing to do: he would have to make the journey on his own.

While Jem went to fetch some ale and Mistress Foster fussed over Edward, he took his chance. Slipping out quickly through the back yard, he set off for home.

As he turned into their street, he stopped in his tracks. He'd only been gone an hour, two at most, and already someone had scrawled a grinning death's head and the words 'papist traiturs' in chalk across their front door.

A shadow in the window of the house next door caught his eye. A face pressed against the glass grinned at him then melted into the darkness behind. His chest tightened. He pushed the door open, crept inside and darted upstairs to his bedchamber.

He checked Jago was safe in his box and bundled him into a blanket together with a change of clothes. Then, snatching up his waist-pouch, he shoved Father's knife and the old silver tinderbox Mother had given him inside it and dashed downstairs. On his way out through the kitchen, he stuffed some cheese and bread into an old flour sack.

He had an idea of where Cowdray lay from what Jem had told him: he'd said it was a day's journey by horse and cart. But on foot, if he kept moving, there was a chance he might make it by sundown.

He took one last look behind him, then darted across the courtyard, slid through the gates and set out on the London road.

As he passed the church, his mother's last words to him echoed in his head. 'Put courage in your heart.' A knot formed in his throat. Courage! He hadn't shown much of that when Constable Skinner had come calling. And, now, because of him, Father was running for his life.

But he couldn't think about that now. Not if he was going to stand any chance of helping him. He took a deep breath and marched on.

The road was harder going than he'd thought, full of puddle-filled ruts and holes. And he soon found out he wasn't welcome in the villages he passed through either. There were cries of 'Beggar!' and 'Thief!' and in one tumbledown place, the local children chased after him flinging handfuls of mud and dung.

A ragged man stinking of ale stopped him outside a

tavern and made a grab for his sack. It was only because the man was drunk that Tom managed to get away. After that, he did his best to avoid meeting anyone else on the road, hiding in bushes until they'd gone by.

As he trudged on, the daylight faded and the shadows lengthened. Besides the ache in his legs and shoulders, his boots were pinching, and he knew without looking he'd sprouted a giant blister on the sole of his right foot. His stomach was growling too. It was no use; he was going to have to stop. He stumbled across to an old oak tree and slumped down next to it, resting his back against its mossy trunk.

Rummaging inside his bundle, he pulled out Jago's box and slid the lid a quarter open. A whiskery nose nudged at his fingers. 'You must be hungry too, boy.' He reached inside the sack for the bread and cheese. 'Here we go.' He broke a small piece of cheese off and dropped it into the box then sank his teeth into what was left.

Jago gave an excited squeak.

'You can have a run around when we get there, I promise.' Tom pushed the mouse back inside, closed the lid and stuffed the box into the bundle. At least he could let Jago out. But what about Mother: all alone in some dark, stinking gaol cell with only the rats and Weasel Face for company?

He shuddered, then remembered the prayer book. He pulled it from his jerkin and pressed the soft cover to his cheek. It smelt of old leather and lavender. *Please Lord, protect her and keep her safe, please.*

He flipped the book open and peered at the inscription inside. What kind of man was this new uncle of his? Mother had said the Montagues were rich and powerful and Jem Foster had called them grand. As he went to close it, a piece of paper fluttered to his feet. He picked it up. There was a date scrawled on it. Beneath it someone had marked a cross. He stared at the writing. *The twenty-first day of June 1604.* The day William had died.

He squeezed his eyes tight shut. But it was no use. Try as he might, this time he couldn't block the pictures that bubbled up in his head. The sweat on his brother's pale forehead. The red flush of his cheeks. His shivers and groans as the sickness took hold. The pus-filled black buboes which meant only one thing. Plague. And then the dark, panic-filled time after, when they were locked up inside the house to prevent it from spreading. Finally, the cries of pain and tears of grief as William breathed his last, rattling breath.

He shivered and flicked his eyes open. Everything had changed after that. No more games of leapfrog and stopping the sinking of old King Henry's flagship, the *Mary Rose*. No more beachcombing on the shore for Spanish treasure and playing at being fish in the shallows. And no more William to stick up for him in fights with the other boys in their street.

Mother and Father had changed too. Mother had become nervous and sad, wanting him to stay at home and help her with the chores. As for Father, he'd barely been able to look at him in those first few weeks after William had died. Even now, a year and more later, he was always so stern-faced, as if judging him and finding a lack.

Tom sighed and slid the prayer book back inside his jerkin. Time to go. Taking a last mouthful of bread and cheese, he picked up his bundle and scrambled down on to the road.

Slowly the sun sank below the horizon. The hoot of an owl sounded from a nearby copse of trees. Night was drawing in. It couldn't be much further, could it? He shivered and plodded on, willing himself forwards step by painful step. Just when he thought he couldn't go any further and would have to bed down in a pile of leaves, a string of distant lights came into view, winking out across the fields.

Midhurst: the town closest to Cowdray. It must be! His stomach fluttered. Now all he had to do was find his uncle's house. Then with his and God's help, he would make everything right again.

Chapter Seven

The blister stung more with every step Tom took. He gritted his teeth and hobbled on, past a row of half-timbered cottages, some in darkness, others with windows lit by flickering candles. Further on, he came to a crossroads. He stopped and looked about him. Which way now?

'Lost, are you?'

He spun round.

A figure pulled away from the porch of a building opposite. ''Tis not a night for a boy to be travelling alone.' The man's voice was flat and iron-edged: not like the soft country burr of the locals.

The sound of music and merrymaking wound through the air from the half-open door behind him.

'Where are you bound?' The man towered above him, blotting out the night sky.

Hugging his bundle, Tom took a step back and peered

up at him. The man wore a thick, curling beard. That much he could see. But the rest of his face was in shadow, hidden by his hat and the upturned collar of his cloak.

'What's wrong, boy? Lost your tongue?'

He licked his lips. 'To – to Cowdray, sir, to see my uncle.'

'Your uncle, eh? And who is he?' The man lifted a slim white pipe to his mouth. He sucked on it and blew a puff of grey smoke into the air. A glint of gold shone back from the little finger of his left hand.

The sweet smell of tobacco pricked Tom's nose. He clenched his jaw tight shut. He'd had his fill of roadside encounters.

'Rather keep your counsel, would you? A sound position when there are so many spies and ne'er-do-wells about.' The man gave a low chuckle, swirled his cloak about him and turned back towards the tavern door.

'Wait!' Tom stumbled after him. 'Do you know the way?'

'Hmmm.' The man raised his hand to his chin and raked his fingers through his beard. 'Some might regard me as a stranger in these parts, but as a matter of fact, yes I do.' He pulled on the pipe again and blew a smoke ring at him. 'What's it worth?'

Tom stifled a cough and gripped his bundle tighter still. 'I – I don't have any money.'

The man's eyes flashed black in the glow of embers from his pipe. He looked him up and down and laughed. 'If we meet again, you can repay me then. Your thanks will do for now. Cowdray lies up yonder.' He pointed up the street with the stem of his pipe. 'There's a causeway at the edge of town. Follow it across the water meadows. You shall come on the house, by and by.'

'Thank you, sir.' Tom nodded and limped on up the road. When he glanced back, the man had vanished.

He had been so outlandish, and had disappeared so quickly, that he wondered if he'd imagined him. He shook his head. He was so tired he couldn't be sure. But the man's directions proved real enough. Just beyond the last cottage, he spotted the start of a gravel track. He followed it up on to a causeway, lined on each side by a row of tall, leafless trees.

The meadows beyond were dotted with shimmering pools. A scattering of early stars reflected in them like strange, ghostly jewels. The dank air clutched at his face and neck, sending a cold shiver down his spine. He swallowed. *Courage. I must have courage.*

A muffled squeak came from his bundle. His heart lifted. He opened it, pulled out the box and pushed back the lid. Jago peeked out, beady eyes shining and sniffed the air. Tom stroked his head. 'Not far to go now, boy.'

They came to a small stone bridge which carried the track across a river of rushing black water. Beyond it, a building loomed above them, floating like a great grey ship on a sea of grass.

Tom jerked to a stop and stared open-mouthed at its soaring walls, the rows of gleaming black windows and the clumps of twisted chimneys dotted across its roof. Was he seeing things again? He blinked and shook his head, but the walls of the house stayed where they were. Mother had said his uncle was rich, but Tom had never dreamt anyone could be as rich as this. And she had lived here too, once. He frowned. Why would she ever have wanted to leave?

'Best keep out of sight for the time being, boy.' He stroked Jago's head again, then shut him back in the box and pushed it inside his bundle.

He gazed up at the turreted gatehouse in front of him. Time to meet this mysterious uncle of his. As he started towards the pair of heavy-looking entrance gates, a light flashed from the top of the right-hand turret. He dashed over to the nearest bush and crouched down behind it. As he peered up through the tangle of twigs and branches, a small figure dressed in a cape and carrying a lantern appeared on the battlements.

A sudden gust of wind tugged the figure's hood back revealing a pale oval face and a head of blonde ringlets. He drew in a breath. A girl. What was she doing up there?

The girl raised the lantern above her head and swung it to and fro, shining the light up and down the causeway. After a few moments, her shoulders slumped. She pulled the hood over her head, lowered the lantern and disappeared back into the darkness.

He frowned. A servant? No, she couldn't be. Not with curls and ribbons like that. He shrugged and got to his feet. He'd find out who she was soon enough.

As he neared the gates, there was a rattle of metal and a creak of wood. A small door in the left-hand gate opened and the figure of a man slid out. Tom's heart lurched. What if the girl had seen him hiding there and raised the alarm? He backed away, getting ready to run. But something about the way the man moved, keeping his head low and his body stooped, made him hesitate. It looked like he didn't want to be spotted either.

The man skirted round the side of the gatehouse and along the wall of the house. Then, with a quick glance over his shoulder, he darted towards a nearby tree. As he reached it, a figure stepped out from the shadows to meet him and the pair disappeared from view.

Tom shot a look back at the door. The man had left it ajar. He should get inside, while he had the chance. But it was strange, two men meeting in secret like this right outside his uncle's walls. What were they up to? He rubbed a hand across his forehead. There was only one way to find out. Ducking down, he crept as close as he could to the tree and held his breath.

'What news?' A man's voice muffled, as if by a cloth. Impatient-sounding too.

'The Viscount is still away in London, but there have been sightings of two strangers in town.' The second voice scraped through the air like the point of a knife being dragged across glass.

'Any names?' The first man spoke again.

'No. And they kept their faces hidden so my informant could not give me a description.'

The first man made a clicking sound with his tongue. 'A pity. Have you found any evidence inside?'

'Not yet. But I will keep on searching. I am expecting the

usual crowd at My Lady's not-so-secret Mass tomorrow. And I will be on the lookout for any new faces, of that you can be assured.' The man hissed the last word like a snake.

'Well, keep alert. I will make mention of the strangers in my next report to the Master. It might be nothing, but our friends in London have been getting more active of late – and this place isn't known as Little Rome for nothing.'

'So, I stay at my post?'

'Of course.' The first man sounded vexed. 'Make no mistake about these papists. They are as slippery as eels. They will wriggle free unless we weave our basket tight enough to hold them. The Master has always been clear on that point.'

'Yes, sir.' There was disappointment in the other man's voice.

'Meanwhile, I will visit the local taverns and see what I can find out about the strangers. There's always some slack-jawed fool ready to blabber for a groat or two.'

A figure emerged from beneath the tree and headed towards where Tom was crouched. Heart racing, he flung himself down behind a clump of marsh grass. What would he say if the man discovered him? The crunch of boots grew louder. He pressed himself into the mud. The man paused a few feet from where he was hiding, then marched on past. Tom heaved a sigh. That was close. He waited until his footsteps had faded into the distance, then lifted his head and peered back through the grass stalks at the house. He was just in time to see a second dark shape slip in through the gatehouse door.

He frowned. The men were spies. That much was clear.

But what were they doing here at Cowdray? And who were they spying for? The local constable? No, that couldn't be it. The stranger had talked about London and called the man in charge the Master.

He waited a few moments longer then jumped up. A cold breeze blew across the meadows. He shivered and stared down at his jerkin. It was covered in a layer of stinking black marsh mud. The prayer book! If he'd got it wet . . . He rammed his fingers between the buttons, felt for it, then heaved a sigh of relief. Still dry. Without it, looking like this, he'd have a job convincing the Montagues he was anything other than a beggar-boy.

'Come on, Jago. Let's go and meet my uncle.' He shouldered his bundle, took a deep breath and set off for the gatehouse door.

Chapter Eight

The door was shut when Tom reached it. He twisted the metal ring handle but it wouldn't shift. The man must have drawn the bolt on the other side. He thumped on the wood with his fist and waited. Nothing. He tried again. Still nothing.

'Hey! Is anyone there?' He rattled the ring. From somewhere inside came the thud of heavy boots. The footsteps got closer then stopped.

'Who goes there?' It was a man's voice, gruff and unfriendly.

Tom let the ring drop. He swallowed hard then drew back his shoulders and stood tall. 'A visitor. For Lord Montague.'

'We aren't expecting any visitors.' The man sounded suspicious.

'It's urgent. I have news from his sister.'

'Sister?' A bolt rattled. The door opened a crack and a pair of eyes glinted back at him. The door opened wider. A man stepped out, flaming torch in one hand, spiked halberd in the other. 'Lord Montague is not at home. Who are you, boy?' He thrust the torch under Tom's chin.

'Watch out!' He dodged the lick of the sooty flame. Best to try and stay on the guard's right side. He took a deep breath. 'Please, sir. I'm Lord Montague's . . . I'm his nephew, Tom Garnett.'

'Tom Garnett? Never heard of him! Now be on your way, rascal, unless you want to get better acquainted with my weapon.' The man jerked up his halberd and pressed the cold blade against the side of Tom's throat.

His knees buckled. He glanced back at the causeway. If he made a run for it now . . . But no. He curled his fingers into fists. He wasn't going to let the man beat him. Not when he'd come this far.

'Wait, please. I've got something to show you.' He shoved his hand inside his muddy jerkin and pulled out the prayer book.

The man's eyes narrowed. 'And what would I be wanting with a battered old book?'

'It's my mother's. She's Lord Montague's sister. He gave it to her, before she left. Here, look. He signed his name inside.' He flipped to the page with the inscription and held it out.

The man lowered his halberd and peered at the writing on the page. 'Hmmm. Very pretty, but seeing as I can't read . . .' He raised the weapon again.

'But you've got to believe me. It's the truth. Look, here's his signature.' Tom jabbed at the page.

'Sergeant Talbot, what is going on?' It was a girl's voice, clear and strong. The sort of voice whose owner got what she asked for.

The guard looked over his shoulder. 'Why, young Mistress Cressida, whatever are you doing out at this hour? I hope you haven't been up that tower again. You know My Lady doesn't approve.'

Tom followed his gaze. A figure in a deep blue velvet cape and hood stood in the doorway behind them, a lantern clutched tightly in her milk-white hand.

The girl from the battlements. So he'd been right. She wasn't a servant.

'You are not my keeper, Sergeant Talbot. I am free to climb the tower if I choose.' The girl raised the lantern and ran the light over Tom's face. 'Who is this?'

'I'm afraid 'tis a ruffian come here with mischief on his mind.' The sergeant shoved his halberd against the door and grabbed Tom by the arm. 'He claims he is His Lordship's nephew, sent here by his mother.'

Tom tried to wriggle free but the sergeant's grip was too strong.

'Nephew?' The girl threw back her hood and shook her curls free.

Tom raised his eyebrows, surprised. From her tone she'd sounded older. But seeing her face in the lantern-light, she looked more his age.

'He claims this is the proof.' Sergeant Talbot jerked his

head at the prayer book.

The girl frowned. 'Give it to me.' She stepped through the door, put the lantern down and held out her hand.

Reluctantly Tom handed her the book. She scanned the inscription, then looked up, eyes gleaming gold in the torchlight. 'How did you come by this?'

'Like I said, it's my mother's.' He made to snatch it back.

The sergeant yanked him close. 'You cheeky snipper-snapper. Stand clear, mistress. It's time I sent this young cur packing.' His grip tightened.

The girl's frown deepened. 'Hmmm. It *is* the lord my father's writing.' She put her head on one side and fixed Tom with a hard stare.

His cheeks burned. He looked away.

'Let him pass. I will take him to Great-Grandmother. We will see what she has to say.' Before he could stop her, the girl slid the prayer book inside her cape.

The sergeant shook his head. 'I'm not sure that's a good idea, Mistress Cressida.'

The girl glared at him. 'I did not ask for your opinion, Sergeant.' She glanced at Tom. 'Follow me and we'll see if Granny believes your story.' She picked up the lantern and with a swish of her cape, turned and glided back inside.

Tom clenched his jaw. 'It's not a story.' He hesitated, then made to follow.

The sergeant grasped him by the collar. 'You're lucky, boy. But the Viscountess is a shrewd one. If she suspects you of lying, make no mistake, she'll call the constable and he'll throw you into the town gaol.' He shoved him through the doorway and in beneath the gatehouse arch. 'Hurry along now. You don't want to keep your sweet little *cousin* waiting.'

Tom stumbled after the girl, stomach churning. He'd only just got here and already he'd let Mother down. She'd told him to give the prayer book to no one but his uncle. What if this Viscountess person refused to believe him and had him locked up like the sergeant said? What chance would he have of rescuing Father then?

Stepping through the arch, he found himself in a large courtyard surrounded by high walls studded with rows of candlelit windows and topped by more great stone battlements. In front of him, water splashed from the statue of a man holding a pitchfork into a polished bronze bowl.

'Over here!' The girl's voice rang out above the noise.

He spun round, but there was no sign of her. If this was some kind of trick . . . He turned back to face the fountain. Then he saw her, a dark shape hovering beneath the shelter of a stone porch.

She put her hands on her hips. 'Keep up, or I will have to get the sergeant to escort you after all.'

He paused, took a deep breath and limped across the cobbles towards her. 'Where are we going?'

She frowned. 'I told you. To see my great-grandmother. Hurry up! It is nearly eight o'clock. She will be taking her supper soon and doesn't like being interrupted.' She pushed on the oak door behind her. It swung open with a creak and she disappeared inside.

Tom followed. A cold dark passage stretched away in front of him, its walls lined with heavy wood-panelling, its floor paved with large slabs of stone. His nose pricked at the smell of soot and beeswax.

'This way.' The girl led him along the passage before stopping at a fancy metal gate set into a stone arch. She lifted the latch and gestured for him to go through. The room beyond was in shadow, but from the great swoop of the window arches and the echo of his boots on the polished floor, he knew it was big. As big as the nave in St Thomas's church. Maybe bigger. He glanced about him. A row of dark panels hung on the walls beneath the windows. He guessed they must be portraits, though it was too dark to make out the faces. In between them, sitting on slabs of stone, were a line of carved stags, each with a set of spiked horns and a pair of glittering black eyes.

'This is the Buck Hall, for obvious reasons.' The girl pointed at the stags then lifted her arms and spun round on the spot. She seemed to have forgotten he wasn't to be trusted. She pointed at a bow and quiverful of arrows slung round the neck of the nearest stag. 'And those' – she said, sounding particularly pleased with herself – 'were a gift to my great-grandfather from Good Queen Bess to thank him for the excellent hunting when she was his guest here.'

Tom's eyes widened and for a moment, he couldn't help being impressed. 'Did you see her? The old Queen, I mean.' Even though she had persecuted Catholics, he had heard tales of her bravery, how she had rallied the troops when the Spanish Armada was threatening to invade.

The girl rolled her eyes. 'No, silly! That was in ninety-one, the year before I was born.'

Somewhere outside a bell tolled eight times.

'Come on, we don't have much time!' She marched on past a giant stone fireplace, heels clicking on the marble floor.

It was all right for her. She wasn't the one with blisters. Tom gritted his teeth and hobbled after her.

At the far end of the hall, they passed through an arch into another passage. The girl walked towards a heavy wooden door set into the wall. She pulled off her cape and threw it over the carved chest next to it. Smoothing her gown and patting her curls, she turned and looked him up and down.

'You might claim to be our relative' – she wrinkled her nose – 'but you look and smell more like a pig-herd to me.'

A surge of anger rose up inside Tom, but before he could say anything, she pointed at his bundle.

'You can leave that out here.'

'I'm keeping it with me.' He gripped it to him.

She tossed her curls. 'All right. Suit yourself!' She narrowed her eyes. 'What do they call you anyway?'

He lifted his head and jutted out his chin. For all her grand ways, she was just a girl. And girls didn't scare him. 'Tom. Tom Garnett.'

'She can see straight through a lie, you know.'

He clenched his fists. 'I'm telling the truth.'

The girl sniffed. 'Great-Grandmother will be the judge of that. Well, Tom Garnett' – she gave a sly smile, then raised a white knuckle to the door – 'let us see whether you can convince her to keep you out of gaol.'

Chapter Nine

'Come!' The voice behind the door sounded strong and used to commanding.

The girl turned the handle and stepped inside. Tom drew in a breath and followed.

The room was low-ceilinged and dark, lit only by the light of a fire which burned in a stone fireplace opposite. A smell of wood smoke and dried rushes spiked his nose. He blinked and looked around him. The panelled walls were carved with thick ropes of ivy. Faces peered out between the pointed leaves. Strange creatures with sharp fangs, horns and wild staring eyes that seemed to follow his every move. He shivered. The sooner he could get help for Mother and Father and get out of here, the better. But where was she, the old woman? He glanced around nervously.

'If that is you, Joan, you can tell master cook I shall be taking supper alone this evening. I have had quite enough of company today.' The voice, clipped and frosty, came from behind a high-backed chair pulled close to the fire.

The girl sidled forward, signalling him to follow her. 'Not Joan, Granny, but me.'

'Well, and why are *you* here?' There was a rustling sound and the tapping of fingers on wood.

The girl stepped round the side of the chair. 'We have a visitor.'

'At this late hour? Why did Sergeant Talbot not send them away? I have had my fill of our tenants complaining about the poor harvest and begging for more time to pay their rent. What can the man be thinking of disturbing my peace and entrusting a visitor to your care? You are a Montague, not a messenger.'

Tom stiffened. If she was as sharp-tongued and impatient as this, what chance was there she'd listen to him?

'But, Granny, I think you will want to meet this one.'

'And why, pray, do you say that?'

'He claims he is the son of the lord my father's long-lost sister.' The girl frowned at Tom and gestured him to move closer.

'What?' A bony white hand gripped the chair arm. The silhouette of a woman rose before them like a spirit rising from the grave. Tom planted his feet further apart, determined to stand his ground.

'What is your name, boy?'

'Tom Garnett, of Portsmouth.'

'Garnett?' The woman froze for a moment, then reached for a silver-topped cane propped against her chair.

She walked slowly towards him, black skirts rustling. A sudden whiff of something bitter-sweet stung his nostrils.

As she approached, the shadows fell away revealing a sharp curved nose, marble-carved cheeks and a pair of flint-grey eyes. She wore a black velvet cap on top of her head and beneath it a lace caul pulled tight over a twist of parchment-coloured hair. A jewelled crucifix swung on a chain below the ruff at her neck, its gold arms gleaming in the firelight. She stopped suddenly and slid her head towards him, like a river heron about to spike a fish. Tom licked his lips and edged backwards.

'I am Magdalen, Viscountess Montague, widow of Lord Montague's grandfather, the first Viscount, and while My Lord and his wife are in London, mistress of this household. Explain yourself, boy.' She struck the floor with her cane.

'I . . . er . . .'

The girl darted forwards. 'I took this from him, Granny.' She waved the prayer book in the air.

'Give it back!' Tom made a swipe for it.

She jerked it out of his reach, gave him a triumphant smile, then curtseyed and handed the prayer book to the Viscountess. 'There's an inscription inside. He claims it's from the lord my father to his mother.'

He glared at her.

'Bring me my eyeglasses, girl.' The Viscountess shot out a bony hand.

The girl hurried over to a large leather-topped table next to the fireplace. She rummaged through the rolls of parchment and piles of books stacked on top of it.

'Hurry, will you?' The old woman clicked her fingers.

'Here they are, Granny.' The girl bobbed back to her side and held out a piece of curved horn with two circles of glass fixed beneath it.

The old woman perched the strange-looking object on the end of her nose and scanned the page with a pointed nail. Tom was sure for a moment her eyes widened.

She removed the eyeglasses from her nose, hooked them over the black cord at her waist and snapped the book shut. 'And how can I be sure you did not steal it?'

His cheeks flushed. What right did she have to accuse him of being a thief? Just because he wasn't rich like them. If he had the choice, he'd march out of the room right now. But he needed her to believe him, for Mother and Father's sake. He gritted his teeth.

'Mother told me she was Lord . . . I mean Uncle Montague's favourite sister. She said he gave the prayer book to her for her sixteenth birthday, the day before she left here for good. She said . . . she said he used to call her his own dear Nan.'

The Viscountess narrowed her eyes. 'And did she say why she left?'

He frowned. 'She mentioned some troubles between them. She seemed sad . . .'

'As well she might.' The Viscountess sounded bitter. She shook her head. 'Such a waste.'

A surge of hope flashed through Tom. 'So you believe me?'

'I admit the evidence you give is compelling. But why

are you here?'

'To get help. Mother is in gaol . . .'

The girl gasped and put her hand to her mouth.

The Viscountess struck the floor with her cane again. 'In gaol? Why?'

Tom hesitated. Could he trust her with the truth? He glanced at the cross hanging from her neck. The conversation between the two men outside the gate about 'My Lady's not-so-secret Mass' echoed in his ears. He clenched his fingers tight against his palms. He'd have to. How else was he going to get the Montagues' help?

'She and Father they . . . they sheltered a priest, and now the constable is hunting Father down.' His bottom lip trembled.

'What?' The Viscountess's eyebrows arched in horror.

He swallowed. Now wasn't the time to confess what a coward he'd been. But at least, with the old woman's help, he'd have a chance to put it right. 'Mother said Uncle Montague was friends with the King and would be able to stop the constable and—'

'Fools! The pair of them!' The Viscountess clutched the prayer book against her crucifix. 'What were they thinking?' She groaned, then, letting her cane slide between her fingers, she closed her eyes and pinched the top of her nose.

What was she saying? Tom tugged at her sleeve. 'Please, mistress . . . I mean, My Lady. You've got to help them!'

She snapped her eyes open. 'It is not as simple as that! Unlike your father, we Montagues have our reputation to think of. One false move . . .' She shook her head and gestured to the girl to pick up her cane.

'But they might die.' His eyes blurred with tears. He scrubbed at them with his sleeve. He mustn't cry. Not now.

The Viscountess stroked the worn cover of the prayer book then gave a deep sigh. 'Your mother, although estranged from us, is of our blood. I will send word to Lord Montague in London about her plight. Let us hope he can use his influence at court to secure her release. As for your father . . .' Her mouth hardened into a thin white line. 'He is a lost cause.' With a rustle of skirts, she turned, walked back to her chair and sat down.

'What do you mean?' Tom stumbled after her.

The Viscountess fixed him with a granite stare. 'Many years ago, he brought great grief to this house. Now, once again, he has shown himself to be a man of poor judgement.'

He frowned. 'I don't understand.'

She shook her head. 'For a town-bred boy, you are very naive. Your father should know better than to try his hand at priest-smuggling. With watchers everywhere, it is a dangerous business, even for those with the means to support it.'

Anger whirled up inside Tom. How dare she talk about Father like that? He glared at her, but her eyes gazed past him into the fire.

His jaw tightened. All right, if she wanted him to beg . . . He knelt down and clutched at her skirts. 'Please. Help him. In the name of Our Lord . . .'

She pulled back and frowned. 'No. Your father will have known what the stakes were. He must take his chances and pray that God will be merciful.' She dropped the prayer book in her lap and smoothed the front of her gown with the palm of her hand.

A bitter taste flooded Tom's throat. Without the Montagues' help, what chance did Father have? He shot a look at the girl. She turned away quickly, fixing her eyes on the carving of a two-headed dog next to the fireplace. He jumped to his feet and strode towards the door.

'Where do you think you are going?' The Viscountess's voice was iron-hard.

'Home.' He clenched his fists and kept walking.

'To what? An empty house and a mother in gaol? Don't be foolish, boy. You must stay here until your uncle returns. Then he can decide what to do with you. Besides, it is past the curfew now and Sergeant Talbot is under strict orders to let no one pass through Cowdray's gates.'

Tom stopped in his tracks, shoulders slumped.

A pair of footsteps crunched slowly across the rush mats behind him. 'Here.' Something sharp prodded him in the back.

He spun round. The old woman lowered her cane and held out the prayer book. He snatched it from her and slipped it inside his jerkin.

The Viscountess turned to the girl. 'Ask Joan to prepare one of the bedchambers in the North Range for him, then take him to the kitchen so he can be fed.' She waved them away with her hand.

The girl tugged at his sleeve. Tom yanked it free and marched to the door. He'd stay here tonight, but if the high and mighty Montagues thought he was going to sit around waiting for Father to be hunted down and thrown in gaol, they were wrong.

Chapter Ten

Sunday 27 October

For a moment when Tom woke, he thought he was back in his bedchamber at home. But the silver candlestick by the bed, the heavy tapestries hanging from the walls and the sharp sting of the blister on his foot soon reminded him of the truth. His heart sank. What use was it being related to these Montagues when they refused to help? They might be going to get Mother free, but what about Father? He bit his lip and dug his fingers into the soft velvet coverlet spread across the bed. A brush of whiskers tickled his toes.

Jago. He must have left the box open last night after he'd fed him. Just as well his little friend hadn't decided to go exploring. He pushed back the coverlet and scooped him up in his palm. 'Hello, boy. Let's see where we are.' Hauling himself out of bed, he hobbled over to the window and peered through the pale green glass. The room looked down on to the courtyard and across to the gatehouse opposite. Beyond it stretched the water meadows, their pools and grasses wound about with tendrils of mist. To the left, rising above them, was a low hill, topped with trees and a huddle of grey stone ruins.

Jago raised his head and sniffed the air. Tom tickled him between the ears.

'There must be another way to help Father, boy.' He frowned. 'We just have to think of it, that's all.' A distant bell sounded the hour. He felt a stab of guilt. He hadn't said his prayers yet. He closed his eyes and began to mutter the words.

A knock at the door made him start. Sliding Jago into the sleeve of his nightshirt, he leapt back into bed and pulled the covers up under his chin. 'Who's there?'

The door swung open. The girl stepped into the room with a bundle under her arm. She was wearing a blue silk gown decorated with red bows. A pair of blue velvet slippers peeped out from beneath her skirts.

He scowled at her. 'What do you want?'

'I've brought you some clothes.' She held up a mustard-coloured silk doublet, a pair of brown velvet breeches, a stiff white ruff and some black silk slippers. 'They belonged to my elder brother when he was a boy.' She tilted her head and looked at him. 'They should fit. Although' – she sighed – 'they are not today's fashion.'

'I'll wear my own, thanks.'

'Those grimy old things?' She pulled a face like a cat sniffing a bowl of sour milk. 'Joan fetched them away when you were sleeping and put them on the fire.'

'What?' He stared wildly around the room. His boots were still there, and so was his waist-pouch, but everything else was gone. 'She had no right!'

'You are a Montague, so you must dress like one.' She gave a prim smile. 'Besides' – her eyes took on a distant look – 'it's fun to dress up and pretend to be someone else. Actors do it all the time.'

He snatched up the ruff and hurled it across the room. 'I'm a Garnett, not a Montague!'

She blinked and arched her eyebrows. 'Tsk. What a temper! I'm surprised you want to stay a Garnett, when your father is being hunted down like a common criminal.'

'Don't you talk about Father like that!'

She frowned. 'I didn't mean anything by it.' She twisted a blonde curl round her little finger. 'Anyway, you had better get dressed. Granny says you must join us for prayers in the chapel.' With a swish of her skirts she turned and walked back to the door. 'I will wait for you outside.'

Tom waited until she had gone, then fished Jago out from his sleeve. He held his soft, silky body against his cheek and breathed in his mousy smell. 'If they think they can keep us prisoner here, they're wrong, boy.' He glanced down at his nightshirt then back at the over-stuffed doublet and puffed-up breeches and groaned. Right now though, it looked like he didn't have much choice.

Tom sat in the candlelit pew next to Cressida. He gawped up at the chapel's stained-glass windows and the ceiling decorated with gold stars and flying angels. The pleats of the ruff dug into his throat. Stupid fancy clothes. He stuck a finger behind it and stretched his neck. He felt like a pheasant, pinned and stuffed for the cooking pot.

A finger poked him in the ribs. 'Keep still! Granny doesn't approve of people fidgeting during the service.'

'And she doesn't approve of girls climbing up towers either, does she?'

A look of panic flashed across Cressida's face. 'If you dare tell . . .'

'What? You can't make things any worse for me than they already are. What were you doing up there anyway?'

'Nothing.' Cressida pursed her lips then clasped her hands together and bent her head.

Tom sighed and shot a look at the statue-still back of the Viscountess in the pew in front. Was there anything she *did* approve of? He slid his tongue between his teeth and pulled a face. As if sensing it, the Viscountess swung round. He jerked his head down quickly and pretended to pray.

The sickly-sweet smell of candlewax and incense enveloped him, tickling his nose and making his eyes water. A low murmur started up in front of him. He sneaked another look up. The Viscountess sat with her neck craned forwards, head pressed against her hands, muttering a prayer. He frowned. How could she call herself a Christian when she'd refused to help Father? He stared at the golden cross on the altar and the row of grim-faced saints set in the niches behind it. They looked as angry as he felt. The sooner prayers were over and he could get out of here, the better.

His waist-pouch jiggled against his hip. He stole a quick glance at Cressida; she was busy praying too. He undid it, slid his fingers inside and let Jago climb out on to his palm. What would 'Granny' do if she knew he'd brought a mouse into church? He stroked the top of Jago's head and smiled. *Our secret, boy. Our secret.*

He dropped him back in the pouch and was about to retie it when a shuffle of footsteps and a whisper of voices sounded in the passageway outside. He jerked his head up. A crowd of men and women had appeared in the chapel doorway. At first he thought they must be servants, but some of the women were carrying babies and there was a bunch of children with them too.

He watched open-mouthed as they shuffled their way down the aisle to the empty pews in the main part of the chapel. Now it was his turn to nudge Cressida. 'Who are they?'

She threw a glance at them and shook her head.

'Come on, tell me.'

She hesitated then heaved a sigh. 'Townsfolk. People who have stayed true to the faith.'

'What are they doing here?'

'They've come to hear the Mass, of course.'

He frowned. So the man outside the gate last night had been speaking the truth. He licked his lips. 'But that's forbidden.'

'We have our own rules here at Cowdray. You'll find out soon enough.' She gave him a sly smile. 'Look, here comes

Father Chasuble now.' An elderly black-robed man with stooped shoulders stood in the doorway a silver chalice draped with a white cloth in his hands. Head bent low, he tottered down the aisle towards the altar.

A priest! What was he doing here? Tom glanced nervously back at the doorway, half expecting a troop of soldiers to come clattering through it. But no one else appeared. The room fell silent as Father Chasuble reached the altar and bowed. He placed the chalice on the altar top and bowed again, then made the sign of the cross with his right hand.

'Why hasn't he been arrested?' Tom whispered above the drone of the priest's voice.

'Arrested?' Cressida arched a pale eyebrow. 'That will never happen. Don't forget, we are Montagues.' She stuck her nose in the air and tossed her curls.

A fresh jab of anger spiked him. 'But that's not fair!'

'Fair? What on earth do you mean?' Cressida gave him a puzzled stare.

Tom shook his head. What was the point? He glanced at the back of the Viscountess's bowed head. How could she get away with harbouring a priest right under the nose of the law, when ordinary people – people like the Cresswells and his parents – were being so cruelly persecuted? And she'd accused Father of showing poor judgement for helping Father Oliver. He balled his fingers into fists. If those men last night were spies and they reported her, it would serve her right! After a few nights spent in a gaol cell with only the rats for company, maybe she'd think twice about refusing to help him. Not that that would be any use to Father. He slumped against the back of the pew.

A white furry body scooted across his knee. *Jago! No!* He jolted up and made a grab for him. But it was too late. Jago sprang to the floor, jumped over his feet and disappeared beneath Cressida's skirts.

Tom flashed her a look. She had gone back to praying. He stared at the silk folds of her dress, willing Jago to reappear.

But he didn't.

Suddenly Cressida's cheeks flushed pink. Her head flew up and she let out an ear-piercing scream.

Father Chasuble stopped in mid-sentence. Everyone turned and stared.

Cressida jumped to her feet. She clawed at her dress and screamed again.

Father Chasuble dropped his prayer book and made the sign of the cross. A baby started crying. The people in the congregation began whispering to each other. Some of them made to leave.

Tom dipped down and shook the bottom of Cressida's skirts. A white shape plopped out next to his feet. Quick as a hawk, he snatched the mouse up by the base of his tail and dropped him back in his waist-pouch. *Got you!* He tied the strings tight, raised his head and looked around. No one else had seen. They were all too busy staring at Cressida.

'Get it off, get it off!' She bounced up and down beside him, tears streaming down her cheeks.

An ice-cold voice rang out from the pew in front of

them. 'Silence!'

Everyone froze.

The Viscountess stood up slowly, then turned and fixed Cressida with a hard, grey stare. 'How dare you interrupt our service?' Two spots of red glowed on her chalk-white cheeks.

'But, Granny, I mean My Lady . . . There . . . there was something crawling up inside my dress.'

'Enough of your play-acting, girl! Mister Mandrake?'

A sallow-faced man dressed in a schoolmaster's black gown emerged from the shadows at the far end of their pew. He gave the old woman a simpering smile.

'Yes, My Lady?'

Tom shivered. That wheedling voice. He'd heard it somewhere before . . .

The Viscountess pointed the tip of her cane at Cressida. 'Please devise a suitable punishment for my granddaughter at the end of tomorrow's lessons.'

''Twill be a pleasure, My Lady.' Mister Mandrake swept down into a low bow. Strands of greasy black hair swung forwards to reveal a patch of scaly red skin in the centre of his crown. As he raised his head, his yellow-brown eyes locked with Tom's. The look he gave him was a cold, knowing one, as if he had sliced him open and discovered all his deepest secrets.

A trickle of fear slid down Tom's spine. He knew now where he'd heard the voice before. Last night at the gate. Which meant . . . which meant that the tutor was one of the spies.

'Now go to your room, girl, and do not show your face again until morning.' The Viscountess swept round to face Father Chasuble. 'My apologies for the behaviour of my granddaughter, Father. Her attention-seeking ways will receive due punishment on Earth, if not in Heaven too. Pray continue with the service.' She tapped the front of the pew with her cane and lowered herself in her seat.

Cressida let out a sob. The congregation bent their heads again. Tom bit his lip. He couldn't help feeling sorry for her. It was his fault Jago had escaped and now she was getting the blame. He reached out to touch her arm.

'Leave me alone!' Fumbling at her sleeve, she pulled out a lace kerchief and dabbed at her eyes. She gave a loud sniff, then, head held high, stepped down from the pew and glided out through the chapel door.

Chapter Eleven

Thursday 31 October

The rain rattled like nails against the schoolroom window. Tom hugged his arms to his chest and tried to blot out the sound of Mister Mandrake's voice as it scratched and whined its way through endless Latin verbs. He'd been forced to spend another four days here, with Joan and the other servants watching his every move. Each morning he'd woken up hoping there'd be news about Mother, but it never came.

He stared through the windowpane at the slate-grey clouds. All the while he was trapped here, Father was out there somewhere on the run – or worse. These people, they lived in another world. He glanced at the back of Cressida's ribboned head. She hadn't spoken to him since the business in the chapel on Sunday. But from the black looks she'd been giving him when they met for lessons, she must have guessed it had something to do with him. He couldn't risk losing his only friend so he'd made sure all week to keep Jago safely tucked up in his box in the bedchamber, only letting him out when they were on their own.

'Isn't that right, Master Garnett?' Mister Mandrake's birch rod cracked down against the desk, narrowly missing Tom's left ear.

He jerked up, heart thumping. 'What?'

Cressida swung round in her chair.

'What, *sir*?' Mandrake bent over him, stroking the tip of the rod with a skinny finger. 'Something tells me that you have not been paying attention to my lesson.' A waft of mustiness rose up from the tutor's gown. Tom wrinkled his nose. It was worse than the smell down in the crypt of St Thomas's.

'Sorry . . . sir.' He dipped his head to avoid the tutor's gaze. There was no way Mandrake could know he'd eavesdropped on his secret meeting with the other spy because Tom hadn't told anyone about it yet. And the way he felt about the Montagues, he wasn't sure he was going to either. So why was the man paying him so much attention?

Mandrake scowled. 'I do not like your tone, Master Garnett. It has a touch of insolence about it. So, now.' He tucked the birch rod under his arm, stretched out his long, pale hands and examined his fingernails one by one. 'How best to punish you?'

Tom's chest tightened. He stared at the pattern of wood grains in the desktop and waited for his sentence.

'I know.' Mandrake raised a thin black eyebrow. 'How about a little extra Latin translation at the end of the lesson? You will be in good company, after the unfortunate episode at Sunday's Mass. The young mistress is still only halfway through her penance.' His eyes flicked snake-like to Cressida. She flushed and shoved her nose back into her book.

The tutor gave an oily smile. 'Yes, that will do very nicely. Now, on with your work.' He flexed his rod and strode back to his desk.

Tom hung his head and stared at the never-ending list of Latin verbs in front of him. He hated it here. He had to find a way of escaping. If he went back home, at least he would be there for little Ned. And with Jem Foster's help, if he could get news of Father . . .

The rest of the morning was taken up with repeating the names of the Kings and Queens of England, and yet more Latin grammar. He was grateful Mother had insisted on giving him lessons. He'd never have been able to keep up if she hadn't. He had given up hope of ever finishing when a knock sounded at the door.

Mister Mandrake hooked the ends of his greasy black hair behind his ears and adjusted the sleeves of his gown. 'Come!'

The door swung open. A red-faced woman dressed in an apron stepped inside. It was Joan.

'I have come for Master Garnett. My Lady wishes to see him.'

Tom's heart leapt. News from home. It must be! He

rammed his quill back into the ink pot and scrambled to his feet.

'Sit!' Mandrake shot out an arm and snapped his fingers. 'And did she say why, Joan?'

'She did not.' Joan clamped her fleshy lips tight shut.

'Hmmm.' He tapped a bony finger against his own thin lips. 'Well, I will send him along directly we have finished the lesson.' He waved Joan from the room.

She stood her ground. 'My Lady says Master Garnett is to come at once.'

Mandrake's eyes narrowed. 'Really? Then it must be something urgent?'

Joan folded her arms across her chest and looked him straight in the eye. 'Begging your pardon, sir, but 'tis none of your concern.'

Cressida stifled a giggle.

Mandrake spun round. 'Do you find something amusing, Mistress Cressida?'

She shook her head.

'Good, then get back to your work.' He turned back to Tom and frowned. 'Very well. You may go, Master Garnett. But rest assured, your punishment will be waiting for you on your return.'

Tom glanced at Cressida but she had her nose buried in her Latin grammar book again. He was almost at the door when a hand grasped him by the shoulder.

'You were lucky today.' Mandrake's clammy fingers tightened their grip. 'But don't forget, only cats have nine lives.'

He twisted free. Cats? Nine lives? What was he talking about? Well, one thing was for sure; he wasn't going to sit through any more of the slimy tutor's lessons. Not if he could help it. He scrubbed his neck with his sleeve and followed Joan outside.

'Quickly, we mustn't keep the mistress waiting.' She let out a puff of air, then bustled down the passage, skirts flapping.

He ran to catch her up. 'Is it about my mother?'

She shrugged. 'How would I know? A messenger arrived on horseback this morning from London. That's all I can tell you.' She set off again.

London? A message from his uncle. It had to be. Tom closed his eyes. *Make it good news, Lord, please.*

At the end of the passage, Joan took a left turn across a narrow landing and plodded up a small flight of stairs. He followed her through a door and into a long gallery. He gazed around him at the rich tapestries and fine portraits which decorated the walls. Had Mother walked here too? It was hard to imagine her among all this grandeur.

'This is no time for daydreaming.' Joan stood at the far end of the gallery, hands on hips, foot tapping the floor.

He jumped and hurried towards her. As he passed the final window, a small portrait jolted him to a stop. It was the likeness of a young woman, so lifelike she looked like she might be flesh and blood. He frowned. There was something else about her too. Something familiar. He stepped closer.

She wore a fine lace ruff around her neck. Beneath it a

gold crucifix shone out from the black velvet of her gown. Her fair hair was pulled back, piled on top of her head and decorated with a band of pearls. But it was her sad-looking eyes which drew Tom most. Bright blue and almond-shaped. The same eyes that had filled with tears as he left for the Fosters nearly a week ago.

Mother? He touched a finger to her pale cheek.

'Master Garnett. Please!'

'I'll find a way to help Father, I promise.' He dropped his hand, then, giving the portrait one last look, he turned and scurried after Joan.

The servant bustled out on to another landing, down a polished wooden staircase and along a passage, stopping at a door halfway down. She put her head on one side, ran her eyes over Tom's clothes and pulled a face. 'No matter how much you dress it up, a sparrow is always a sparrow.' She batted his shoulders and the front of his doublet with her rough, red hands.

'Leave me alone!' He shook her off.

She sighed, then raised her fist to the door and gave a sharp rap.

'Enter.' The voice behind it rang out hard and cold as ice.

Tom gritted his teeth. Hopefully this was the last time he'd have to face the old black crow.

Joan turned the handle, opened the door and pushed him inside. The door banged shut behind him. He blinked. The chamber was in semi-darkness, the light from the windows blocked by the thick pieces of oiled cloth which hung across them. But he could make out enough to know it was the same room he'd been taken to that first night. He peered at the fireplace. The grate was cold and dark and the chair in front of it empty. The air smelt of old smoke and rushes and, above it, that same strange bitter-sweetness from before.

Suddenly Tom knew what it was. Two Yuletides ago, when William was still alive, Father had come back from the harbour with a basket of flame-coloured oranges he said came all the way from Spain. There had been one each for all of them. How excited they'd been as they peeled the glowing skin and sank their teeth into the juicy sweet-sharp flesh. And how happy too.

A rustle of silk brought him back to the room with a start. He spun round. The Viscountess stood before a small alcove next to the door, her face caked with white powder. She gestured with her cane for him to join her.

He edged towards her, eyeing the black stick nervously. What if he was wrong? What if she'd sent for him because she'd found out about Jago and wanted to give him a good whipping?

She stepped into the alcove and nodded at a large silver crucifix on a table set against the wall. 'I have been praying.' She picked up a string of jet-black rosary beads from a glass dish and raised them to her lips. 'It is only the Lord God who can help us at such times.' Her voice was quieter than before: cracked-sounding.

The hairs on Tom's neck prickled. A sudden surge of sourness hit the back of his throat. Something was wrong. He swallowed hard, trying to force the taste back down.

The Viscountess took a deep breath and fixed him with her flint-grey eyes. 'There is news.'

'Of Mother?'

'No, boy. Your father.'

His heart jolted. 'Where is he? Can I see him?'

The old woman shook her head. 'I am afraid that will not be possible. He and the priest . . .' She ran the beads clicking between her fingers. 'They are taken.'

A loud rushing noise filled his ears. 'Wh-what do you mean, taken?'

Viscountess Montague gathered up the beads. Then turning back to the crucifix, she raised a bony hand and crossed herself. 'Your father is in London, imprisoned in the Clink.'

Chapter Twelve

Tom's knees buckled beneath him. He fell against the table, head spinning. The crucifix wobbled then toppled and hit the floor with a clang.

A hand gripped his arm. 'Sit.' The Viscountess steered him to her chair by the fireplace and pushed him down.

His fingers sank into the softness of the cushion beneath him, but it might as well have been a bed of nails. He slumped forwards and buried his head in his hands. *Please, God. Don't let it be him. Let it be someone else. Please!*

'Look at me boy.'

He raised his head. The Viscountess stood over him wearing the same grim look as before. A stab of pain shot up from the pit of his stomach and rippled through his chest. So it was true.

'I – I want to see him.' He made to stand, but his legs were too shaky to hold him. He collapsed back in the chair.

The Viscountess sighed. 'That is impossible. Your father is accused of treason and held on the orders of the King's chief minister and spymaster, Robert Cecil. He may receive no visitors before his trial.'

Hot tears scalded his cheeks. 'It's my fault. It's all my fault.'

'Your fault? How could it be?' Furrows appeared in the white powder covering her forehead.

'I told the constable.'

'Told him what?'

'Which way . . .' He bit his lip to stop it from trembling. 'Which way Father and the priest went.'

She shook her head. 'That's as may be, but the truth is your father has brought this on himself. And with the King so stirred up on religious matters by Cecil, he is set to pay the highest price.'

His heart lurched. 'What do you mean?'

'Cecil hates all Catholics with a vengeance and has convinced the King we mean to kill him and put a Catholic king on the throne of England instead. There have been two plots against the King already, one hatched and led by priests. For anyone found harbouring a priest . . . and worse, a Jesuit, which this Father Oliver appears to be . . . the sentence can only ever be one thing.'

The floor began to sway. A black mist swirled up in front of him. He scrunched his eyes tight shut, but the mist seeped under his eyelids. It twisted and writhed into the shape of a man swinging from the end of a rope. Father . . .

'No!' His eyes snapped open. But he knew what she said

was true. And now the worst had happened. He gave a low groan.

'Let it be a lesson to you, boy. These are dangerous times. If you want to live through them, you must be cautious. You can never let your guard down.'

Her words spun around him like leaves in a storm. Lessons, caution. What did any of that matter when Father might hang?

'But . . . can't my Uncle Montague help him?'

'He has already secured your mother's freedom, thank the Lord. I believe she has been taken in by some friends of yours, the ones caring for your younger brother. But as for your father . . .' The Viscountess shook her head again. 'My grandson would risk too much.'

'Please . . .'

'You must understand the world we Montagues live in.' Her lips pressed into a thin, hard line.

A ball of anger tore through Tom. He understood all right. A palace filled with gold and silver and a whole army of servants, but still they wouldn't lift a finger to save Father.

The Viscountess turned to the fireplace and prodded at the cold, grey ashes with her cane. 'When our Protestant King came to the throne, he was well disposed to your uncle, in spite of their differences in matters of faith. But as every Catholic knows, he was persuaded by those who would destroy us to bring in new and harsher laws. Your uncle himself spent some time in prison for objecting to them until eventually, thank the Lord, the King agreed to his release. Now Cecil and his lackeys are sowing rumours that Catholic plotters are seeking to make mischief again and relieve the King of his throne. If your uncle was seen to be pleading for the life of a suspected traitor at a time like this . . .'

'Traitor?' Tom leapt to his feet. 'But he's not! He was just trying to help the priest find the right road. And what about Father Chasuble? He's a priest. So if Father's a traitor, that must make you one too.'

The Viscountess's back stiffened. She swung round and fixed him with dagger-sharp eyes. 'How dare you!'

'It's true though, isn't it?' He glared back at her.

'Silence!' She raised a hand. 'I will suffer no more of your insolence. You should be grateful we have given you shelter.'

Grateful? He snorted. That was the last thing he felt. 'I hate it here. I'm leaving.' He shoved the chair aside and made to barge past her.

'No!' She swung her cane out in front of him, barring his way. 'You will stay here at Cowdray in our safekeeping until your uncle comes back from court. She reached for a small silver bell on top of a nearby chest and shook it. 'Joan!'

The door creaked open and the servant stepped inside. 'Yes, My Lady.'

'Keep watch on Master Garnett while I summon one of the other servants to help. Then take him to his room and lock him in.' She gave Tom a cold-eyed stare. 'We will see what time spent in quiet reflection does for his manners.'

Tom sat on the edge of his bed, staring into the gloom. The worst had happened. Father had been taken and thrown into gaol. But in spite of everything, the Viscountess had made it clear the Montagues still weren't going to help.

Which meant it was down to him to save Father.

A tide of panic surged through him. What was he going to do? He took a deep breath. *Courage, Tom Garnett. You've got to show courage.*

A rustling noise came from Jago's box. He pulled back the lid and lifted the mouse out. He stroked his head then pressed Jago's damp nose to his own and stared into his beady eyes.

'Mother's safe with the Fosters, but Father needs my help more than ever. We've got to get out of here now, boy.'

He glanced at the locked door and frowned. There had to be another way. He darted over to the window, opened it and peered into the gathering shadows below. It was a long way down. Too far to jump. He sank his shoulders. He was about to shut the window again when a pale gleam of metal caught his eye. A drainpipe. Hope bubbled up inside him. He pushed the window open wider to get a better view. It was within reach – just – and it looked as though it ran all the way down to the cobbles below. It was dark out there, but if he took it slowly . . .

'Come on, boy.' He scooped Jago back into his box. 'We've got some climbing to do.' He bundled the box up in his nightshirt along with the candle from his bedside and the bread and cheese Joan had brought up earlier, then glanced down at his doublet and fancy breeches and frowned. He was going to need something warmer and less conspicuous for the journey.

A wooden chest stood at the foot of the bed. He opened

it and rummaged through the pile of linen inside until his fingers closed round the ends of a brown, wool blanket. He yanked the ruff from his neck, threw the blanket round his shoulders and knotted the ends together. Then, kicking off his thin silk slippers, he slid his feet inside his own boots and fixed his waist-pouch on to his belt. At least now he didn't look like a puffed-up gamecock.

Slipping the prayer book inside his doublet, he slung his bundle over his shoulder and crept back to the window. No sign of anyone. And in the poor light, he'd be harder to spot. All the better to make his escape.

'Let's go, boy.'

He hoisted himself up on the window sill and swung his legs out so they were dangling over the edge. The secret to climbing is not to look down. William had told him that once when they'd scaled the old oak at the end of their street looking for a woodpecker's nest. Now, keeping his eyes fixed on the opposite wall of the courtyard, he shuffled his bottom along to the end of the sill, pulled up his feet and lifted into a crouch. He reached for the drainpipe. The tips of his fingers brushed the cold lead. He reached again . . . Got it! He tightened his grip and counted to ten. Keeping his right foot planted firmly on the sill, he swung his body out, then in again towards the wall. Clutching the drainpipe with both hands, he felt for a gap in the stonework with his left foot and rammed his toe in hard.

He puffed out a breath. So far, so good . . .

Steadying himself he dropped his right leg down and searched for another toehold. Nearly there . . .

'Arrgghhh!' His boot slipped. He jerked backwards, legs flailing, head spinning. The square edges of the drainpipe dug into his palms. His fingers cramped and his grip began to loosen. *Hold on. You've got to hold on!*

He took a deep breath, counted to three and jabbed at the wall with his right boot. It bounced off. He licked his lips and jabbed again. This time it held. He toed over the stones with his left foot. After what seemed like an age, he found a gap. He shoved his boot in and tested it. It stayed where it was. He sucked in another breath. What if someone had heard him? He shook his head. He'd worry about that later. He gritted his teeth and fixed his eyes on the drainpipe. Then, placing one hand below the other, he started to make his way down.

As soon as his feet touched the cobblestones, he ducked and peered about him. No one. He mopped his forehead with his sleeve and heaved a sigh. A loud squeak sounded from his bundle.

'It's all right, boy. We made it!' He patted the side of Jago's box.

The clock in the gatehouse tower chimed five. Staying low, he edged along the wall, then made a dash for the gatehouse arch. Still no sign of anyone. He crept up to the door in the gate, slid back the bolt and pushed it open. His heart leapt at the glimpse of the causeway beyond. He gathered his makeshift cloak to him.

'This is it, Jago. We're free!'

He was about to step over the threshold when a thud of boots outside pulled him up short.

Chapter Thirteen

Tom yanked the door shut and stole back into the shadows. He couldn't risk getting caught and locked up again. He'd have to hide and wait for whoever it was to go away. But where? He scanned the courtyard. There was a low arch to the right of the gatehouse, half stacked with wood. He darted over to it. He was about to slide beneath it when a set of footsteps pattered across the cobbles behind him.

'What are you doing, skulking about like a common thief? I thought Great-Grandmother had sent you to your room?'

His heart sank. Cressida! Slowly he turned to face her.

'Nothing. I . . . I felt sick and Joan let me out to get some air.'

'Really?' Her face wore a disbelieving frown.

He bit his lip. He had to put her off the scent. 'Aren't you meant to be doing extra Latin?'

She tossed her curls and sniffed. 'I finished that *hours* ago.' She glanced at the bundle and the blanket tied around his neck. Her frown deepened. 'Going somewhere?'

He flushed and slipped the bundle off his shoulder. 'No … I … er …'

A rattle of metal and the creak of wood made them both jump. In a moment, whoever it was would enter the court-yard and spot them and he'd be back under lock and key.

'Quick! In here!' He grabbed her by the arm and dragged her behind the wood pile.

Footsteps echoed beneath the gatehouse and an orange light spilled across the cobbles. 'Who's there?'

Cressida made to stand but he dragged her back down. 'It's only Sergeant Talbot.'

'Keep quiet.' Tom spoke through gritted teeth.

'Who's there, I say?'

He pressed a finger against Cressida's lips and shook his head then closed his eyes and waited.

Silence, then an annoyed-sounding growl, the marching of footsteps back beneath the gatehouse and the creak and bang of a door.

He snapped his eyes open and heaved a sigh. 'That was close. What's he doing?'

'Making his patrol. He does it every evening to frighten off any vagabonds that might be lurking outside.' Cressida narrowed her eyes and gave him a meaningful smirk.

He clenched his fists. If she was laughing at him … But what did it matter? He slumped back against the wall. With

Sergeant Talbot on the prowl, there wasn't much chance of getting away from here tonight.

She tapped him on the knee. 'What's wrong?'

'Nothing.' His throat tightened. He reached inside his bundle and pulled out Jago's box. As he slid back the lid, the mouse leapt free. He sprang on to Tom's right arm and skittered up on to his shoulder.

'What's that?' Cressida shrank back, hands clutched to her chest.

'A friend.' *My only friend.* He lifted Jago off gently and cupped him in his palms.

She wrinkled her nose. 'A mouse for a friend? Whoever heard of such a thing?' Her eyes flashed with sudden anger. 'So it *was* you in the chapel!'

He'd felt guilty then, but he didn't now. 'Better a mouse than no friends at all.'

'What do you mean?' Her face wore a hurt expression. 'I'd have plenty of friends – the Princess Elizabeth, the King's own daughter, included – if the lord my father would let me join him at court.'

'Why doesn't he then? Here, boy.' Pulling a small lump of cheese from his bundle, Tom dropped it in front of Jago and watched as the mouse gobbled it up.

Cressida fiddled with one of the bows on her dress. 'I . . . I don't know. Because he wants to keep me safe.' She shot him a look. 'Not like your father who seems to have done everything he can to put you in danger.'

Anger sparked inside him. 'You don't know anything about my father. He'd never hurt anyone, least of all us. He doesn't deserve to han—' He clamped his mouth shut. If he didn't say the word, maybe it wouldn't happen. His eyes blurred. He rubbed them with the back of his sleeve. 'Come on, boy.' He put Jago back inside the box, retied his bundle and ducked back out into the courtyard.

A rustle of skirts sounded behind him. 'Cousin.' Warm fingers clutched his arm. He stiffened. 'I'm sorry. About your father, I mean. Granny told me earlier.'

He raised his shoulders. He didn't care a fig what she thought.

'But what good will it do if you run away?'

He sighed, then turned to face her. 'You don't understand. It's because of me Father's in prison. I came here to put things right and get help. But your precious granny won't lift a finger, even though Father's so-called crime is no worse than hers.'

'What do you mean?' Cressida arched her eyebrows.

'My father helped a priest because he was sick and needed shelter. Your granny has a priest living under her roof and leading the Mass every Sunday. So why isn't she in prison too?'

She gave a small shrug. 'Because she's a Montague.'

'That's your answer for everything, isn't it?' He kicked at a pebble. It bounced across the cobblestones and smashed into the wall opposite.

She frowned. 'But I don't understand? Why was it *your* fault your father was captured?'

Tom's stomach twisted. The scene in the kitchen flashed in front of him. Constable Skinner's jeering words. Weasel

Face's fist ready to strike. And the look of horror in Mother's eyes as he blurted out the road Father and the priest had taken.

He shook his head. 'It doesn't matter!' He shouldered his bundle. If he didn't go now he might not get another chance. He turned and marched beneath the gatehouse arch.

'Where are you going?' Cressida's voice echoed after him.

'To find someone who *will* help Father.'

'Who?'

He clenched his jaw. Why was she asking him all these questions? 'I don't know. I'll work it out along the way.'

'But what about the sergeant?'

'I'll take my chances.' He reached the door, took a deep breath and made to pull it open.

'Wait.' She drew alongside him and tugged at his hand. 'There's another way.'

He rounded on her. 'What?'

'Let me show you.'

He narrowed his eyes. 'If this is some kind of trick?'

She widened hers. 'Do you doubt the word of a gentle-woman?'

He snorted. There she went again, making out she was better than him.

'Look, Tom Garnett, I'm trying to help you, but it's your choice. If you would rather tangle with Sergeant Talbot and his blade . . .' She swept up her skirts and turned to go.

A distant clump of boots sounded outside.

Tom licked his lips and grabbed her sleeve. 'All right! All right! Show me.'

Chapter Fourteen

As they ran across the cobbles, Tom glanced up at the windows above them. They glittered down on him as if following his every move. He shivered. What if behind the glass, there were real eyes watching? The eyes of a spy. He pulled his cloak tight around him and hurried on.

'In here!' Cressida darted beneath a low doorway.

'Where are you taking me?'

'You'll see. Fetch a light, will you?' She jerked her head at the stand of flickering candles in the passage behind.

He frowned. 'Fetch one yourself.'

'What, and have hot beeswax burn my hands?'

He raised his eyebrows. 'But it doesn't matter if I burn mine?'

She glared at him. 'Look. Do you want me to help you or not?'

What choice did he have? He puffed out his cheeks,

strode over to the stand and lifted one of the candles from its spike.

'You first.' She pointed to a flight of stairs which wound down into the floor behind her.

Marching over to it, he shone the candle into the gloom. The light reached as far as the third step, then beyond it, nothing but blackness.

The sound of giggling echoed behind him. 'You're not scared, are you?'

He flushed. 'Don't be stupid!' He gripped the candle tighter and began to descend. He'd gone fifteen steps, maybe twenty, when the stairs ran out. He lifted the flame above his head. A stone passageway stretched in front of him.

A hand shoved him in the back. 'Keep going.'

'Get off me!' He jerked away and stomped along the passageway, boots crunching on the grit-covered flagstones.

'Stop. You've gone too far.'

He spun round. She was standing in front of a door set into the brick-lined wall. As he trudged back to her, she brushed her curls from her face, smoothed her skirts and raised a fist to the wood.

'Wh–what are you doing?'

'Making sure Grimwold, our cellar-keeper, isn't down here.'

'But what if he is?'

'Then I'll tell him he's wanted upstairs.' She rapped on the door.

He held his breath. Silence, except for the thump of his

heart against his ribs.

'It looks like we're in luck!' She flashed him a smile, lifted the latch and stepped inside.

Tom glanced up the passageway. What if Grimwold came back and found them in here? He'd like to see what excuse his clever cousin could come up with then. He frowned, then slipped in after her, shutting the door behind him. The candle flame jumped and flickered before settling to a steady glow. He peered around him. They were standing in a long, narrow room, its lime-washed walls studded with rows of brick shelves. On each shelf rested a line of large wooden barrels. A smell of overripe berries laced with a hint of leathery sourness hung in the air.

Cressida spread out her arms. 'Our wine cellar.'

Tom raised the candle and shone the light along the length of the room. There were at least a hundred barrels. Maybe more. He let out a whistle. 'There's enough wine in here to sink the whole English Navy.'

Her face took on a dreamy look. 'Why that sounds just like something from one of Mister Shakespeare's plays.'

He frowned. 'Mister who?'

She rolled her eyes. 'England's greatest living playwright, of course. But this is nothing. The cellar is much better stocked when the lord my father is at home.'

'Why do you call him that?'

'What?'

'The lord-my-father?' He mimicked her voice.

She blushed. 'Because . . . because . . . it's the proper thing to do.'

'The proper thing?'

She poked her nose in the air. 'I wouldn't expect someone of your position to understand.'

He scowled. These Montagues. They thought they were so much better than anyone else. He peered into the darkness beyond the shelves. 'I thought you said there was another way out.'

'There is. Through a tunnel.' Her eyes flashed in the candlelight.

His breath caught in his throat. He hadn't been expecting that. 'A tunnel?'

'Yes.' She sniffed. 'It runs from here to the town. I've never been inside it myself, but . . .'

'So how do you know where it goes?'

'The townspeople who attend the Mass use it. It saves any embarrassment with the local constable.'

Of course. It made perfect sense. It would be risking too much to have the common folk arrive for Mass on a Sunday at Cowdray's front gate. He glanced around him. 'So where's the entrance?'

Cressida pressed her lips together and frowned. 'It's here somewhere. I'm sure it won't take too long to find.' She turned and skipped her fingers daintily along a blank stretch of brickwork then stopped and pulled a face. 'It really is horribly dirty down here.' She dusted the front of her dress with her hand.

He shook his head. This cousin of his, she wouldn't last long in the world outside Cowdray's grey walls. An image of Father bruised and bloodied and lying in a stinking gaol cell flashed before him. He shivered and blinked it away before it could take a stronger hold.

They needed more light. Wedging the candle into a gap in the bricks, he fished inside his bundle for the one he'd taken from his room and lit that too.

'If the tunnel leads to the town, it's more likely to be on *this* side.' He ran the flame along the opposite wall, skimming the bricks with his left hand. Nothing there. He moved on past another shelf of wine barrels to the next clear space. His fingers brushed against something soft and sticky. He snatched them away and held them up to the candlelight. They were plastered in spiders' webs, peppered with the husks of dead flies.

A warm breath tickled the back of his neck. 'What on earth is that?'

'A bit of Grimwold's leftover breakfast.' He wiped off the mess on the leg of his fancy breeches.

She pulled another face, but this time, her eyes flickered with the trace of a smile.

He was about to turn back to the wall when a scratching noise came from his bundle. Jago! Of course! He'd always had a good nose for escape.

'Take this!' He thrust the candle at her.

'What are you doing?'

He fished Jago out of his box and dropped him on to his upturned palm.

She raised a hand to her mouth and took a step back. 'Put that . . . that creature back in its box.'

Ignoring her, he stroked Jago's head and set him on the

floor at their feet. 'Find me that tunnel entrance, boy, and when we get home, I'll get you the biggest cheese you've ever seen.'

The mouse gave a squeak and scampered off. Tom grabbed the candle from Cressida and hurried after him, tracking his every movement. Halfway along the next section of wall, Jago stopped. He twitched his nose and whiskers then squeezed himself flat against the dusty floor and disappeared.

Cressida let out a cry and wrapped her skirts tight around her legs. 'Where did he go?'

Tom grimaced. 'I don't know.' He crouched and traced his fingers along the bottom of the wall. The surface here had been lime-washed too, but it wasn't brick. It was wood. His fingertips caught a draught of cool air. He ran them in a straight line up from the floor. They snagged against something halfway up. A loop of rope.

'I think I've found something.'

She bent down next to him. 'What?'

'It looks like some kind of handle.' He tugged on the rope but it held fast. Ramming the candle into a nearby crevice, he gripped the rope with both hands and pulled. The section of wall lurched forwards. A cool rush of air flowed through the gap.

Jago had done it!

'It's a door.' He yanked again, but it was stuck fast. He glanced over his shoulder. 'Help me, can't you?'

She pouted. 'But I'll ruin my gown.'

'I'm sure the lord-your-father can buy you another.'

She hoisted her shoulders and gave him an icy stare. 'Are you mocking me?'

'We don't have time for this. What if Grimwold comes back?'

She didn't move.

'Come on. Please . . .'

She let out a sigh. 'All right, but just remember, I'm not one of your peasant playfellows.'

There she went again. Still, not long now and he'd be free of her and 'Granny' for good. 'Put your arms round me and hold on tight.'

Her arms circled his waist. He drew in a breath and braced himself. 'One. Two. Three. Pull!' He yanked on the door.

Nothing happened.

'Harder!'

Her fingers dug into his stomach. They pulled again. With a rickety groan, the door juddered then swung towards them.

Tom staggered backwards and thudded to the floor. There was a moaning sound behind him. He rolled over and looked up. Cressida lay flat on her back in the dust, curls plastered to her forehead.

He scrambled up. 'Are you hurt?'

She blinked then took a deep breath and sat up. 'I . . . I don't think so.'

'Here.' He hauled her to her feet.

She stared at the front of her dress. It was covered with smuts of dirt and cobwebs.

He felt a twist of guilt. 'I'm sorry.'

'It wasn't your fault.' She sniffed and shook out her skirts. A cloud of dust puffed up around her making her sneeze.

'You were right about the tunnel.' He jerked his head at the door.

'I was, wasn't I?' She gave a small smile.

'Er, well ... Goodbye then.' He grabbed the candle closest to him, slung his bundle over his shoulder and turned to go.

'Wait. I'm coming too.'

'What?' He spun round. If she thought he was going to take her with him ...

'Only as far as the other end.' She dabbed her nose with her kerchief. 'I want to see where it comes out.'

'But won't your granny be missing you?'

She twisted the kerchief in her hands. 'No, I don't think so. In fact, I doubt anyone would really miss me much, even if I left Cowdray for good.' Her bottom lip trembled.

He widened his eyes. 'What about your mother and father?'

She shook her head. 'The lord my ...' She glanced at him. 'I mean, *Father* spends most of his time at court these days. And now my brothers and sisters are married, Mother has no reason to stay here either.' Her eyes glistened. 'That's why I climb the tower each night.'

He frowned. 'What do you mean?'

'To watch for Father. In case he comes home. Except he never does.' She raised the kerchief to her cheek and turned away.

Was this a girl's trick to try and make him feel sorry for her? Tom wasn't sure. The tears looked real enough. But how could she be unhappy when she had everything anyone could ever want?

'Anyway' – she blew her nose and turned to face him again – 'I thought you might need some help getting your mouse back.'

Jago! She was right. He needed to track him down and quickly.

'All right.' He frowned. 'But just to the end of the tunnel. From there, I'm going on alone.'

She dabbed at her eyes again and nodded.

'Come on then, quick. Before Grimwold finds out we're here.' He took a deep breath, pulled his cloak around him and stepped through the door.

Chapter Fifteen

'Eugghh!' Cressida pressed her kerchief to her nose. 'How could anyone bear the smell?'

The light from the candle danced across the entrance of a rough-hewn passageway casting serpent-like shadows across its walls. A waft of dankness and the sound of dripping water came from somewhere further inside.

Tom cupped his hand round the candle flame and shone it over the jagged outcrops of rock above his head. 'I wonder how long it's been here?'

She shivered. 'Years from the look of all that green slime on the walls. Great-Grandfather probably ordered it to be dug when he had Cowdray built.'

'What for?'

Her eyes gleamed back at him cat-like in the darkness. 'Granny has always been a priest-squirreller. Father told us that when things got bad for the Catholics under the old

Queen, Granny would give them shelter and stow them away in secret hiding places until they could be got to safety overseas.'

He frowned. 'I thought you said Queen Elizabeth stayed here once?'

'She did. She and Granny were the best of friends.'

'But I don't understand. How could they be when they were on opposite sides?'

She shrugged. 'Granny is a Catholic, but she was always loyal to the Queen. At least that's what Father said.' Cressida fluttered her eyelashes and sighed. 'I suppose it's a bit like being an actor really.'

He shook his head. Typical Montagues. Saying one thing and doing another. That carving of the two-headed dog he'd seen in the Viscountess's room suited them well. But why was he wasting his time thinking about them? He needed to find Jago. He clicked his tongue against his teeth and made a chirping noise. The sound bounced away along the tunnel walls.

'Here, boy!' He set off into the darkness, candle held high, eyes scouring the ground for any sudden movement.

They kept on going, taking it in turns to call Jago's name. He had nearly given up hope when a shriek rang out behind him.

'Look! There!' A flash of white shot in front of them and disappeared into an opening on their left. Cressida clung to his elbow. 'Where did he go?'

Tom jerked up the candle and shone it into the space. 'In here.'

'What is it?' She peered over his shoulder into the velvety blackness.

'Some kind of cave, I think.' He stepped inside. As the candle flame steadied, its light fell on a row of wooden barrels stacked neatly against the back wall. There, on top of the nearest one, front paws raised, eyes shining like a pair of tiny red rubies, sat Jago. 'Hold this.' He shoved the candle at her and rummaged inside his bundle for a piece of cheese. 'Here, boy.' He held it out and crept towards him.

Jago sniffed the air and reached for the cheese with his paws.

'Got you!' Tom grabbed the base of the mouse's tail and scooped him up in his palm. He yanked his cloak to one side and nodded at his waist. 'Open my pouch.'

Cressida fumbled with the strings then flashed him a look. 'There's a knife.'

'Take it out.'

Gingerly she lifted his father's knife out and dropped it on the nearest barrel top.

He slipped Jago inside the pouch next to the silver tinderbox.

Cressida held the flame close. 'Where did you get him?'

'I rescued him from a trap, didn't I, Jago?' He reached in and tickled the mouse's whiskers.

'Jago? What made you call him that?'

'He's named after an old sailor me and William met down at the harbour once. He was a Cornishman, from a place called Mousehole. His hair was pure white, just like Jago's.'

She glanced up at him. 'Who's William?'

His chest tightened. He tied the strings of the pouch and snatched back the candle. 'Stop asking me all these questions, will you?'

She raised her eyebrows. 'Why? What's wrong?'

'Nothing! I don't want to talk about it. Let's go.'

'Tom?'

He spun round. 'Leave me alone!'

'But . . .' Her voice shrank to an urgent whisper. 'But I heard something.'

He held his breath. She was right. A grinding sound echoed up the main tunnel. He stuck his head out of the cave and peered in the direction they'd been heading. A pinprick of orange light bobbed in the distance. A torch. And from the dragging and grunting noises, whoever it was, they were shifting something heavy.

He turned. 'Grimwold?'

She stared past him, lips trembling, face white as chalk. 'Maybe . . . but wait. There's more than one of them.'

He twisted back. A second light had appeared behind the first. One was bad enough, but whoever they were, with two of them, they wouldn't stand a chance.

He snatched up his bundle. 'Come on! Let's get out of here!' He blew out the candle, then grabbed her by the hand and jerked her out into the tunnel. As they stumbled back up the way they'd come, she tripped and let out a moan.

'Shhh!' He steadied her, then tugged her after him, feeling his way with his free hand.

A crack of light appeared up ahead. The door!

'We've made it!' Shoving her through the opening, he turned and glanced back down the tunnel. The torches had disappeared. For a moment he thought he could hear muffled voices. Then . . . silence.

'I think . . . I think they've gone.' He snatched in a breath.

Cressida fanned her face then pulled out her kerchief and dabbed at her forehead. 'That was close. Who do you think they were?'

He took another breath. 'I don't know. Maybe Grimwold's got some smuggling friends.'

'What?' Her eyebrows shot up. She shoved her kerchief up her sleeve and turned on her heel.

'Where are you going?'

'To find Sergeant Talbot, of course. If these men are trying to steal our wine, they must be stopped at once and punished.'

'No, wait!' He seized her arm and swung her back round. If the sergeant came stomping around down here, he might as well forget about trying to escape now, or ever.

'Ow! You're hurting me!'

'Sorry.' Reluctantly he let his hand drop. 'But what's going to happen to me when your precious granny finds I've escaped?'

She narrowed her eyes. 'You've got a knife, haven't you? I'm sure a boy like you knows how to pick a lock and get back inside your chamber again before you're found out.'

He clenched his fists. She was still trying to put him down, even now. But wait. A bolt of panic shot through him.

'Where is it?'

'What?'

'My knife.'

Her eyes widened. A red flush spread across her cheeks. 'I . . . er . . . I must have left it back in the cave.'

He rolled his eyes and groaned. How could she have been so stupid? He snatched up the candle they'd left burning on the shelf and darted back to the tunnel entrance.

'You can't go back in there. What if one of the smugglers catches you?'

'I've got to. It's Father's.' He clenched his jaw.

'Suit yourself.' She gave a loud sniff. 'I'm going to find the sergeant.' She marched towards the cellar door, yanked it open and, with a swish of skirts, she was gone.

Tom sucked in a breath. He had to act quickly before she managed to raise the alarm. He peered into the tunnel and listened. The noises had stopped and there was no sign of the torches. The smugglers must have gone. Gripping his bundle tight against him, he slipped through the door and made his way back along the tunnel to the cave. All he had to do now was find the knife and get back upstairs before Sergeant Talbot arrived. As he shone the candle into the hollowed-out room, a glint of silver caught his eye.

Relief rushed through him. He snatched up the knife from the barrel top, raised the worn leather handle to his lips and kissed it. *I'm going to save you, Father, I promise. I don't know how, but I will.*

He was about to turn back into the tunnel when he heard a chinking sound. His heart lurched. He snuffed out the candle and dashed back into the cave. He groped towards the row of barrels. He'd almost reached them when something snagged his foot. He tripped and fell, stifling a groan.

The chinking sound grew louder.

'Who's there?' It was a man's voice. Gruff and hard.

He scrambled up into a crouch and held his breath, keeping a tight grip on his knife. A ball of flame shot up in front of him. As he staggered backwards, a rough hand grabbed him by the neck and yanked him off his feet.

'What are you doing snooping around in here, boy?' The hard, flat tones of the man's voice sounded familiar.

Dropping his bundle, Tom rammed the knife behind his back and swallowed hard. 'I – I – I was just . . .'

The smuggler thrust the burning torch up to his face. 'Just what?'

He jerked his head away from the heat. The man's grip tightened. The knot in Tom's cloak dug into his throat. The walls of the cave began to spin. 'P–p–please. I c–c–can't breathe.' He scrabbled at his neck, trying to free himself.

The smuggler loosened his grip and Tom dropped face first into what tasted like a pile of old sacks. He rolled over quickly, sucking in great gulps of smoky air. Slowly the walls of the cave stopped spinning. Keeping the knife pressed against his back, he made to stand.

A hand shoved him down again. 'Not so fast! Now explain yourself, Master Spy.'

Tom blinked, then sat up slowly. A pair of coal-black eyes glowed back at him from the shadows. He shuddered.

He'd seen smugglers once before when he'd peered through a spyhole in the wall of the Mermaid Tavern, but this one was more fearsome than all of them put together. Tall as a giant and wide as a ship's mast, with red-brown hair that hung in tangles to his shoulders and a beard and moustache to match. As he swung his head towards Tom, the flame flared across his face revealing an ugly red scar on his left cheek.

Tom gasped.

The smuggler crumpled his forehead into a mock frown. 'I am not a handsome subject for a portrait, 'tis true. But that's what a life of adventure does for you.' As he raked his fingers through his beard, a glint of yellow metal caught the light. The smuggler's mouth twisted into a half-smile. 'Pretty, eh?' He held up the little finger of his left hand.

Tom stared at the ring. It was fashioned from gold with the image of a bird's head stamped into it; its beak was curved like a hook, its eye picked out with a gleaming white stone.

'Know what the bird is?'

Tom shivered and shook his head.

'It's a falcon. A loner. Lives in the cliffs above the sea. So quiet and careful you wouldn't know he was there.' The man's eyes glittered. 'But if he's hungry and he gets you in his sights, watch out!' He balled his fist and shot it at Tom's head.

He ducked just in time.

The man threw back his head and laughed. 'With quick wits like that, Master Spy, you may yet live to fight another day. But' – he dug the torch into the ground between them and squatted down on his haunches – 'if your story does not please me, be warned.' He sliced a finger across his throat. 'For I will show you no mercy.'

Chapter Sixteen

Tom's heart pounded against his ribs. He looked over his shoulder. There was no way out. He still had the knife, but if he pulled it on the smuggler now, he'd easily overpower him. And what if his friend was on his way back to join him? He had to think of something and quickly. He glanced at the smuggler's frayed brown cloak and worn leather jerkin. Money. That was what men like him wanted. He would try and strike a bargain with him. Being a so-called Montague had to be worth something. He wiped a hand across his forehead and took a deep breath.

'My name's Tom. Tom Garnett.'

The smuggler raised his right shoulder in a shrug. 'Should that mean something to me?'

He stuck out his chin and tried to look brave. 'No. But I am the nephew of Lord Montague, the owner of this house. My uncle . . . he's very rich. He'd pay you well if you let me go.'

'Your uncle, eh?' The smuggler's eyes glinted gold in the torchlight.

Tom held his breath. Did he believe him, or was he working out the best way to kill him?

The smuggler's voice cut like a blade through his thoughts. 'We have met once before, I think.'

'Have we?' Tom frowned.

'A few nights ago, in the town. You were looking for the right road to Cowdray.'

Of course! It was him. The man outside the tavern.

The smuggler scratched his forehead. 'So if your uncle is Lord Montague, what are you doing skulking down here when you should be upstairs at his table feasting on roast beef, stuffed swan and the like?' He jabbed a finger at the rocky roof above them.

Tom reached for his bundle. 'I – I lost something. I thought maybe I might have left it here.'

The smuggler's eyes narrowed. 'You've been here before? And when, pray, was that?'

He licked his lips. 'A few moments back. I was with my ... my cousin.'

'Your cousin?' The smuggler thrust a hand beneath his cloak. 'And where is he now?'

Tom pressed his back against the cave wall. If he knew the truth, that Cressida was fetching the sergeant, he would slit his throat then and there. 'She ... she's gone, sir. She was afraid of the dark.' He blinked and looked away.

The smuggler laughed. 'And the spiders, no doubt. Well,

'tis no place for folk of noble blood, least of all their children.' He relaxed his arm.

For a moment Tom forgot his fear. 'I'm not a child. I'll be thirteen this Sunday.'

The man gave a low whistle. 'Thirteen, eh? Well, Master Spy, where I come from, you must earn the right to be called a man. And creeping about in tunnels, poking your nose into what doesn't concern you, is not the way to go about it.'

His cheeks flushed. 'I told you, I'm not a spy! I was looking for something.' He caught a sudden whiff of peppery smoke as the smuggler pushed his face up close.

'So tell me. Was it a wasted journey?'

Tom gripped the knife even tighter and dropped his gaze.

In one swift move, the smuggler reached behind and seized it from him. 'I see it was not.' He ran a sooty finger along the blade and whistled again. ''Tis a serious weapon for a boy. What do the initials stand for?'

Tom hesitated.

'Come now. It is a fair question.'

'Richard Garnett. My . . . my father.'

'And where is he now? Upstairs carousing with your grand relations?'

'No. He . . . he's in London.'

'On business?'

Tom shook his head and bit on his lip.

'What, then?'

He slid his knees up and hugged them to his chest. 'He's

in a place called the Clink.'

The smuggler cocked an eyebrow. 'Prison, eh? What's his offence?'

'He sheltered a man who needed his help.'

'That is no sin.' The smuggler frowned. 'There must be more to it.'

Tom pulled his cloak tight around him. The old Viscountess was right. He needed to be careful. What if this smuggler was a Catholic-hater too? He clamped his jaw tight shut.

Rough fingers lifted Tom's chin up. 'Tell me.' The smuggler's grip was firm but there was a flicker of warmth in his eyes.

His shoulders slumped. He was tired of trying to hide things. He opened his mouth and let the words spill out.

'The man was a priest. Father said he'd come in secret by ship from France.'

'A Jesuit . . . I see.' The smuggler pursed his lips. The skin beneath his right eye jumped and twitched as though some creature was burrowing beneath it, trying to get out. 'And how did he and your father meet?'

'By accident. Down at the harbour in Portsmouth. We live there. Father works for a merchant. The priest was sick. Father rescued him and brought him back home.'

'So what are you doing here at Cowdray?'

His chest tightened. 'Father tried to get the priest to safety. After they'd left, the constable and his men came for Mother, me and Ned – I mean Edward; he's my little brother. The constable questioned us and threw Mother in gaol and . . .' He shivered again at the memory of the treacherous words he'd spoken that had sealed his father's fate. If he confessed the truth, the smuggler would surely run him through. Not just for being a spy and a Catholic, but a coward too.

'Go on, boy.' The smuggler's tone had changed, grown quieter, softer even. 'I have no quarrel with papists.'

Tom drew in a breath and carried on. 'He . . . he let me and Edward go. Mother told me to come here and ask my uncle for help. Except . . .' He curled up his fists. 'Except, he's away at court and the old lady, the Viscountess, is in charge.'

'So?'

'She's arranged for Mother to be freed, but she won't help Father.'

'Why?'

'She says he's shown poor judgement.' He looked down and began picking at the knot on his bundle. The man might not hate Catholics, but it didn't feel right to share his new-found family history with a stranger.

The smuggler clicked his tongue against his teeth. 'The Viscountess was always a hard one.'

'You know her?' Tom jerked his head up.

The smuggler shifted on his haunches and grimaced. 'I was once in the employ of the old Lord Montague, the present lord's grandfather. I came here as a young man seeking to make my way in society by working for a noble family. But we didn't . . . how shall I put it? Warm to each other. He dismissed me after a few months' service. When he died, I returned for a while to work for your uncle. And after that'

– his eyes took on a faraway look – 'I followed a different path. But that's another story.' His gaze sharpened and focused back on Tom. 'Well now, Master Spy, I find myself in a fix.'

'Wh-what do you mean, sir?'

The smuggler flipped Tom's knife in the air and caught it by the handle. 'Your story sounds plausible enough. And the offer of payment for your freedom is an attractive one. But unless you happen to have some gold stashed in that pack of yours, I don't see how you can keep to your side of the bargain.'

Tom struggled to his knees. 'But if you'll just wait, I can go and get it.'

'From the Viscountess?' The smuggler snorted. 'I think that unlikely. As I said before, she is no friend of mine. No.' He tapped the side of his sharp, beaked nose. 'Another course of action is required.'

Tom's stomach twisted inside him. So the man was going to kill him after all. He closed his eyes and steeled himself for the blow.

Laughter echoed around him. A hand slapped him hard across the back. He flicked his eyes open.

'You misjudge me, Master Spy. I'm not going to run you through. Rather tie you up awhile. And don't worry. That old rascal Grimwold will find you eventually, though you must pray he beats the rats. Now' – he pulled the torch up from the ground and got to his feet – 'I have wasted enough time blathering. London is at least two days' hard journeying and I have an urgent appointment to keep there.'

London! A bolt of excitement shot through Tom. If he could get the smuggler to take him with him, he could seek out his uncle and beg him to save Father himself. But could he trust him? He glanced at the man's smoke-stained hands and scarred face. His stomach knotted again. He knew what Mother would say.

The smuggler pulled a length of rope from his belt.

Quick, Tom. Decide!

'Wait!' Heart thrumming, he grabbed his bundle and jumped to his feet.

'What is it?'

'The other night, you said . . . you said if we ever met again, I might repay you for the favour of setting me on the right road to Cowdray.'

The smuggler nodded slowly as if remembering. 'You are right, Master Spy. I did.' He shot him a glance. 'So what did you have in mind?'

'If you take me with you, I'll . . . I'll keep watch, fetch firewood, find water, look after your horse, get supplies for you and the other smugglers.'

'Smugglers, eh?' A smile curled across the man's lips. He gestured at his bundle. 'What's in your pack anyway?'

Tom held it close. 'Clothes and some things from home.'

The smuggler frowned. 'Planning on making a journey, were you?'

He shrugged.

The smuggler tugged on his beard and sighed. 'The business with your father troubles me. And it would seem the mistress of this place has been less than kind to you. I do not like injustice. Besides' – he raised the torch and looked him up and down – 'you may be of use to me after all.'

Hope sparked inside Tom. 'Do you really mean it, sir?'

The smuggler tilted his head to one side, then gave a quick nod. 'I will take you with me to London and in return you will work your passage as you have promised.'

'Yes, sir!'

'And if you prove yourself a worthy travelling companion, I'll do what I can to assist you in this business with your father.'

His heart jolted. 'You mean . . . help get him free?'

'I can make no promises.' The smuggler threw him a mysterious look. 'But, God willing, there might be a way . . .'

Tom's jaw dropped. This was even better than he'd hoped for. A wave of happiness surged through him. At last something good had happened. 'Yes, sir! Thank you, sir!'

The smuggler nodded and handed him back his knife. 'No need for "sir".'

'What shall I call you then?'

The man ran a finger over his ring and gave a crooked smile. 'The Falcon.'

'The Falcon?'

The man's eyes took on a distant look. ''Tis the bird on my family's crest, and a reminder to me of happier times.'

Tom frowned. A smuggler grand enough to have a family crest?

'Is there a problem?'

He shook his head. 'N-no . . .'

'Good. Now, time we were going.' The smuggler turned and ducked out into the main tunnel.

Tom held back for a moment. It wasn't too late to change his mind. If he was quick, he could make a dash back to the cellar. He rubbed his forehead. But what if the man – this Falcon – could really help him rescue Father? And even if he didn't, at least he'd be in London and could look for his uncle there. It was the only real chance he had. He couldn't let it slip. He took a deep breath, shouldered his bundle and ran after him.

The tunnel sloped uphill. As they crept along it, he thought he heard something above the chink of the Falcon's spurs. What if it was Cressida come back with Sergeant Talbot? She'd been gone long enough. He ran his tongue over his lips and glanced back in the direction of the cellar door.

A hand clamped his arm. 'Not having second thoughts, are you, boy?'

'No, but my cousin . . . she went off to get the sergeant . . .'

'The sergeant?' The Falcon's eyes flashed with anger. 'Why didn't you say so before?' He growled, then doubled his pace and hauled Tom deeper into the gloom.

Chapter Seventeen

As the slope of the tunnel got steeper, Tom struggled to keep up with the Falcon's great strides. At last, a faint blue circle showed ahead of them. The way out. It must be! Chest heaving, he kicked up his heels and put on a final spurt.

The circle of light grew steadily bigger and a gust of cold air stung his cheeks.

The Falcon jerked to a stop. 'This is it. Out you go.' He thrust him through an opening in the dark hewn rock.

Long, bony fingers snatched at Tom's head and shoulders. He twisted free and spun round, fists raised.

The Falcon snorted. 'It's not the undergrowth you should be afraid of, boy.' He swept the thick ropes of ivy to one side and pushed past him.

Tom followed, face burning. But the nip of the frost-chilled air soon cooled him down. He shivered and drew his cloak tight against him.

'Come on. And keep the noise down. We don't want the nightwatchman finding us.' Turning the torch upside down and ramming it into a mound of earth, the Falcon marched off down a narrow snaking path towards a clump of trees.

Tom stumbled after him. They passed beneath a tumble-down arch, its stones shining white in the moonlight. These must be the ruins on the hill he'd seen from his window. He darted a look behind. The tunnel entrance was set into the side of a steep wooded slope. He could just make out the meadow and the grey-green walls of the house beyond. How much longer before Sergeant Talbot came after them? He turned and hurried after the Falcon.

The path broadened out into a track beyond the trees. Halfway down it stood a horse and cart. Tom peered about him. So where was the other smuggler – the one he and Cressida had heard in the tunnel?

'Hurry, boy. This is no time for sightseeing. Not if your cousin has managed to raise the sergeant.' The Falcon snatched a pair of leather gloves from beneath his cloak. He pulled them on and strode towards the cart.

Tom hoisted his pack over his shoulder and sprang after him. The back of the cart was stacked up high, its contents hidden beneath a heavy grey sailcloth fixed with ropes to its sides. His shoulders sank at the sight of the lumbering great carthorse and the cart's giant, iron-rimmed wheels. He could already feel the bumps and jolts they'd have to suffer on the journey to London.

The Falcon nodded at the cart as if reading his mind. 'Fret not. There is a more civilized way for gentlemen.' He leapt up the side of the bank and disappeared into the trees. A moment later he scrambled down again leading a grey horse by the reins. He rubbed his gloved hand along the horse's charcoal-coloured nose. 'Meet Shadrach.'

The animal snorted and tossed his black mane. Tom sprang back as Shadrach's front hoof pawed the ground.

The Falcon gave a low chuckle and reined the horse in. 'A fiery name for a fiery steed.' Grasping the pommel of Shadrach's saddle, he slid his left boot into the stirrup then swung himself up on the horse's back. 'Come.' He bent down and held out his hand.

Tom glanced back the way they'd come.

'A problem, boy?' The Falcon fixed him with a glittering stare.

He flushed again. 'No, I ... er ...'

'Good. Then jump up behind me. Unless' – the Falcon jerked his head at the carthorse – 'you would prefer to jolt along like a bag of bones behind old Goliath there?'

Tom shook his head, then frowned. If they were on horseback, who would be driving the cart?

A rustle of leaves sounded on the track behind them. He twisted round. A tall, bearded figure in a black cloak and hat strode down the slope towards them, a sack slung over his right shoulder. As he approached he lifted his hat and a tumble of grey-streaked hair fell about his shoulders. Tom raised his eyebrows. He moved fast for an old man. But as the newcomer reached them and the moonlight clipped his face, he realized he'd been mistaken; he looked only a few years older than the Falcon.

'You took your time, Mister Browne. Any trouble?'

The man shook his head. He heaved the sack on to his left shoulder, wiped a sheen of sweat from his forehead then shot Tom a look and frowned. 'Who's this young jackanapes?' It was the voice of a gentleman, but terse and ice-hard. 'I wasn't expecting we should have company.'

The Falcon tightened his grip on Shadrach's reins. 'Truth to tell, neither was I. But as we both know, plans can change. Young Master Garnett is a friend of mine. He will be joining us on our trip to London.'

'Oh, he will, will he? Good of you to consult me!' Browne's eyes flashed silver in the moonlight.

The Falcon shrugged. 'I did not have the opportunity. He has promised to be useful to us on the journey. I have offered him safe passage in return.'

Browne shook his head again and scowled.

The Falcon shifted in his saddle. 'You needn't worry, Mister Browne. He will be my responsibility.'

The other man rammed his hat back on. 'He had better be. But if he steps out of line, and you do not deal with him, rest assured I will.' He fixed Tom with a menacing stare. Then, marching over to the back of the cart and raising the sailcloth, he swung the sack from his shoulder and thudded it down inside.

Tom shivered.

The Falcon reached down and patted him on the shoulder then trotted Shadrach over to Browne. 'What's in the sack?'

'Provisions.' Browne fastened down the sailcloth.

'I thought we had all we needed.'

'Not these ones. They're a rare sort.' He shouldered the horse away, stalked to the front of the cart and climbed up on the seat.

'How did you come by them?'

'I'll tell you later. Now can we go? The longer we sit here conversing, the more likely some prying telltale will discover us.'

The Falcon rode back to Tom, leant over and held out his hand again. 'Though it pains me to say it, Master Garnett, my friend is right. We must away from here at once, before the sergeant catches up with us. Come.'

Tom paused a moment, then blew out a breath and gritted his teeth. He could do this. He had to. Father was depending on him. He glanced at his waist-pouch, desperate to check on Jago, then shook his head. It would have to wait. He slid the pouch round on his right hip then let the Falcon haul him into the saddle.

The Falcon gestured for him to put his arms round his waist, then with a click of his tongue, he spurred Shadrach's flanks. The horse twitched and trotted forwards.

Tom stole a quick look back at Browne as they set off down the track. The man was a bad-tempered sort. Best to keep a wide berth of him. But, in spite of the doubts he had about his two travelling companions, he couldn't help feeling a sudden rush of excitement. He was on his way to London at last.

*

They passed through the town without disturbance. As they turned on to the main highway, the Falcon shook his head. ''Tis a pity we must travel at this snail's pace. But with a full load, we don't have much choice. The sooner we put some distance between ourselves and Cowdray the better.'

'What's in the cart, sir?'

The Falcon said nothing.

'Sir?'

He cleared his throat. 'Supplies. Courtesy of Mister Grimwold. Now keep your wits about you, Master Garnett. This stretch of road is notorious for cutpurses, highway robbers and the like.'

Tom tightened his grip.

The Falcon laughed. 'Not scared, are you?'

'No, sir.' He glanced over his shoulder. Beyond Browne and the cart, the road dwindled into shadows, its edges blurred by a line of bushes. He was about to turn back when a dark shape flitted across it.

'What was that?'

'Where?' The Falcon jerked Shadrach to a stop.

'Back there.' Tom pointed into the gloom.

The Falcon twisted in the saddle. 'See anything, Mister Browne?'

The cart rumbled to a halt. Browne rose from the seat and peered behind him. 'Nothing. The boy wastes our time with his lily-livered fancies.'

Tom flushed with anger. 'I'm no coward!'

The Falcon sighed. 'Pay no heed to my companion's

manners. 'Tis good that you keep a lookout, Master Garnett. But try not to see ghosts at every turn, or we'll not make London before Yuletide.' He kicked his heels against Shadrach's belly and they set off again.

Tom dragged his eyes from the bushes and focused on the white ribbon of chalk ahead of them. Whatever the Falcon and Browne thought, someone or something was tailing them, he was sure of it. And if they attacked – his fingers closed round the handle of his knife – he'd be ready for them.

Chapter Eighteen

Tom did his best to stay awake, but the warmth of the Falcon's body and the swaying of the horse rocked him to the edge of sleep. He leant his head against the Falcon's back and closed his eyes.

He woke with a start to find himself slumped across an empty saddle. He jerked up and twisted round. The horse and cart stood driverless some way back. Men's voices floated over the top of it. The Falcon's, then Browne's.

'Why take such a risk?'

'You dare to question my judgement when it was your foolhardy decision to bring that shrimp of a boy along? Anyway, like I said, I didn't have a choice. And besides, we might need something to barter with if things don't go to plan.'

Tom's stomach fluttered. What were they talking about? He gripped hold of the pommel and raised himself up in the saddle.

''Tis an insurance of sorts, but if we are caught with such a cargo . . .'

There was a muffled squealing.

'Zounds! We can't afford to have that with us all the way to London.'

A sudden thud and the squealing stopped.

'Wait, I didn't mean—'

'It worked, didn't it?'

'Yes, but not for long. We must find another solution, and soon.' The Falcon's voice was strained.

Tom sank back into the saddle and frowned. From the sound of it, Browne must have captured a wild hog. But why would the Falcon call that an insurance?

The sudden snap of a twig made him jump. Shadrach reared up on his hind legs, whinnying. Tom scrabbled for the reins. He missed and lurched backwards.

Oof! He slammed down on to the highway's rutted surface. He lay there for a moment, eyes closed, all the breath knocked out of him.

Footsteps crunched towards him. If the Falcon saw him like this . . . He gulped in a draught of frosty air, blinked and made to sit up. A cold point of metal dug against his throat, forcing him back down.

He froze. What if the Falcon had changed his mind and decided to kill him after all? He blinked again. The cloaked figure of a man loomed above him. But it wasn't the Falcon.

'Where's yer money?' The man's voice was muffled by a stained kerchief which covered the lower half of his face.

'I – I – I don't have any.' Tom made to swallow, but his tongue was solid as a lump of chalk.

'Don't lie.' A heavy boot rammed into his ribs. 'All travellers has some tucked away somewheres.' The man's eyes gleamed fox-like at him over the top of his mask.

Tom twisted his head. Where was the Falcon? He opened his mouth to cry for help.

'Keep quiet or I'll slit you from ear to ear.' The silver blade arced across his throat.

Tom flinched and snapped his mouth shut again.

'What's this?' The thief leant forwards and wrenched Tom's waist-pouch from his belt.

'Leave it alone!' He grabbed the man's boot with both hands and tried to topple him.

'Quiet, rat!' The thief shoved his foot down harder, undid the pouch strings and rummaged inside. 'Argghhh!' He flung the pouch to the ground, ripped the kerchief from his face and stuffed his finger in his mouth.

The pouch twitched and squeaked.

The thief's eyes widened. 'What devilry is this?' He jerked his boot up from Tom's chest and staggered backwards, nursing his finger.

A chink of spurs sounded behind them. 'None but of your own making.' The voice was low and menacing.

A flush of relief flooded through Tom. The Falcon. So he hadn't deserted him!

The thief spun round.

'Drop your weapon!'

There was a clink of metal against stone.

Tom rolled clear and hauled himself to his feet. He snatched up the pouch and felt inside. Jago's damp nose pressed against his palm. He heaved a sigh and looked up. The thief stood with his arms pinned behind him, the point of the Falcon's dagger pressed against his whiskery cheek.

'Now, cur, you are going to take a short walk with my friend here.' The Falcon swung the man round to face the shadowy figure of Browne.

The thief dropped to his knees and clasped his hands across his chest. 'P–p–please, sir. I'm just an old soldier, wounded in the Dutch wars. I didn't mean nobody any harm.'

The Falcon scowled. 'I dislike thieves. But a liar is even worse.' He nodded at Browne. 'I'll leave you to deal with him as you see fit.'

Browne grimaced then threw a loop of rope round the thief's neck, tied it in a noose and yanked him to his feet. He tugged on the rope. The man had no choice but to follow him like a dog on a leash.

A dark cloud swallowed up the moon and the pair of them disappeared from view.

Tom licked his lips nervously. 'He's not going to hurt him, is he?'

The Falcon furrowed his brow. 'Why so much concern? That trickster would have slit your throat and thought nothing of it.'

'I know . . . but still . . .'

'Listen. All Mister Browne is going to do is to truss him to a tree and leave him. If he's lucky, the local constable will find him before the wild hogs do. Either way, he will have learnt his lesson.' He tousled Tom's head with a gloved hand. 'Well done, Master Garnett. You were right after all. Someone *was* on our tail.'

A warm glow spread through him. The Falcon might be a smuggler, but he had a heart too.

'Now' – the Falcon glanced back up the road – 'we must go on. We have fifty miles to cover at least, and thanks to that scavenger, we have already lost valuable time.'

Tom followed him over to where Shadrach stood, cropping a patch of grass at the side of the road. 'How long have you had Shadrach?'

'Five years, maybe six. We've been on many an adventure together, haven't we, boy?' The Falcon patted the horse's muscled neck. 'It's thanks to his fleetness of foot I am still here today. He is a Spanish jennet. The best for a battle, though I know some who might disagree.'

'Battle?' Tom frowned. 'Were you a soldier?'

The Falcon looked up and narrowed his eyes. 'A soldier? Yes, and a real one. Not like that ruffler there.' He jerked his head over his shoulder.

'Ruffler?'

'A scoundrel who dupes poor travellers into thinking he's a military man fallen on hard times, then relieves them of their money and whatever else he can make off with.'

The cloud cleared and the moon lit up the road again. Tom turned. Browne and the thief were nowhere to be seen. A shiver rippled through him. He reached up and stroked Shadrach's ears.

'Where did you fight?'

'Over the sea in Flanders.'

'What was it like?'

'Hard and dirty.'

'Did you . . . did you kill anyone?'

The Falcon ran a gloved finger across the scar on his cheek. His face took on the same faraway look it had worn back in the tunnel when Tom had asked him how he knew the Viscountess.

'Sir?'

The Falcon started. His eyes flicked back to him. 'So many questions. A boy like you would do well in the King's spy service.'

An image of Mandrake meeting in secret with the stranger outside Cowdray's gate flashed into Tom's head. He was about to mention it when a piercing shriek ripped through the air behind them. Shadrach jerked his nose up and whinnied again.

Tom grasped the Falcon's sleeve. 'What was that?' He snatched a look in the direction of the trees.

'My, you two are jumpy as a pair of crickets in a pot. 'Twas nothing but an owl.' The Falcon mounted the horse and hoisted Tom up behind him. As he steered Shadrach back on to the track, there was a crunch of twigs and a tall, black-cloaked figure appeared from beneath a giant yew tree at the side of the road.

'Is he strapped up good and proper, Mister Browne?'

The other man gave a tight laugh. 'Let's just say he has learnt a lesson he will not forget.'

'Good. Then let us be off.' The Falcon clicked his tongue against his teeth and Shadrach started forwards.

What kind of lesson had Browne taught the ruffler? Tom glanced back at the Falcon's companion. He was standing by the side of the cart wiping something flat and shining against the sleeve of his doublet. After a few moments, he slid it down the side of his boot then pulled a length of rope from his belt, wound it round his elbow and threw it into the cart. As he climbed up on to the seat, he lifted his head and their eyes locked.

Tom shuddered and turned away. The threat Browne had made earlier to deal with him if he stepped out of line rang in his ears. And what about the argument he'd just overheard the two men having? If it was a hog Browne had caught, why had the Falcon been so angry?

He wiped his forehead and tucked his legs tight against Shadrach's warm flanks. One thing was true. If it hadn't been for the Falcon, he'd be dead by now. But Browne? He shivered. He didn't trust him. Not one little bit. The sooner they parted company with him the better.

Chapter Nineteen

Friday 1 November

They journeyed on in the moonlight, the clip-clop of hooves and the creak of cart wheels the only things to break the silence. From time to time, Tom looked back the way they'd come. The black ridge of the downs rose up behind them like a sleeping dog. The road was empty. Why hadn't Sergeant Talbot caught up with them yet? Perhaps Viscountess Montague didn't care about a few missing barrels of wine? After all, they had a cellar full of them. Would it be the same when she discovered he was gone too? Probably. She'd never pretended he was anything but an annoyance.

He sighed and wrapped his cloak tight around him. Who cared? He might be tied by blood to the Montagues, but they weren't family. The Falcon had shown him more kindness. In less than two days they'd reach London and then, with his help, he would work to get Father released.

The rocking of the horse lulled him into a doze. When he opened his eyes, the stars had faded and there was a soft, pink tinge to the sky. A blackbird struck up a tune. Another answered. Soon the air was filled with birdsong. Tom yawned. He ached all over and his legs and feet were numb with cold. Riding on horseback might be the way gentlemen travelled, but it was just as uncomfortable as sitting on a hard wagon seat. He stretched his arms and flexed his knees, trying to get some feeling back in them.

They travelled on, stopping at a chalk stream to water the horses and again in the afternoon to dine on some bread and a hunk of game pie the Falcon produced from one of his saddlebags. Tom was grateful for the chance to slip Jago some crumbs and a few drops of water when the others weren't looking. As the sun moved westwards, a line of hills rose ahead of them. The sound of a church bell rang out across the fields.

Tom sat up in the saddle and peered over the Falcon's shoulder. 'Where are we?'

'Outside the town of Guildford. We'll break there for a while and then travel on. It's another thirty or so miles to London and we need to get across the bridge by dusk tomorrow before they shut the city gates.' The Falcon tugged on Shadrach's reins, wheeled him round and trotted back to the cart. 'I'll go on ahead and get what is needed, Mister Browne. We'll meet again in the old chalk quarry next to the crossroads on the other side of town. You know the spot?'

Browne tipped the brim of his hat back and glared at him, grey eyes flashing. 'I do. But I don't see why you should have the pleasure of riding on horseback for the whole journey. We both know who the true gentleman is in this party. Let me take the jennet into town.'

The Falcon laughed. 'You ride Shadrach?' He shook his head. 'I'm afraid not. My horse is a wild one and would not take kindly to another man's weight on him.'

Browne jerked up from the seat. 'Do you doubt my horsemanship?'

'Not at all. All I meant is that we cannot afford any accidents. Now, down you get, Master Garnett.'

'What?'

'You will travel this next bit of the road with Mister Browne and Goliath.'

Tom's chest tightened. 'Can't I come with you?'

'No. We don't want to attract any undue attention. A man and a boy on a cart will pass unnoticed in the bustle of the marketplace. A man and a boy on a horse will not.'

Tom glanced at Browne. The black scowl on his face showed he was as pleased as he was at the news.

The Falcon twisted round in his saddle. 'Come now. We're wasting valuable travelling time.'

Slinging his bundle over his back, Tom slid down from the saddle and hobbled over to the cart.

'Until later then. Yaaa!' The Falcon flicked Shadrach's reins, dug in his spurs and set off in the direction of the town.

Tom looked up glumly at the empty seat next to Browne. He was about to climb on board when the tail of a whip flashed across Goliath's back. The horse and cart lurched forwards leaving him standing in the middle of the road. He curled his fingers tight against his palms. Why did the man have to be so mean to him? He shook his head. Folding his arms across his chest, he stumbled after them.

They travelled in silence in the dull grey afternoon light, past fields of ragged grass and hedges filled with brambles. As Tom found his stride, his legs and arms loosened up and he began to feel less stiff. The church bell rang out again. Three strikes. Back at Cowdray lessons would be nearly over for the day. He didn't miss them one little bit, or that slimy snake, Mandrake – in spite of his bad-tempered travelling companion.

The cart rumbled past a line of cottages and splashed through a shallow, sandy ford. Tom jumped across the river using a row of stepping stones. He was cold enough already without giving his feet a soaking. The grey flint bulk of a church rose up on their right. The town looked busy for the time of day, although some of the shopkeepers were already pulling in their goods and closing the shutters.

As they turned into the main street a rosy-faced woman walked past them, a basket strapped to her back. 'Apples,' she called. 'Come buy my sweet apples.' A grey-whiskered man stepped out of a shop and lifted up a tray of pies from the wooden window counter. Tom's stomach churned. It seemed an age since they'd last eaten. He'd give anything to sink his teeth into a juicy bit of spiced meat and pastry and let Jago have something tasty too. But he had no money. Browne and the cart trundled on ahead of him. No point asking him.

He swallowed back the saliva and plodded on up the hill, past women carrying baskets of eggs and men driving geese and cattle before them. The cart picked up pace as it crested the hill, threatening to leave him behind.

'Wait for me.' He ran alongside it, gasping for breath.

Browne glanced over his shoulder and shrugged. ''Tis no concern of mine if you can't keep up. I never wanted you along anyway.' He pulled a lace kerchief from his sleeve and mopped his forehead and the back of his neck, then flicked the whip across Goliath's back. The cart groaned on.

At the first crossroads out of town, Browne turned Goliath down a small, stony track, through a copse of birch trees and into a chalk-walled hollow in the hillside. He tugged hard on the reins, jumped down from the seat and strode round to the back of the cart.

Tom's mouth filled with water again. He was so hungry! Thirsty too. Perhaps Browne was fetching some provisions? He hesitated, then followed.

Browne had the sack laid out on the ground and was halfway through untying it. He jumped up as Tom approached. 'Keep away!' He planted himself in front of it, arms clamped across his broad chest, daring him to come closer.

'I . . . I thought there might be something to eat.'

Browne's eyes grew hard and narrow. 'Well, you thought wrong. I don't like your prying ways, boy. If it were up to me,

I'd have left you to the mercy of that ruffler. But luckily for you, my friend seems to think himself your protector. While we are getting our cargo to safety, I will humour him. But be assured' – he curled his top lip to reveal a row of dog-like teeth – 'things will change when we meet the others.'

Tom frowned. 'Others? What others?'

Browne untied a large leather bottle from the side of the cart. 'You'll find out soon enough. That's if your protector doesn't tire of you first.' He thrust the bottle at him. 'Enough talking. There's a spring further down the hill. Make yourself useful and fetch some water.'

Tom grabbed it and trudged off down the track. It wasn't fair. What had he ever done to Browne? And who were these *others*? Or was he just trying to scare him off? He gritted his teeth. Another day's travelling and they'd be in London. He'd bear it until then, for Father's sake. But the sooner the Falcon was back with them, the better.

He crunched over piles of dead leaves and twigs, squinting between the lines of thin white tree trunks. Where was this spring anyway? Or had Browne made it up to get him out of the way? A gust of wind carried a faint gurgling sound up from the hillside. Leaving the track, he slipped down a chalky slope and into a dank hollow filled with willow and alder. A smell of mould wafted up from the soft, boggy ground beneath his boots. He shivered. It was colder down here. Darker too. It would be a perfect place for an ambush . . .

A splash of silver caught his eye. He squelched through the mud and bent down next to a pile of moss-covered rocks. Water bubbled up from between the stones. Dipping his hand in, he scooped it to his lips. Cold and sweet. He scooped another mouthful then uncorked the bottle and positioned it beneath the flow.

He'd almost filled it when a crack of dead wood and a rustle of leaves sounded behind him.

He pulled out his knife and spun round.

'Steady, Master Garnett. 'Tis a friend, not a foe.'

'I . . . er . . . I know.' He jerked back his shoulders and stuck out his chest. The last thing he wanted was for the Falcon to think him a shadow-jumping coward.

'Good. Then put your blade away before you do me an injury and let's go and eat.' Seizing the bottle, the Falcon strode along the track to where Shadrach stood waiting beneath a large beech tree.

Tom rammed the knife back in his belt and hurried after him.

Chapter Twenty

Browne sat slouched against a mossy grey rock, the brim of his hat pulled over his eyes. He leapt to his feet as Tom and the Falcon approached and reached for his knife.

'No need to excite yourself, Mister Browne. 'Tis only us.'

Browne pushed back his hat and shot the Falcon a cold-eyed look. 'Did you get it?'

The Falcon slid a small stoppered jar from Shadrach's saddlebag. He ran a finger across the lid and frowned. 'The apothecary said it should be used sparingly to avoid lasting harm.'

Browne cracked his knuckles and thrust out a hand. 'Let me have it then.'

The Falcon considered for a moment, then tossed the jar to him. Browne caught it and marched round to the back of the cart.

'What's it for?'

'Mister Browne has an attack of the toothache, but it's nothing a little oil of mandrake won't cure.'

Tom pulled a face.

'Does something ail you too, Master Garnett?'

'No, but Mandrake was the name of the tutor we had at Cowdray.'

'He did not treat you well?'

'He didn't, but it's not that.' He licked his lips.

'What then? Come on, boy, spit it out.'

'Nothing, it's just that, well, I think he's a spy.'

'A spy?' The Falcon's eyes darkened. 'Why d'you say that?'

'I saw him meet with a stranger outside the gates the night I arrived at Cowdray. The stranger asked Mandrake if he'd found any evidence.'

The Falcon stiffened. 'Evidence? What kind of evidence?'

'I don't know. Something that could be used against the family I think. He talked about papists and setting a trap.'

The Falcon frowned. He gripped Tom by the arm. 'Did you catch sight of him, this stranger?'

'No. He kept to the shadows.'

'A pity.' The Falcon let his hand fall.

'There . . . there was something else.'

'What? Tell me.'

'The stranger talked about reporting back to a man called the Master.'

'The Master, eh?' The Falcon raked a hand through his

red-coloured locks.

Tom's eyes widened. 'You know him?'

'Not personally, no. But by reputation; although there are other less flattering names for him.' The Falcon gave a bitter-sounding laugh.

'Who is he?'

The Falcon's scar twitched. 'Robert Cecil, the Earl of Salisbury, the King's most powerful minister and servant.'

Tom's heart skipped a beat. 'The Viscountess told me it was Cecil who put my father in prison.'

The Falcon's eyes glowed with a sudden fire. 'Cecil is the Catholics' greatest enemy. Pouring venom in the King's ear about so-called papist rebellions and plots, all to turn him against the true faith.'

'So you are a Catholic too?'

The Falcon flashed Tom a look then thumped his fist against his chest. 'Yes, boy. Through and through.'

A moaning sound came from the back of the cart. The Falcon jerked round. 'Is everything all right, Mister Browne?' His voice was knife-sharp.

Browne stuck his head above the sailcloth. 'It will be when this potion kicks in.' He dipped out of sight again.

More moaning. Muffled this time. Tom allowed himself a secret smile. It looked like the mandrake oil was as unpleasant as the man who shared its name.

The Falcon's jaw twitched.

The moaning stopped.

'At last.' He let out a sigh. 'Now, food. A soldier cannot fight on an empty belly. Here.' He reached inside the saddlebag and threw Tom a leg of cooked chicken and a hunk of bread. "Twill build your strength for the rest of the journey. We won't be stopping again until we reach the Duck and Drake.'

'The Duck and Drake?'

'An inn in London, just off the Strand. We are set to meet some of our friends there.'

The hairs on the back of Tom's neck prickled. So Browne had been speaking the truth.

'No need to look so worried, Master Garnett. My comrades are good fellows.' The Falcon cast a glance in the direction of the cart and frowned. 'With one or two exceptions.' He put an arm round Tom's shoulder and pulled him close. "Tis through them I hope to do what I can to get your father freed.'

A tingle of happiness spread through him. So the Falcon still meant to help him. 'If you could, sir, I'd do anything to pay you back.'

'I might take you up on that.' The Falcon's teeth flashed white against his beard. 'Now eat.' He dropped his arm and turned back to the saddlebag.

Tom kicked a pile of dry leaves together, threw himself down and sank his teeth into the chicken. It tasted of melted butter and herbs. He took another bite. Something wriggled against his waist. Jago. He'd forgotten all about him. He must be hungry too. He glanced at the Falcon. He was busy pressing a pinch of tobacco into a long clay pipe. Tom reached inside his waist-pouch and scooped Jago out. The mouse blinked in the light. 'Here, boy.' He broke off a piece of bread and dropped it on to his palm.

A shadow fell over them. 'So, you *do* have a friend?'

Tom's fingers closed over the mouse's small white body.

'Let me see.' The Falcon squatted down next to him.

Tom hesitated, then dropped Jago into his outstretched hand.

The Falcon held him up by the base of his tail. 'He's a curious-looking fellow.' He stroked the mouse's back with his little finger. A late burst of evening light caught his ring. The bird's eye sparked. Jago let out a squeak and pawed at the air.

'Twitchy, isn't he? A bit like his master.' He winked and dropped the mouse back into Tom's palm.

Tom flushed and looked at his boots.

The Falcon settled down against a nearby tree. 'Where did you find him?'

He looked up again. 'In a trap in our stable. I wouldn't have been allowed to keep him normally, but things changed after . . .' A lump rose in his throat. He swallowed against it.

'Go on.'

He took a deep breath. 'After my brother William died.' He dropped his gaze again.

'What happened?'

'He caught the plague last summer.' Tom drew in another breath and let it out slowly. Speaking the words had hurt, but not quite as much as he'd thought they would.

The Falcon clicked his tongue and shook his head. 'I'm sorry to hear it. But the Lord will have his reasons for taking him so young. Perhaps he was too good for this earthly life?'

Tom's chest tightened. He didn't know about God, but William was Father's favourite, of that he was sure. And with good reason. His brother would never have betrayed him. Not like he'd done. His eyes pricked. He blinked and gritted his teeth. He was going to put that right though. He was determined.

The Falcon busied himself making a flame with the contents of his tinderbox. Soon the sweet smell of tobacco swirled through the twilit air. 'Ahhh! Nectar.' He pulled on the pipe and blew an apple-sized smoke ring above his head. 'So what sort of trade is your father in, Master Garnett?'

'Wine and woollen cloth from Flanders.'

'Flanders, eh? Scene of my soldiering days.'

'Who did you fight with?'

'The Spanish, against the heathen Dutch.'

'Do you mean the Protestants?'

'They go by that name too, yes.' The Falcon puckered his lips as if the taste of the tobacco was no longer to his liking. 'I had some scores to settle.'

'What sort of scores?'

The Falcon sighed and ran a finger round the smooth white clay of the pipe bowl. 'I was not born a Catholic. I became one when my father died and my mother married a man of the true faith. Since then, like you and your family and so many other believers, I and my kinfolk have suffered great persecution and injustice for our beliefs. So when the Spanish King put out a call for men to help defend his territories in the Low Countries against the heretic

Protestants, I knew I must answer it. Though I did not bargain for the souvenirs I might pick up along the way. This one' – he tapped at the scar on his cheek – 'was courtesy of a Dutchman's sword. Though, in the end, my own blade had the better of him.' He gave a grim smile.

'Does it hurt?'

'Now and again.' His face clouded over. 'But nothing compared to the pain I feel daily for the suffering of honest, God-fearing men and women. People like your father, treated like a common criminal because he dares to stay true to the faith. We believed things might get better after the death of the old Queen – no doubt your father hoped the same?' He shot Tom a look.

He nodded, remembering the conversations between his parents at mealtimes.

'But in spite of fine promises, they have not.'

'Promises? From who?'

'Those in power.'

'You mean the King?'

The Falcon shrugged. 'Those that advise him.'

Tom's heart jumped into his throat. He glanced over his shoulder. This was treasonous talk and they both knew the penalty. 'But you wouldn't take up arms against him?'

The Falcon frowned. 'Although he gave us reason to hope otherwise before he took the throne, King James has proved this past year he is no friend of the Catholics. Mark my words' – he shook his head – 'only trouble will come of it. But I have said enough.' He tapped the bowl of his pipe against the side of his right boot, stretched out his long legs and closed his eyes. 'Get some sleep, Master Garnett. We will be starting off again as soon as night has fallen.'

Tom lifted Jago from the front of his doublet, opened his bundle and slipped him into his box. Then, covering himself with his cloak, he pulled out the prayer book and re-read the inscription in the dying light. Mother wouldn't approve of what he was doing. Joining up with a band of smugglers. Men who were thieves and, in Browne's case, maybe worse. But he'd done it for the best of reasons. And although the Falcon might have his grudges and secrets, he could trust him, he was sure of that now. With his help, God willing, he'd get Father freed and give him and Mother a reason to be proud of him too.

Chapter Twenty-one

Saturday 2 November

'Wake up, boy. We're almost there.'

Tom's head lolled forwards. He blinked. A line of misty grey hills stretched across the horizon, studded with speckles of milky orange light. London. After another night and day's riding it must be! His skin prickled. Somewhere down there lay the Clink and Father locked away inside it. He closed his eyes and clasped his hands together. *Please, God, keep him safe.*

As they drew closer, scatterings of low cottages gave way to two- and three-storey houses which pressed in on both sides like snaggles of black teeth. The stink of rotting vegetables and manure rose up from piles of rubbish strewn across the road.

'Welcome to Southwark,' the Falcon called back to him.

'The lawless side of the river. Brawls and killings happen here in broad daylight. Why, even a playwright or two has committed murder in these very streets.'

Tom tightened his grip round the Falcon's waist.

He laughed. 'Fear not, boy. You will be safe with me.'

A tide of mist surged towards them. It swallowed up houses, taverns and churches, sucking everything it touched into its clammy grey depths. Fingers of damp twisted through Tom's hair and trailed across his cheeks. He shivered and clutched his cloak tight about him.

''Tis only a river fog.' The Falcon's voice sounded muffled. 'We will be clear of it once we reach the high ground about St Paul's. In the meantime we must go carefully. The streets are full of vagabonds and drunkards. And in this smoke it is easier for them to make their mischief.'

As if conjured by the Falcon's words, shadowy figures sprang up out of the fog and lurched towards them, their voices rising and falling like the calls of ghostly sea birds.

'Help a good man fallen on hard times, sir.'

'Take pity on a poor woman. Ten mouths to feed and not a penny in her purse.'

A bony hand shot out and grabbed Tom by the leg. 'Show charity, noble captain. Give me a halfpenny so I may slake my thirst.'

'Get off me!' He jerked away, but the hand gripped tighter, threatening to topple him from the saddle.

The Falcon wheeled Shadrach about. 'Stay back, ruffian!' A flash of silver sliced through the fog. The shadow shrieked a curse and melted away.

The Falcon rose up in the saddle and peered into the mist. 'Are you still with us, Mister Browne?'

A muffled creak of wheels sounded in reply and the lumbering grey shape of Goliath appeared like a spirit horse before them.

'We must get to the bridge and through the city gates before they shut them for the night.'

'I am as aware of that as you.' Browne cracked his whip against the tired horse's rump.

The Falcon steered Shadrach round again and urged him on. The stench of muck hung heavy in the air, and cutting through it, something sharp and salty, like the smell of the harbour at home. They passed a great church, its tower twice the size of St Thomas's. A small distance on, a gatehouse loomed out of the mist.

The Falcon nodded at the battlement-topped walls. 'Pass through the gatehouse and we are on the bridge.'

Tom leant back in the saddle and peered up at it. 'What are those?' He pointed to a line of stakes, topped with what looked like giant turnips.

The Falcon gave a deep sigh and shook his head. 'Rather ask who. The heads of so-called traitors. Put on spikes that the crows may feast on their soft bits and men may learn a lesson.'

A surge of bitter liquid flooded Tom's throat. What if Father was dead already, his head up there now, his eyes picked clean by the birds? He swallowed hard. No. It couldn't be true. He wouldn't let it be. Father was alive, and with the Falcon's help, he was going to save him. He gripped his bundle tight against him and focused on the road ahead.

Halfway across the bridge, at a gap between the houses and shops that lined it, the Falcon jerked his head upstream. 'A wherry-ride up river is the place where the King and his ministers make their laws.'

Tom craned his neck.

'You cannot see it from here, but 'tis not far from where we are bound, so you may yet get your chance.' The Falcon pulled on Shadrach's reins and nodded at the inky black current which shone through gaps in the fog below. 'Men have died trying to shoot the rapids beneath the bridge for fun at turn of the tide. Down below in the river mud is a graveyard full of their bones.'

Tom shivered. Riding horseback might be uncomfortable, but at least you couldn't drown doing it.

Once across the bridge, the Falcon reined Shadrach to a stop and waited for Browne to catch them up. As the cart rumbled into view, Browne stood and waved them on. 'You go ahead. I will stow the cargo in the place we discussed.'

'What about the provisions?'

'Don't worry, man. I will see to them later.'

'As you wish.' The Falcon dipped his head. 'Now, Master Garnett, we must hurry. My friends are waiting.' With a quick jab of his heels, he urged Shadrach along the road ahead.

Tom heaved a sigh of relief. He'd be happy if he never saw Browne again. Why the Falcon kept company with him was a mystery.

They followed a route of winding alleys that led up out

of the river fog and past the great cathedral of St Paul's. The street widened out beyond it and Shadrach's hooves struck stone. Tom gaped at a series of great houses, each one more magnificent than the last. As they drew level with a particularly grand set of gates topped with golden spikes, the Falcon slowed Shadrach to a walk. Tom peered through the iron bars. Beyond them stood a palace complete with turrets and rows of glittering black windows set around a fine stone courtyard.

'Is this where the King lives?'

The Falcon snorted. 'No. But it might as well be. Remember we spoke about that Catholic-hater, Cecil?'

He nodded.

'Well, this grand house belongs to him.'

'So why does he hate us so much?'

The Falcon's jaw clenched. 'Because if we were to restore England to the truth faith again, he would lose everything his tyrant ways have gained for him. Position. Riches. Power.' His eyes narrowed to two black chips. 'In all likelihood, his life too. Be assured, Master Garnett, that hunchbacked toad will not rest until he has rooted us out and killed every one of us.' He shot a look back through the gates then gave a grim smile. 'It is some small comfort that my friends and I meet hard by his palace, yet he and his watchers have not yet discovered us.'

Tom frowned. 'What do you mean?'

''Tis of no matter.' The Falcon kicked his heels hard against Shadrach's flanks. 'Onwards, Shadrach. We are already late for our meeting.'

They set off again at a light trot. A few moments later, the Falcon steered Shadrach away from the grand paved road and down a side street of dingy-looking houses.

They were halfway along it when a door on their right burst open, shedding a pool of yellow light on to the mud-slicked cobbles. A man stumbled out followed by a storm of jeers and cock-crows.

The Falcon laughed. 'Our destination betrays itself.'

They rode past him and pulled up in front of a large gate set into a wall. The Falcon leant forwards and banged against it with his gloved fist. With a jangle of metal and a scrape of wood, the gate swung slowly open. A pale-faced boy gripping a flickering candle peered up at them.

'We're closed.'

'You know me, lad. I have business here.' The Falcon leant down. His face and beard glowed orange in the light from the flame.

The boy's eyes widened. 'Yes, sir.' He leapt smartly to one side.

They passed beneath an arch and into a cobbled court-yard, lit by a line of blazing flares. Two rows of crooked galleries, one stacked above the other, ran round the inside of the yard with space against the back wall for stabling.

The boy darted alongside them and held out a grubby hand. 'Take your horse, sir?'

The Falcon dismounted, tossed the boy a coin and handed him Shadrach's reins. Clutching his bundle, Tom slid down from the saddle and made to follow.

The Falcon raised a hand. 'Wait here, Master Garnett.

My friends are not expecting you. I must prepare the way.' Spurs chinking, he strode across to a small oak door set into the wall of the arch. As he opened it, a low hum of voices spilled into the yard. Then the door slammed shut and both man and voices were gone.

Tom took a step and winced. His legs felt stiff as a pair of skittles. He clapped his arms round his chest and peered at the row of doors and windows set into the gallery walls.

'Those be lodgings for gen'l'men.' The boy stepped out in front of him wiping his hands down the side of his breeches. 'Your master sometimes takes a room here.'

He bristled. 'He's not my master.'

'Begging yer pardon, I'm sure.' The boy's eyes flashed over his clothes. 'You might want to clean yourself up a bit before you goes in there. Mister Hackett, the landlord, he ain't much keen on beggars.' He scooped up a fistful of straw from the ground and offered it to Tom with a cocky grin.

Tom glanced down at his dusty makeshift cloak and mud-spattered boots. The boy was right. He was a mess. He hesitated then snatched the straw and used it to scrub off the worst of the muck.

'Your master and his friends – they seem like a fine bunch of fellows.' The boy shoved a piece of straw in his mouth and chewed on it. 'Secretive, though.' He narrowed his eyes.

'What d'you mean?'

'Nothing. Just, well, they don't mix with the other drinkers. They're in there now.' The boy tipped his head towards the inn. 'Tucked up in their usual dark corner, like rats in a hole.' He gave him a sly smile.

Tom balled up his fists. 'What are you saying?'

The boy raised his hands and took a step back. 'No need to take offence.' He flicked the coin the Falcon had given him into the air and caught it one-handed. 'I'm mighty thirsty, so if you'll excuse me, good sir . . .' He gave a mock bow then pushed past him towards the inn door and disappeared inside.

Tom wished he could follow the boy into the warm, but the Falcon had said to wait. He kicked at the straw, then trudged over to the stables. Shadrach stood in one of the stalls feeding from a leather pail. Tom's stomach grumbled. He'd give anything for a slice of pie and something to drink. How long was the Falcon going to be? He shot a look back at the door, but it stayed firmly shut. He sighed and slumped down in a pile of fresh straw. A tapping sound came from Jago's box.

'I'll get you out in a moment, boy.' He buried his face in his cloak, closed his eyes and drifted into a fitful sleep.

A crunch of footsteps woke him.

'This is no time for napping.'

He blinked. 'I wasn't . . . I was . . .'

The Falcon yanked him to his feet, black eyes sparking. 'Save your excuses for another time.' He strode over to Shadrach and unhooked the bags from the saddle. 'Now hurry, we have kept my friends waiting long enough.'

Chapter Twenty-two

The Falcon led Tom inside and down a narrow, wood-panelled passage. A warm glow of orange light spilled from a doorway up ahead. As they drew near it, the hum of voices became a buzz. A man in a velvet doublet and breeches stumbled out into the passage and lurched past them, hand pressed to his mouth.

The Falcon clicked his tongue. 'A gentleman in his cups is a sad sight indeed. Come. This way.' He steered Tom through the door and into a low-ceilinged hall lit by the sooty flames of dozens of candles.

The stink of tobacco smoke, hops and stale sweat made Tom's head spin. He muffled his nose with his sleeve and glanced around. A handful of well-dressed men stood propped against a low wooden counter on his left. Behind the counter, two potboys in aprons ran up and down filling jugs of ale from barrels on a rack. To his right, groups of men sat at long tables lifting mugs of beer, drawing on clay pipes or sinking their teeth into crusty brown pies dripping with meat juice. His mouth watered. If he could only have a bite . . . He scanned the men's faces wondering which of them were the Falcon's friends.

'We have a private room at the back,' the Falcon called over his shoulder. 'You can't hear your thoughts in here, let alone your words.' He walked swiftly towards a low wooden door set in a wall next to the fireplace. He raised his fist, rapped three times and paused, then lifted the latch and stooped inside.

Tom faltered for a moment, then took a deep breath and darted in behind him. He blinked. The room was in darkness, save for the glow of an oil lamp set on a table at its centre. Round the table four hunched figures sat deep in conversation, their voices low and urgent-sounding.

'Give me your bundle and your cloak.' The Falcon held out his hand.

'But . . .'

'You can have them back when we leave.'

Reluctantly Tom unhooked his bundle from his shoulder then tugged the blanket over his head. The Falcon stowed them behind the door next to the saddlebags. He rejoined Tom carrying the leather water bottle and cleared his throat. 'Here is the boy.'

The conversation stopped. One by one the men raised their heads. Shadows leapt like black and gold serpents across their faces.

The Falcon nudged him. 'Step closer. They'll not bite.'

Tom licked his lips. The frowns the men wore suggested otherwise.

The man nearest to him pulled out his stool and stood. He was tall and square-chested with shoulder-length fair hair. A neat gold moustache and beard forked over the top of his starched white ruff. The front of the black leather doublet he wore glinted with a scattering of silver-painted stars.

'Come.' He beckoned with his finger.

Tom didn't move.

The man raised an eyebrow. 'Are you a man or a mouse?'

One of the others made a squeaking noise and the room filled with laughter.

Tom crossed his arms and stuck out his chest. He wasn't going to stand there and let them call him a coward. Not after all he'd been through. He took a step forwards. 'A man, sir.'

'The right answer, for I am Robin Cat and it would grieve me to have to eat you before we had become properly acquainted.' The man's green eyes twinkled and a smile flickered across his lips.

Tom's cheeks flushed. 'I'm not a fool, sir.'

'Well said, Master Garnett.' The Falcon gripped his shoulder and gave it a reassuring squeeze.

'Zounds, man!' one of the others muttered. 'Anyone would think you were his father.'

The Falcon fixed the speaker with a hard stare. 'The boy has spirit and should be commended for it.'

'We admire spirit, don't we, friends?' Robin Cat walked

up to the Falcon and slapped him on the shoulder. 'Come and join us. You and the boy must be hungry after so much time on the road.' He led them over to the table, pulled out two stools and signalled to one of his companions to pour the Falcon a mug of ale.

The Falcon passed Tom the bottle of water. He uncorked it and took a swig.

'Eat!' Robin Cat gestured at a dish piled high with wedges of spicy-smelling meat pie.

Tom held back but then hunger got the better of him. He grabbed a slice and crammed it in his mouth. The taste of beef and onions exploded on his tongue and a trickle of warm meat juice ran down his chin. He wiped it off with the back of his hand and took another bite.

'Good, eh?' Robin Cat winked at him and sat back down. 'Now, Tom, is it?'

He nodded and gulped down another mouthful of water.

'My friend here, the Falcon I think you call him, tells me your father is in trouble?'

'Yes, sir, Mister Cat.'

'Robin, please.'

'Er, yes, sir, Mister Cat.'

The other men sniggered. Tom clenched his jaw, cursing his mistake. Robin Cat ignored them and nodded for him to go on.

'My father . . . he rescued a priest and now he's locked up in the Clink. I came here to . . . to save him. The Falcon said you might be able to help.'

The man next to him made a choking noise, as if a piece of pie crust had stuck in his throat. The Falcon banged his mug down and glared at him. The man flushed and fell silent.

Robin Cat frowned. 'Hmmm. I see. Well, I am mighty sorry to hear of your father's misfortune, but I don't quite see how . . .'

Tom's heart felt suddenly heavier than a sack of stones. He glanced at the Falcon, but he was staring at the oil lamp, his mouth fixed in a hard line. They had to help . . . 'Please, sir.' He clutched at Robin Cat's sleeve. 'I've come all this way. You're' – his voice quavered – 'you're my last chance.'

Robin Cat's frown deepened. He stroked his moustache and turned to the Falcon. 'What were you thinking of?'

The Falcon took a swig from his mug, then cleared his throat and looked up. 'As I told you before, I have made no promises to the boy. But if he agrees to help us in our mission, then surely it will be possible to secure a royal pardon for his father?'

Tom's heart lurched. Mission? What mission?

The man next to him jerked up from his stool. 'Are you mad? How do you know we can trust him?'

'Wait!' Robin Cat held up his hand. 'There is a lot at stake for this boy. His father's life.' He narrowed his eyes. 'Perhaps his own too.'

Tom loosened the collar of his doublet and glanced round the table. What was he talking about? And why were the others so angry?

'The boy says he is no fool. So, here is my proposition.'

Robin Cat turned back to face him. 'We will let you in on our plans, Tom, but first you must agree to help us.' His eyes grew narrower still. 'And you must swear never to reveal them to anyone.'

Tom chewed his top lip. Robin Cat was trusting him with a secret. But what if, once he knew it, he didn't want to be part of it?

A low muttering started among the other men.

Tom flashed a look at the door. It wasn't too late to leave and seek out his Uncle Montague. But London was a big place. What if he couldn't find him, or he refused to help? Then he'd be worse off than he was now. Alone on the dark dangerous streets full of murderers and cutpurses. Miles from home . . . He glanced at the Falcon. A bubble of hope sprang up in him. He wouldn't put him in danger. He was trying to help him. That's why he'd let him ride with him to London.

The muttering grew louder.

'Enough!' Robin Cat thumped the table with a gloved fist. 'Or have you forgotten who is the captain here?' He glared at his men, jaw muscles twitching. They fell silent. 'Now, Tom, do you agree?'

Tom took a deep breath and met Robin Cat's gaze. 'Yes, sir, Mister Cat. I mean, Robin.'

'Good. But remember, it will not go well for you if you betray us. Will it, lads?'

The others were quick to growl their agreement.

A line of sweat pricked Tom's forehead. He wiped it away with his sleeve. 'On my mother's life, I swear I'll keep it secret.'

Robin Cat threw him a sharp-eyed look then gave the Falcon a quick nod. 'Proceed, my friend.'

The Falcon turned. He gripped Tom by the shoulders and fixed him with a coal-black stare. 'Remember we spoke earlier of Robert Cecil? Of his evil influence over the King? And how he wages war against us Catholics?'

'Yes, sir.' Tom had heard enough about that man to be convinced what he said was true.

The Falcon let his hands drop, then clasped them together and twisted the ring on his little finger. 'Our plan is simple. To purge both King and country of his poison so that we can be free to worship openly again without fear of persecution.'

Tom's jaw dropped. 'But how?'

'We intend to kidnap him and send him to the Spanish King to deal with as he sees fit.'

A lump formed in Tom's throat. He swallowed against it. 'But . . . but won't King James be angry?'

The Falcon's eyes flashed orange in the oil lamp's glow. 'Once rid of that black spider and his web, the King's sight will clear and he will see the justice of our cause. Besides, we have an ally in the Queen. 'Tis no great secret that, in spite of outward appearances, she is a follower of the one true faith.'

Robin Cat furrowed his brow and cupped his chin in his palm. 'So tell me, where does our young friend here fit in?' But the curl of his lips and the amused look in his eyes told Tom he already knew the answer.

''Tis obvious. He can help us dig the tunnel that will take

us beneath Cecil's house and up into his cellar.'

A tunnel? Tom's eyes widened.

'Ah yes, the tunnel.' Robin Cat's smile broadened. 'The Falcon is right. We are full-grown men and not accustomed to such confinement. Whereas you, on the other hand . . .' His eyes flitted over him. 'You are nimbler and will fit better into tight spaces.'

The man next to Tom grunted. 'Puny, more like.' More sly laughs.

'Manners, friends!' Robin Cat shot them a warning look. 'I did not mean that at all.' He clutched Tom's arm. 'You are both brave and strong. We have heard of your exploits on the road. Standing up to cut-throats and the like. A man after my own heart.' He gave him a playful punch on the shoulder.

Tom frowned. 'But what about my father?'

Robin Cat laughed. 'And shrewd too! Fear not. The first thing the King will do when we have freed him of that crookback Cecil's influence will be to pardon all those who have been imprisoned for their faith, your father included. Eh, my friend?'

The Falcon hesitated for a moment, then nodded.

'So, Tom.' Robin Cat fixed him with his sharp green gaze. 'Are you with us?'

The others watched him, waiting for his answer.

Tom's frown deepened. It wasn't what he had expected. But this Cecil was the cause of much misery. Everybody said so, even the Viscountess. It was because of him Father and the priest were locked up in prison. For England to be rid of him would surely be a good thing. And if Robin Cat was speaking the truth, once Cecil was out of the way, Father would be a free man. He clenched his fists and took a deep breath. 'Yes.'

'Good lad.' Robin Cat lifted the jug and recharged everyone's mugs. 'A toast. To our mission. May it be the success we all hope and pray for.'

The Falcon ruffled Tom's hair. 'Well done, boy. You'll not regret it.'

Three short raps sounded on the door.

'Who's that?' The Falcon leapt to his feet and drew his dagger.

'Hold, man.' Robin Cat jumped up and put a hand on his arm. ''Tis a friend. They have given the signal.'

The Falcon frowned. He sheathed his dagger, strode to the door and opened it. Two men stepped inside. The first Tom didn't recognize. He was dressed in a black cloak and tall felt hat, the lower half of his face covered by a muffler. But his stomach knotted at the sight of the second's grim face and silver-grey locks.

'Mister Browne!' Robin Cat gave a tight smile. 'And this must be Mister Hunt. Though he is so well wrapped against the November chill, it is hard to be certain.'

The Falcon gave the newcomer a black look. 'Mister who?'

'George Hunt. Our newest recruit.' Browne pulled off his hat and threw it down on the table.

The man called Hunt touched a pale finger to the brim of his own hat, but left it and the muffler on.

The Falcon narrowed his eyes. 'I thought for security's sake we had agreed to stick at the numbers we already have.'

'You can talk.' Browne mopped his face with his kerchief and helped himself to a mug of ale. 'You gave us no warning about this one.' He scowled at Tom, then turned to Robin Cat. 'I trust you will be sending our little friend back where he came from with all due haste.'

Robin Cat's eyes sparked with a green-gold fire. 'You are mistaken, Harry. The boy has agreed to join us on our mission. The one to save the King from the clutches of that fox Cecil. His small hands will prove most useful to us in our tunnelling work.'

'What?' Browne spat out the mouthful of ale he'd just taken and stared at Robin Cat in disbelief.

'I will explain more later. Now come. Take some refreshment.' Robin Cat pushed the pie dish towards him.

But Browne wasn't finished. He slammed his mug down, strode over to the Falcon and jabbed a finger at him. 'If I had my way, sir, you would be locked up in Bedlam, for only a madman would risk bringing such a mewling babe into our company.'

The Falcon unsheathed his dagger again. 'Insult me one more time, Harry Browne and you won't live long enough to regret it.'

Browne's eyes narrowed to two iron-hard points. 'Scoundrel! It's time you learnt to show some respect for your betters.' Tossing his cloak to one side, he pulled his own blade free from his belt, flashed it up and lunged.

The Falcon sidestepped and Browne careered into the

tabletop, sending the pie plate and ale jug flying.

'Arrghh!' Browne rebounded and twisted round, but the Falcon was quicker. He grabbed Browne's dagger-arm, thrust it up behind his back and pointed the tip of his blade at the other man's sweat-slicked throat.

'Steady now, lads. Steady!' Robin Cat sprang forwards and pushed the Falcon's dagger down. 'You are entitled to your opinions, Harry, but the decision has been made. Our young friend stays. Come, put your weapons away. We are all comrades here.'

The Falcon grunted, then released his grip and slid his dagger back in his belt.

Browne jerked free. He sheathed his blade, shook out his cloak and wiped his kerchief across his neck.

Robin Cat nodded at the other man, waiting patiently in the shadows. 'And Mister Hunt stays too. He has promised us as many horses and pistols as we need. I think you will agree, my friend, we would be fools to turn down such a handsome offer.'

The Falcon shot Hunt a suspicious look, then gave Robin Cat a stiff bow.

'Good. Now, why don't you take the boy to the lodging house and get him settled in? Time is against us and work must begin again on the tunnel first thing tomorrow, so he'll need all the sleep he can get.'

'Come.' The Falcon snatched up their things. Then, thrusting Tom's bundle and cloak at him, he strode towards the door.

Tom hurried after him, stuffing the piece of half-eaten

pie up his sleeve. At the door, he cast a quick glance behind him. The new man had joined the others at the table, but Harry Browne stood glaring after them, his eyes cold as shards of winter ice.

He shivered. Not a man to make an enemy of. Except – the knot in his stomach grew even tighter – for some reason, it looked like he already had.

Chapter Twenty-three

It was nearly midnight when they finally arrived at the lodging house. The Falcon had taken so many twists and turns in the dark streets and alleys, Tom had no idea how far they were from the Duck and Drake. He rubbed his eyes and stifled a yawn.

The Falcon helped him down from Shadrach then unhooked the bags from the saddle. 'Let's get inside and I'll show you your sleeping quarters. We've a long day ahead of us tomorrow.' He unlocked the door and gestured for him to enter.

Tom was about to cross the threshold when a small square of parchment caught his eye. He bent down and picked it up. There was a message scrawled across it in charcoal.

The provisions are in the attic.

'Here, give me that.' The Falcon snatched the parchment

from him. He scanned the words, grunted and screwed it into a ball.

'Is it from Mister Browne?'

The Falcon gave a brisk nod then pushed past him and disappeared inside. Tom took a deep breath and followed. A dark passageway ran through the middle of the house, with doors to the left and right. The air smelt of soot and damp. The Falcon came to a stop at the foot of a narrow staircase. 'Up here.'

The wooden slats creaked and buckled under their weight. Tom gripped tight to a piece of rope tacked up the side of the cracked plaster wall. At the top of the steps, on a landing of rough floorboards, a rickety ladder stood propped against an open hatch in the ceiling.

'The attic. But you'll not be needing to venture up there.' The Falcon jerked his head at a door opposite. 'And that room is for the use of our out-of-town comrades who have no London lodgings of their own.'

Tom's heart missed a beat. Did he mean Harry Browne? He hoped not. He'd had his fill of him.

''Tis empty at the moment, except for some stores. But' – the Falcon pushed open a door on their left – 'you can join me in here if you like.'

Tom stepped inside. A shaft of moonlight shone through a small square window hole in the opposite wall. The room was about the size of his bedchamber at home and bare, apart from a heavy oak chest in the corner and a straw mattress tossed down on the floor. As he turned, he noticed someone had nailed a rough wooden crucifix above the door.

'How many others are there?'

'I've lost track. Since I've been gone, it would appear Mister Cat has been on another recruiting drive. I doubt you'll meet them all anyway. Not in the time we have left. Here.' The Falcon opened the lid of the chest and threw a rough woollen blanket at him. 'You'll be a mite saddle-sore after our ride. You have the mattress. I'll take the floor.' He pulled off his cloak and boots and unbuckled his belt, lay down on the floorboards and closed his eyes.

Tom took off his own boots, dropped down on the mattress and reached inside his bundle for Jago's box. He slid the lid open, tipped the mouse into his outstretched palm and fished the slice of pie crust from his sleeve. 'Here, boy.' He broke off a piece and held it out to him. 'Sorry it took so long.' He watched Jago eat for a moment then stroked his head. A cold draught blew against his neck. He glanced up at the window. Did Father have a window too? If he did, perhaps the moon's bright face would give him some cheer.

But what if they'd thrown him into one of them rat pits the boys back at home were always talking about? He shuddered. He wouldn't last long in one of those. The sooner they got on with digging the tunnel the better. The sound of snoring filled the room. He glanced at the Falcon. Fast asleep. He'd better try and do the same. He dropped Jago back inside his box. 'I'll let you out for a run tomorrow, boy, I promise.'

He pulled the blanket over his head and closed his eyes. As sleep drifted in, a grey fog rose up and swirled towards him. As it drew closer, ghostly shapes peeled out of it:

ragged men and women with hollow eye sockets and holes where their mouths should be. They snatched at his face and hair with bony white fingers. He spun round then staggered back as a dark hooded figure twisted towards him, hands clutching its neck. The figure moaned and kicked out with booted feet. Then a great shudder ran through it and it fell still. The ghosts swarmed round the figure, yanking its boots and tearing its clothes. Tom made to cry out, but his mouth was stuffed with rags. The air filled with a sudden rush of wings and the shadow of a huge bird darkened the sky. The ghosts shrank back as it swooped down and sank its talons into the man's tattered shoulder. Cocking its head, the bird stared at Tom with a black, glistening eye then stabbed at the man's face with its beak.

'No!' He jerked up with a start and blinked. The moon shone through the window, casting a silver square on the Falcon's outstretched hand and his glittering, bird-headed ring. Tom shivered. Just a dream. Tugging the blanket up under his chin, he rolled over and scrunched his eyes shut. As he slipped into sleep, the moaning started up again. Except this time – he flicked his eyes open – this time it was real.

He lay still and listened. It sounded like it was coming from up above. He tossed off the blanket, jumped up and tiptoed towards the door.

He was halfway there when a hand shot out and clamped his ankle. 'Where are you going?'

'I – I thought I heard something.'

''Twas only the wind. Go back to sleep.' It was clear from

his tone, the Falcon expected to be obeyed.

Tom hesitated, then crept back to the mattress and lay down. He held his breath. The noise had stopped. Maybe the Falcon was right. He closed his eyes and let the sound of the other man's breathing suck him back into sleep.

Sunday 3 November

Watery sunlight shone through the window. Tom blinked and sat up. The space on the floorboards where the Falcon had slept was empty. The sound of church bells drifted in from outside. Sunday. It must be. If he was at home, they'd have had to attend the Protestant church service to avoid being fined, but he doubted that was what the Falcon had planned.

He stretched and yawned then mumbled a quick prayer, opened up Jago's box and fed him the last few crumbs of pie crust. He was about to let him out for a run around when muffled voices sounded below. 'It'll have to wait, boy.' He closed the lid over, rammed on his boots and crept out on to the landing.

'Pah! I don't know what's got into you! You went away a soldier and have come back a sentimental fool.'

His heart sank. Harry Browne. He'd recognize that snarl anywhere.

'Say that again and I'll open your guts.'

'And what good would that serve, except to get you arrested and put our whole venture at risk? Robin's a fool for agreeing to take the boy. Use him for the tunnel, but when the deed is done, I say he's on his own. The rest of us will be too busy with the big fish to have a care about a paltry cloth merchant and his brat.'

A rush of anger surged through Tom. How dare Browne insult Father like that! He was worth ten of him. He curled his fingers into fists.

'Let me pass will you? I have urgent business to attend to with Robin and it will not go well for you if you make me late.' There was the sound of a scuffle then a pair of boots thudded away down the passageway. A few moments later a door banged shut.

He sucked in a breath. Good! At least he wouldn't have to face him. He reached for the rope and made his way down the rickety stairs.

The Falcon stood at the bottom flexing his knuckles. He glanced up as Tom approached. 'Did you hear that?'

'A bit.'

He frowned and tugged at his beard. 'Harry Browne is a hot-tempered fool. He thinks because of certain family connections he can lord and master it over the rest of us. Truth is, he is about as honourable as a fox in a henhouse.'

'So why do you and Mister Cat let him stay with you?'

The Falcon sighed. 'He's an old friend of Mister Cat's, more's the pity. Besides, those lordly connections of his are useful. But enough of him. Let's eat. Then, Master Garnett, you and I have work to do.'

After a quick breakfast in the small, dark kitchen, the Falcon picked up a lantern next to the door and led Tom out into a dirt yard. It was bounded on three sides by a rough-made wall. A huge church with buttresses and spires loomed away to the right. Closer still a high stone building with great arched windows blocked out much of the daylight. Tom wrinkled his nose. The river wasn't far. He'd recognize that stink anywhere.

The Falcon laughed. 'I see you have worked out where old Thames is. But can you tell where the tunnel entrance lies?'

Tom glanced around the yard. There was a stack of wood at the far end, but that was all. He frowned and shook his head.

'The wood pile bears closer inspection. Come.' The Falcon led him over to it. 'We keep it hidden from prying eyes with these faggots and bundles of sticks.' He yanked them away to reveal a black gaping hole beyond. 'They also serve as props to keep the walls and ceiling from caving in where there are weak spots. The soil is a mix of wet clay and gravel. Not good for tunnelling.'

Tom poked his head inside. The air was dank and rivery. He shivered and pulled it out again. 'How close is Cecil's cellar?'

'Not far. 'Tis why we rented this house. For its nearness to our target. And the seclusion too. Once we're inside you'll see what progress we have made. And why we need your help. Do you have a tinderbox?'

He nodded.

'Strike a light, then.' The Falcon pulled a tallow candle from his belt.

Tom fumbled in his waist-pouch. As he pulled out the

box, a shower of black mouse droppings scattered to the ground. He puffed his cheeks. Poor Jago! He'd have to make it up to him later. He opened the lid of the tinderbox, piled scraps of straw into it and struck the flint with the metal fire-striker. A spark flew and caught the straw. He shielded it with his hand.

The Falcon lips twisted into a smile. 'You have the makings of a good fire-starter. A useful skill.' He dipped the candle wick into the flame, slid back the lantern cover and fixed the candle on the spike inside. Leaning forwards, he reached into the mouth of the tunnel and pulled out two shovels.

'Now, Master Garnett, time to show me what you're made of.' The Falcon handed one of the shovels to Tom. Then, shining the lantern into the blackness, he stooped and disappeared inside.

Chapter Twenty-four

At the entrance, the tunnel was big enough to stand up in, but as they went further in, it got lower and narrower, forcing Tom to duck and the Falcon to move into a crouch. They skidded over the greasy clay, round wooden posts and past slumps of flinty black gravel until, finally, the Falcon came to a stop.

'This is where we had got to when we suffered another earth-fall.' Dropping his shovel, he reached for a torch propped against the wall and touched it to the flame inside the lantern. The woody stalks crackled and flared into life.

Tom squeezed between two more wooden props and joined the Falcon in front of a fresh slump of soil and stones.

'As you can see, it was a big one. But we heard the sound of voices just before it happened, a sure sign we cannot be far off our goal. Though as Mister Cat said' – the Falcon's jaw tightened – 'time is against us.'

'Why?'

The Falcon paused, then put down the lantern and turned to face him. 'Cecil is in London now, but in another few days he departs for his estates in the country. So we must strike soon to be sure of getting our bird. See this?' He held the torch up in front of the slump. A slight breeze caught it and blew the flame backwards. Tom nodded.

'It means there is a gap. A gap which, by my reckoning, will lead us through into the Hunchback's cellar. And that's where you come in, Master Garnett.' He slapped him on the back.

Tom stared at the slump. A trickle of gravel slid down from the top and landed at his feet. He licked his lips. 'You mean . . . you want me to climb up there and—' His voice cracked. He swallowed, annoyed at himself for sounding afraid.

'Dig through. That's right. D'you think you can do it?'

He nodded.

'Good! I'll help you up there. Use your hands first. I'll pass you the shovel when you've made some progress.' The Falcon bent and rammed the bottom of the torch into a mound of clay.

'Wh–what if there's another slide?'

'Don't worry. I'll pull you off the moment I hear anything. Now, to work. The sooner we get to Cecil's cellar, the sooner we trap our rat and get your father freed.' Before Tom could change his mind, the Falcon grabbed him round the waist and hoisted him halfway up the slippery mound.

He scrabbled for a moment before he found a foothold,

then clambered slowly up it. As he neared the top, a current of cold air lifted his hair from his forehead. He reached with his fingers into the empty space beyond.

'I've found the gap.'

'Excellent.' The Falcon picked up the torch and ran the flame over where Tom was perched. 'Tell me when you have made it wide enough to crawl through.'

'Yes, sir.' He began to dig. It was dirty work, harder than anything he had ever done before. His shoulder muscles burned, his legs ached and his hands got so caked in clay they looked more like the paws of a bear. But, slowly, surely, the gap grew steadily wider. He paused to scrape the worst of the muck from his fingers then froze. Voices. Men's voices.

'What, boy? Why have you stopped?'

He put a sticky finger to his lips and pointed into the gap.

The Falcon yanked on his ankles. 'Pull back. Now!'

As Tom slithered down the slump, a pair of hands seized him round the middle and lifted him clear. He wiped his face with his sleeve and spat a lump of mud from his mouth. 'What shall we do?'

'Shh!' The Falcon held up a hand, then snatched him by the arm and tugged him back until they were a safe distance from the slump. 'We will have to wait awhile.' He frowned. 'We can't risk digging while they are so close. In the meantime, best take the opportunity for some refreshment. There's a flagon of ale in the kitchen. Go and fetch it while I keep watch.'

Tom wiped his hands on his breeches, picked up the

lantern and scrambled back the way they'd come. He blinked as he stepped into the daylight and took a deep gulp of air. It was good to be out in the open again.

He left the lantern by the woodpile and darted across the yard to the kitchen. There was no sign of the ale flagon so he grabbed the leather water bottle, took a quick swig and headed back to the tunnel entrance. He was about to duck back inside when a crunch of footsteps sounded behind him.

'Flagging, are we, Master Mole?' A gloved hand gripped him by the shirt collar and yanked him round.

Tom stared up into the hard grey eyes of Harry Browne. He opened his mouth to speak, but all that came out was a trickle of water.

Browne gave an unpleasant chuckle. 'Not so full of yourself now, are you? Well, stop standing there like a drowning fish and get back to your work. This tunnel won't dig itself!' He picked up the lantern and shoved him inside.

Tom swung round, free hand clenched in a fist. 'Leave me alone!'

'Or you'll do what?' Browne's shadow loomed above him.

A twist of hate shot through him. The man was a bully, just like Constable Skinner. But stronger, taller and twice as mean. His shoulders slumped. What chance did he stand? Reluctantly he turned and trudged back down the tunnel towards the glow of the Falcon's torch.

The Falcon spun round as he approached. 'Did you find it?'

'No. Only water, but . . .' He glanced over his shoulder. The space behind him filled with the hunched shape of Browne.

'I thought you said you had urgent business to attend to?' The Falcon spoke through clenched teeth.

'It turns out Robin did not need me after all. So I thought I'd come and lend a hand with the digging.' Browne put the lantern down and reached for one of the shovels. 'You should be glad of my help. This one's muscles aren't fit to lift a feather.' He bared his teeth in a dog-like grin.

'Keep it down, man!' The Falcon pointed back to the slump.

Browne raised an eyebrow. 'You've broken through?'

'Yes, thanks to Master Garnett here. So, as you can see, we have no need of your services.' The Falcon's voice was calm, but his left cheek twitched and the scar on it bunched up like a worm.

Browne glanced at Tom then narrowed his eyes. 'But I insist. We can't have your young friend injuring himself, can we?' He peered about him then back at Tom. A sly look stole across his face. 'Stay there, boy and let me show you how it's done.' He wiped his face with his sleeve, then lifted the shovel and sliced it into the section of wall nearest Tom. The blade made a crunching sound as it struck.

Gravel! 'No, stop!' Tom dropped the water bottle and sprang forwards.

Browne shoved him back and sliced again. A rush of stones showered to the floor. A low rumbling noise echoed around them. Browne jumped back, tossed the shovel to the ground then turned and ran.

'Look out!' The Falcon leapt at Tom and threw him to the ground.

He rolled to one side and curled into a ball as a torrent of mud and gravel slammed down from above. He scrunched his eyes tight shut and gritted his teeth. He couldn't die now. Father needed him.

The rushing noise thundered on, like a river in full flood. But at last, after what seemed like an age, it slowed to a trickle and stopped. He raised his head, blinked and coughed. He blinked again, then staggered to his feet and peered into the darkness behind him. His stomach lurched. Where the Falcon had stood a few moments ago, there was nothing now but a great mound of dirt.

'Help!' He jerked round looking for Browne but there was no sign of him. Trust him to save his own skin and leave them to die. Except that wasn't going to happen. Not if he could help it. Tom turned and scrambled over to the mound. If he uncovered the Falcon's head and gave him some space to breathe, there was still a chance he might save him. He glanced over at the slump. What about the men in Cecil's cellar? He shook his head. He couldn't think about that now. All that mattered was saving his friend. Heart thumping, he plunged his hands into the dirt and began to dig.

After what seemed like an age, his fingers brushed against something soft and warm. Matted hair and what felt like an ear. The earth shifted under his hands. *Please, God, let him be all right, please.*

He dug on, clearing a space around the Falcon's mouth and nose. His lips and nostrils were clogged with dirt. He tried to scoop it out but it was no use. He needed water. He twisted round. The bottle? Where was it? He raked the ground until at last he found it. He snatched it up, pulled out the cork and tipped what was left of the water over the Falcon's face.

The man choked and jerked his head away.

Tom heaved a sigh and sank back on his heels. He was alive!

The Falcon blinked and spat a gobbet of clay from between his teeth. 'First buried, now drowned.' He coughed and lifted his head. 'Where's Browne?'

'Run off.'

He growled and spat again. 'What about the men on the other side?'

Tom strained his ears. Nothing. 'I think they've gone.'

The Falcon frowned. 'If they heard the fall . . . Well, 'tis a chance we will have to take. Now for heaven's sake, Soldier, let's get out of this living grave, before it locks us in for good.'

A shiver of pride rippled through Tom. Soldier. No one had ever called him that before. He liked how it sounded.

'Yes, sir.' He reached for the shovel and set about digging his friend free.

Chapter Twenty-five

A fire crackled in the kitchen hearth. Tom huddled beneath a blanket, sitting as close to the curling orange flames as he dared. The coating of mud had tightened on him as it dried, making it feel like a second skin. He shifted to get more comfortable and groaned. Everything ached.

He closed his eyes and imagined himself in the kitchen back at home. Mother would be getting the dinner ready. And when Father got back from the harbour, he might tell them a sailor's tale of the New World or pull an exotic fruit from his sack. Like the oranges at Yuletide, or maybe even a pomegranate. Tom's tongue tingled at the thought.

A thud jerked him back to the small, mean kitchen of the lodging house. A piece of glowing wood rolled towards him across the stone hearth, sending out a shower of sparks. He kicked it away with his boot and frowned. Harry Browne had made the cave-in happen on purpose. He'd been trying to kill him, he was sure of it. Perhaps the Falcon too. And he'd nearly succeeded. What if he'd got plans to come back and make sure the job was done? Tom shivered and hugged the blanket tight against him.

A pair of footsteps clattered down the stairs. The kitchen door swung open and the Falcon strode in, spurs clinking. He was dressed in a fresh shirt and breeches, his hair roughly combed and his face washed clean of all traces of mud. He snatched a grey leather jerkin from a nail on the wall then glanced at Tom and frowned.

'I must go to Mister Cat's lodgings across the water in Lambeth and give him the bad news. Our mission is in grave jeopardy. We need to act swiftly if we are to catch our prey in time.' He shrugged the jerkin on, buttoned it quickly and snatched up his gloves from the table.

Tom scrambled to his feet. 'How long before we can start digging again?'

The Falcon swung round. His frown deepened. 'I don't know. There's a good deal of mud to excavate to get back to where we were. And we'll have to shore up the roof and sides to make it safe. But one thing's for certain, 'twill need more than you and I to get things back on track.'

Tom's heart sank beneath its own load of clay. They had been hours away from capturing Cecil. If he left London before they had a chance to take him, what would happen to Father then? His shoulders slumped.

The Falcon ruffled his hair. 'You saved my life back there. And for that I will always be grateful.'

Tom flashed him a look. He hadn't mentioned Browne yet. But he must know the cave-in was his fault?

The Falcon's eyes narrowed. 'Does something ail you, Soldier?'

'It's nothing. Just that . . . Mister Browne, I think he made the tunnel roof collapse on purpose.'

The Falcon's jaw twitched. 'Why do you say that?'

'He knew it was gravel above us. But he sliced straight into it. I . . . I think he meant to kill us.'

The Falcon rubbed a hand across the back of his neck. ''Tis true Browne and I don't always see eye to eye. And he does not like your joining us – he has made no bones about that. But my skills make me key to the success of our venture. He knows that. And to murder an innocent boy?' He shook his head. 'I don't think even he would stoop that low.'

'So why didn't he stay and help me dig you out?'

'Because for all his bragging, he's a coward at heart. Still' – he raked some stray bits of grit from his beard – 'I will do what I can to keep him away from you. In the meantime, I must to Mister Cat's with all speed.' He slapped his gloves against his thigh. 'And you should get cleaned up before that mud sets and turns you into a marsh boggart or worse.' He turned to go.

'Wait. Could you get this to my mother?' Tom pulled a sheet of folded paper from beneath the blanket. 'It's a message. Telling her I'm safe.'

The Falcon's gaze sharpened. 'What have you said? Nothing about our mission, I hope? If it were to fall into the wrong hands . . .'

Tom shook his head. 'I've told her I've come to London to save Father. And that she mustn't worry. That's all.'

The Falcon snatched it from him and scanned the words. 'Where did you get the tools to write it?'

'I mixed the ink from soot and water and made a quill from a crow's feather I found in the yard. The paper's from this.' He slid his mother's prayer book from his mud-crusted doublet.

'Most resourceful. Well, I will see what I can do. Portsmouth, isn't it?'

He nodded. 'She's staying with the Fosters in St Mary's Street.'

The Falcon slipped the letter inside his jerkin. 'One of my comrades knows a bargeman. He might be able to find a way of getting it along the coast.'

A warm glow spread through Tom's chest. At least now Mother would know he was safe. 'Thank you.'

The Falcon nodded then furrowed his brow. 'It must wait though. I have more urgent business to attend to first.' He pulled on his gloves. 'I'll be back before nightfall. Listen for the signal. Three knocks. You remember? Admit no one who does not use it. And lock the door from the inside with the key when I leave.'

'What about Mister Browne?'

'I will look out for him. But Mister Cat had other duties planned for him, so it would surprise me if he shows up here again today. Besides, having caused the earth-fall, he will be keen to steer clear for a bit, knowing how quick to temper

I and my small pointy friend can be.' He patted the dagger at his waist and gave a grim smile.

Tom locked the door as the Falcon left, then made his way back to the kitchen. He wrapped the blanket around him and stepped out into the yard. A cold wind had got up and the darkening sky was thick with heavy grey clouds. He bundled up some more faggots for the fire. The sounds of the city blew in on the breeze. The clip-clop of horses' hooves, the cries of the wherrymen out on the river, and above everything the mewing of red kites scavenging for scraps of rotten meat. He peered at the roofs of the surrounding buildings. Somewhere beyond them lay the Clink and Father locked up inside it.

He shivered. Jago. He must be starving. Lugging the faggots inside, he filled a bowl from the water pail, tore a chunk of bread from the loaf on the table and hurried upstairs. Scuttling noises came from Jago's box. He pushed the lid back. The mouse gave an angry-sounding squeak and crawled out on to his hand.

'I'm really sorry, boy.' Tom tickled him between the ears then tipped the bowl towards him. Jago dipped his mouth in the water and drank, then nibbled greedily at the bread. 'Now, how about that run.' He dropped Jago on to the mattress and watched as he scampered across it and jumped up on to the wooden chest. He peered up at the window, eyes shining, whiskers twitching. Tom wagged a finger. 'No you don't.' He scooped Jago up and let him run along his arm and on to his shoulder. A damp mousy nose burrowed into the side of his neck. He giggled. 'Stop it, will you?' He cupped him in his hands and flopped down on the mattress.

Rat-tat! Rat-tat! Rat-tat!

He sat up. Was the Falcon back already?

'I'll be back soon, boy.' He dropped Jago into his box, slid the lid shut and ran downstairs.

The banging started up again.

'All right, all right. I'm coming.' He crept along the passageway to the front door. Best check first. He bent down and peered through the keyhole. But all he got was an eyeful of black cloth.

'Who's there?'

'A friend.' The voice was low and secretive.

His heart hammered against his chest. What if it was Browne? He shrank back from the door fingering his knife. 'What friend?'

'George Hunt.'

The stranger at the Duck and Drake. Tom licked his lips. Mister Cat had said they could trust him, but the Falcon hadn't seemed so sure. And he was a friend of Browne too.

'Quickly, lad. I have something important to tell you.'

Tom frowned. He'd not heard the man speak before, but now he did, his voice sounded familiar.

'I don't have much time.' The door handle rattled.

'Why should I trust you?'

'If you don't, you will be making a grave mistake.'

The door rattled again. Tom stayed where he was.

'Very well, you leave me no choice.' A thin metal stick shot through the keyhole and jiggled up and down. The lock clicked and the door swung open. A black cloaked figure filled the frame.

Tom reached for his knife. 'Stop! You can't—'

In one swift move, the man grabbed his arm, tugged the knife from him and rammed it into his own belt. 'Hold still, boy!' Keeping a tight grip on Tom, he banged the door shut with the heel of his boot and locked it fast with the strange metal stick.

Tom glanced over his shoulder. If he could make him think the Falcon was still here . . . He yanked free and dashed towards the stairs. 'Help, sir! Come quick!'

He was halfway up the stairs when a hand clamped his shoulder and dragged him back down. 'Nice try, Master Garnett. But I know you're alone. I watched your friend ride off on that proud horse of his more than an hour ago.'

Chapter Twenty-six

Tom made to twist free but Hunt's grip tightened. A pair of silver-grey eyes shone back at him over the top of the black muffler he wore.

'Has Browne sent you?'

'Harry Browne?' Hunt snorted. 'I do not run errands for that hot-tempered fool.' He steered Tom into the kitchen and pushed him towards the chair by the fire. 'Sit down and I will tell you the reason for my visit.'

Removing his hat, he smoothed a hand over his wispy yellow hair, then rolled back his muffler and pulled up a second chair. He glanced at Tom, then slid the knife from his belt and balanced it on the chair arm. He flicked the blade with his finger. The knife spun like a top.

'You think the man you have journeyed here with is your friend?'

Tom clenched his jaw. 'I know he is.'

Hunt jerked the blade to a stop. 'Well, I am sorry to disappoint you' – he ran a hand over his chin – 'but he is not.'

Tom jumped up, cheeks burning. 'You're wrong! The Falcon saved my life. And he's going to help me get a pardon for Father.'

Hunt's eyes narrowed to a pair of silver slits. 'The Falcon? So that's what he calls himself, eh? But what's this about a pardon?'

The words spilled out of Tom before he could stop them. 'Father's been locked in the Clink by Robert Cecil for helping a priest. But he's a good man. The Falcon says when he and Mister Cat have got Cecil out of the way, they'll ask the King to set him free.'

Hunt sighed and shook his head. 'Why does it not surprise me that this Falcon of yours would give false hope to a child? Listen.' He rose to his feet and placed a hand on Tom's shoulder. 'He and Mister Cat's merry band are not what they pretend. They are planning a grievous blow aimed not just at the King's minister, but at England itself.'

'I don't believe you!' Tom bunched his fingers into fists. Why was Hunt sowing these lies?

'You should. You and your cousin are in grave danger.'

Tom frowned. Cressida? What did she have to do with any of this?

'You remember your cousin, Mistress Maria? Though I believe she likes to go by the name of Cressida when her father is not at home.'

'You're making it up.' Either that or he was mad.

Hunt waved a hand in the air. 'Her play-acting is no

concern of mine. But she's here, Tom.' He peered around the kitchen as if trying to see through the walls. 'And being kept a prisoner, somewhere in this house.'

'That's impossible. She went back to fetch Sergeant Talbot.'

'But she is, I'm telling you.' Hunt picked up the knife and jabbed the blade into the arm of the chair. 'Your friend and Mister Browne shipped her to London in the back of their cart. A contact of mine saw everything.'

'You're lying! If she came with us, I'd have known.'

Hunt levered the knife out of the wood and dangled it between his thumb and forefinger. The blade glowed red in the light from the fire. 'These are ruthless clever men, Tom. They will have kept her quiet by drugging her.' He shot him a look. 'You have intelligence, lad. I can see that. So' – he tapped his forehead – 'use it.' He cleared his throat and frowned. 'During your journey, no doubt you were kept well away from the contents of the cart?'

Tom chewed at his lip. It was true he'd never seen what was under the sailcloth. And there was the time in the chalk pit when he'd caught Browne fiddling with the ties of the sack and been warned off. And the mandrake potion. What if it hadn't been for Browne's toothache after all? But Cressida had gone to fetch Sergeant Talbot. He'd seen her leave with his own eyes. He shot a look at Hunt. For some reason the man was trying to set him against the Falcon. Well, he wasn't going to fall for it. He folded his arms tight across his chest. 'So where is she now?'

Hunt laid the knife back down on his chair arm and

fixed him with a flinty stare. 'I was hoping *you* might be able to shed some light on that, Master Garnett. She will be somewhere under lock and key.'

The doubt bubbled up again. That noise in the roof last night. What if it hadn't been the wind?

'But I don't understand.' He shook his head. 'Why would they want to take her? And who are you anyway?'

Hunt pursed his lips. 'I cannot tell you that, but you should know I go about the King's business.'

'What?' Tom's legs buckled. He sank back down in the chair.

'It's true. But I'm afraid matters are at too delicate a stage for me to say more. I do not yet know all Cat and his gang have planned. Although I worked hard to persuade them to let me join them, they have kept certain crucial facts from me – no doubt because I am a newcomer and have yet to prove myself. But one thing is sure. These men will stop at nothing to get their own way. And as Montagues, you and your cousin are useful bargaining tools to bring others into line.'

'I'm a Garnett, not a Montague!'

Hunt's eyes flashed silver. 'You may have been born a Garnett. But your uncle is a Montague and one of the most powerful lords in the land. Your new friends will not hesitate to use you and your cousin as bait to secure his support and that of the other Catholic nobles. Now tell me.' He bent over him and grabbed him by the shoulders. 'While you were staying at Cowdray, did you come across anything unusual in your uncle's household?'

Tom shrank back in his chair. 'What d'you mean?'

'Oh, I don't know. Perhaps the arrival of strangers or a whispered conversation you weren't meant to hear.'

A sudden spark flashed through him. He knew where he'd heard that voice before. The stranger who'd met with Mandrake outside Cowdray's walls. Hunt was the other spy.

He pulled a face. 'There was a man . . .'

Hunt squatted down in front of him, eyes gleaming. 'Go on, lad.'

'I overheard him talking . . .'

'To who?' Hunt gripped the arms of the chair.

He'd got him now, like a fish on a hook. 'Mandrake, our tutor. They met in secret the night I arrived. He worked for a man he called the Master.' See what he made of that!

Hunt's gaze remained steady, but two spots of pink appeared on his cheeks. 'Interesting.' He dropped his hands to his side and stood up. 'But not what I am looking for.' He pressed his lips into a hard line. 'I have risked a lot in coming here. Too much maybe . . .' His pale forehead creased into a frown.

Rat-tat! Rat-tat! Rat-tat!

Tom jerked his head up. The Falcon. It must be! He leapt to his feet.

Hunt barred his way and fixed him with a stare. 'What I have told you is the truth. You should not meddle in this business. The consequences will be nothing but deadly. Find your cousin and leave this place as soon as you can.' He slid the muffler back over his mouth and nose and pulled on his hat. 'And know this.' His eyes glittered with warning.

'If you follow these men, there can be no hope for your father.' He handed him back the knife.

Tom swallowed hard and looked down at the blade. His father's initials shone back at him in the firelight.

Rat-a-tat-tat!

Hunt glanced over his shoulder. 'There is a back way?'

Tom wavered.

'Quick, lad!'

'Yes, but you'll have to climb a wall . . .'

Hunt nodded, then wrapping his cloak about him, he slid out through the door and was gone.

Tom stared after him, head spinning. If Hunt was one of Cecil's spies, then the Falcon and his friends were in danger of being discovered at any moment. He had to warn them before it was too late. Except . . . He frowned. It was true; Hunt had risked a lot coming here. What if he'd spoken the truth? What if the Falcon and Browne really had captured Cressida? And what if the gang had something far worse than Cecil's kidnap planned? Beads of sweat pricked his top lip. He glanced up at the ceiling. There was only one way to find out.

The hammering at the door grew louder. He gritted his teeth. His search would have to wait until later. He stumbled down the passageway, snatched the key from its hook and unlocked the door.

'Zounds! What does a man have to do to get himself heard?' The Falcon pushed past him into the passageway. 'I hope you have that fire blazing. I've been a-hunting at the butchers and got us something tasty for the pot. Catch!' He turned and swung a brown furry shape at him.

Tom's fingers closed round the coney's limp body. He stared into its sightless black eyes.

The Falcon frowned. 'What's wrong, Soldier? Seen a ghost? Come on.' He slapped him on the shoulder. 'Let's go inside and cook this up. And then you must change into these.' He thrust a bundle at him. 'You and I are going on a journey.'

A flutter started up in Tom's chest. 'What ... what about the tunnel?'

The Falcon shook his head. 'Our plans have changed. I'll tell you more on the way.'

'Where are we going?'

He shot him a mysterious look. 'All in good time, Soldier. All in good time.'

Chapter Twenty-seven

Tom glanced at the Falcon as he busied himself with stirring the coney stew. What was the new plan? And if Cecil was leaving the city soon, shouldn't they be making haste with it? He fingered the handle of his knife. And what about Hunt? Should he tell the Falcon he'd been here? No. He couldn't risk it. Not until he knew for sure Hunt had been lying about Cressida. But what if they didn't come back to the lodging house?

'Here!' The Falcon thrust a bowl of stew at him. 'You deserve this, Soldier.' He helped himself to a bowlful, sat down and began to eat.

Tom's mouth watered at the rich smell of rabbit meat and onions. He dipped his spoon into the steaming mixture.

The Falcon winked at him. 'Good, eh?' He shovelled a final spoonful into his mouth, licked his lips and jumped up. 'Now, I must check on some equipment.' He swiped a bunch of keys from the shelf above the fireplace and ladled some more stew into a fresh bowl. 'I'll take this with me for sustenance. In the meantime, Soldier, change into those clothes I brought you and be ready to leave when I say. No need to bring your mouse.'

'But . . .'

'Trust me. We will only be gone a few hours and he will be safer here.' The look the Falcon shot him told him he didn't have any choice.

Tom frowned. He wasn't happy about leaving Jago behind, but perhaps it was for the best. He glanced at the bundle lying on the table. Where was the Falcon taking him? He sighed. Best finish his stew then change. He'd find out soon enough.

The streets around the lodging house were as twisted and tangled as a rat's nest. The occasional flicker of a candle flame in a window did little to light their way. More than once Tom found himself squelching through piles of stinking black gutter muck. He pressed his nose into the sleeve of the woollen shirt the Falcon had brought him.

'So . . . so where are we going?'

The Falcon shook his head. 'I'll tell you later, once we're across the river. This warren is a breeding ground for eavesdroppers and spies.'

A sudden thought sent an icy prickle down Tom's spine. What if the Falcon knew all about Hunt's visit? Had seen him arrive at the house and, suspecting something, decided to get Tom out of the way before he found Cressida? He bit his lip. No. It wasn't true. It couldn't be. The Falcon was trying to help him. His hoity-toity cousin was tucked up safe in her feather bed at Cowdray and as soon as they got back to the lodging house, he'd prove it.

'Stop lagging behind, or it will be midnight before we get there.' The Falcon waved him on and strode off down a narrow alley on their right.

Tom hurried after him. It was danker down here and the air smelt even more strongly of river. He shivered and pulled his cloak tight about him. In the distance, a night-watchman called the hour of seven. A dog barked. Another answered it and soon the air was full of yips and howls. As they turned a bend, a stretch of glittering black water came into view. He gaped open-mouthed at the lantern lights of a hundred wherries which dipped and darted across it like moths.

'Careful. Watch where you tread. The river mud makes the way slippery.' The Falcon gripped him by the arm and steered him down a set of steps towards the swirling current.

Hunt's words wormed their way back into his head. *Danger. Ruthless. Stop at nothing . . .* His chest tightened. What if the Falcon had brought him down here to drown him?

'No, please!' He jerked away, but the Falcon's grip tightened.

'Keep still or you'll topple us both in.' He raised his right hand as if to strike him.

Tom flinched. He opened his mouth to cry for help but

his tongue was stuck fast to his teeth. He closed his eyes and waited for the blow.

'Over here!' The Falcon's voice boomed across the water. A creak of wood echoed back at them above the slapping waves. Tom flicked his eyes open. A small boat appeared out of the gloom, a lantern bobbing from a stick fixed to its stern.

A wherry. The Falcon had been calling for a wherry. Tom bowed his head and muttered a quick prayer of thanks.

The Falcon released his grip and stepped down into the boat. He turned and held out a hand.

Tom faltered.

'What's wrong? Not a bad sailor, are you?'

He shook his head.

'Come on then. We must make haste.'

He gritted his teeth, took the Falcon's hand and jumped down beside him. The boat rocked from side to side.

''Tis not a long crossing. You have my word on it.' The Falcon turned to the wherryman. 'The stairs by St Mary Overie in Southwark, and sharp about it.'

The wherryman nodded. He waited for them to sit then dipped his oars and turned the boat out into the surging current.

After a good deal of rowing, they neared the arches of the bridge they'd crossed the night before. The rush of the river was louder here and circles of foam spun about them. The Falcon's words about boat wrecks and drowning rang in Tom's ears. He shuddered. Surely the wherryman wasn't going to try his luck riding the rapids? He held his breath and gripped the boat's rough wooden sides.

Suddenly the wherryman raised an oar. The boat swung a half turn. Quick as lightning, he sliced both oars into the inky tide and rowed hard towards the opposite bank.

Tom puffed out a breath and fixed his eyes on the shore. A church tower loomed up before them. It was the one they'd passed last night, before they'd crossed the bridge. At last, after what seemed like hours later, the boat bumped against a set of steps. The wherryman reached for the ring on the wall next to them, ran a length of rope through it and tied it fast.

'St Mary Overie.'

The Falcon handed the man a coin and leapt out of the boat. 'This way.' He nodded at the flight of steps in front of them. Tom followed him up them, legs shaking, grateful to be back on dry land.

When they reached the top, the Falcon turned to him. 'I'll tell you now who I have brought you to see.' He clasped him tight by the shoulder, black eyes gleaming. ''Tis your father.'

Tom's breath caught in his throat. Father? But how? He scanned his face for a sign he was lying.

The Falcon smiled and shook him gently. ''Tis true, Soldier. After I met with Mister Cat in Lambeth, I made some enquiries and discovered your father is still being kept in the Clink.'

A rushing sound filled his ears and bright lights danced in front of his eyes. He stumbled backwards in a daze.

'Steady, Soldier!' A pair of strong hands caught him and

held him fast.

He blinked, took a deep breath and looked up. 'But how will we get in?'

'There's a man. An old soldier friend of mine. He fell on hard times when he came home from the Low Countries and ended up a turnkey at the Clink. He owes me for saving his life from the blast of a Dutch cannon. Just as I owe you.' The Falcon ruffled Tom's head.

His heart swooped up inside him. Father. He was going to see Father. And it was all thanks to this man. His friend. 'Thank you, sir!'

The Falcon's smile broadened. 'One good turn deserves another. But we don't have much time.' The smile faded and his face grew deadly serious. 'As I told you, our plans to trap the Hunchback have changed. Mister Cat has given orders to abandon the tunnel.'

Tom frowned. 'How are we going to catch him then?'

'Worry not, Soldier. 'Tis all to the good. Mister Cat has found another, less risky way. There's a cellar adjoining the one in Cecil's palace available to rent. We will strike from there instead.'

'When?'

'Tomorrow night, once the necessary equipment is in place. Now, we must be on our way. My friend, Mister Jagger, is expecting us.' The Falcon turned down the street ahead of them.

Tom's stomach somersaulted. If what the Falcon said was true, they were only hours away from saving Father. But if Hunt was speaking the truth . . . No. He shook his head.

He couldn't be.

A grey stone wall loomed up on their left-hand side. They followed it until they came to a pair of grand iron gates. The Falcon glanced up at the roof of the great house set behind them. 'The entrance to the bishop's palace. We're not far now.'

A few moments later they arrived outside a heavy oak door. The Falcon thumped against the wood with his fist. After what seemed like an age, a flap banged open and a pair of eyes appeared in the gap. The Falcon gave a nod. 'A friend to see Mister Jagger. He is expecting me.'

The person on the other side grunted. There was another pause, then a scrape of bolts and the door creaked slowly open.

'Wait here. I'll be back.' The Falcon slid inside and the door groaned shut again.

Tom glanced at the row of sharp metal spikes which ran along the top of it. Flickers of doubt crept back into his head. What if this wasn't the Clink after all but some other place where the Falcon could keep him safely shut away? But then why go to the trouble of bringing him here, when he could easily have drowned him or locked him up back at the lodging house?

A cold wind whipped up from the riverbank. Clouds scudded across the face of the moon plunging the street into sooty darkness. He shivered. It was the perfect spot for thieves and cut-throats to lurk.

A sudden creak from somewhere behind him. He pulled his knife and made to spin round. A rough hand grabbed him by the collar.

'Leave me alone!' He kicked out with his boots, but the hand gripped tighter.

'Psssht! Do you want the watch to hear you?' The Falcon's voice sounded low in his ear.

'Sorry. I . . . er . . . I thought you were a thief.' He flushed and slid the knife back in his belt.

The Falcon released him. 'Thief?' A grim smile flickered across his lips. 'That's one thing I'm not. Quickly now. Jagger's shift finishes shortly. After that, our chance will be gone. And remember, say nothing to your father about us or our mission. Like every prison in London, the Clink is infested with Cecil's spies. The less he knows of our venture the better.'

'But what shall I say if he asks how I got here?'

'I am sure you'll think of something. Now, your word as a soldier.' The Falcon held up the palm of his right hand.

Tom paused for a moment. Father didn't approve of liars. But if it was a lie to keep him safe . . . that had to be all right, didn't it? He uncurled his fingers and raised his right hand. 'I swear.'

'Good.' The Falcon gave a sigh then clapped him on the back and pushed him through the door.

Tom stumbled into a small, dark courtyard, enclosed by a set of high stone walls. A burly, wild-haired man stepped out of the shadows to meet them. A lantern swung from his right hand.

The Falcon gave him a brisk nod. 'This is my friend, Mister Jagger. He will take you to your father.'

The man grunted and rattled a set of keys at his belt.

The hairs on the back of Tom's neck prickled. 'Aren't you coming too?'

'No.' The Falcon's jaw tightened. 'You will have much to say to each other and 'tis best done in private. I'll wait outside.' He pulled a small leather pouch from beneath his cloak and handed it to Jagger. 'For your trouble and to keep the prisoner in food and drink.'

There was a chinking sound as the turnkey's great fist closed round it.

'Now go. And don't forget, Soldier: nothing about our mission.'

Tom sucked in a breath and nodded.

The Falcon shook Jagger by the hand, then turned and marched back across the courtyard. A small figure darted in front of him and opened the door to let him pass, then bolted it shut behind him.

Tom glanced around him. There was no way out except through the door. If this was a trap, he was caught good and fast.

Chapter Twenty-eight

Jagger raised his lantern and gave Tom a black-toothed grin.

'Follow me.' He marched through a low archway and disappeared into the building beyond.

Tom wavered then hurried after him, nose pricking at the sour-smelling air. The light from the turnkey's lantern bounced along a narrow passageway, its walls lined with a row of bolted doors. As they passed the first door, it rattled and a low moan sounded from the other side.

'Quiet, wretch!' Jagger pulled a heavy-looking stick from his belt and banged it against the wood.

As if at a signal, a clamour of rattles and moans started up from behind the other doors, pierced by ragged cries of 'Help!' and 'God save us!'

Tom shuddered. It was how he'd imagined Hell to be, but worse.

Jagger struck another door with his stick. 'Troublemakers, the lot of them. Excepting your father. I shall be sad to see him go. A proper gentleman, he is.'

Go? Tom grabbed his sleeve. 'They're letting him out? When?'

A strange look flitted across the turnkey's face. Then his eyes softened. He ran a hand across the line of black whiskers sprouting from the back of his neck. 'Best your father tells you himself.' He lurched on down the passageway, banging his stick against more doors and yelling for silence.

Tom stumbled after him, heart pounding. He couldn't believe it. Father freed? It was more than he could have hoped for. With any luck, in a day or two's time, they'd be on their way home! And it meant other things too. No more having to help Cat and his men kidnap Cecil. And no more keeping clear of Harry Browne. Of course, he'd have to say goodbye to the Falcon. But his friend would be pleased for him. He knew he would. A sudden thought struck him. What if it was because of the Falcon Father was going to be set free? A surge of gratitude flooded through him.

Jagger came to a stop outside the final door in the row. 'This is it. I'll have to search you before you go in. House rules.' He put the lantern down and ran his palms across Tom's shoulders and down his arms. 'Ah! What's this?' He pulled back his cloak and yanked the knife from his belt. 'On a rescue mission, were we?' His eyes narrowed.

Tom clenched his jaw. 'No! My father gave it to me. It

was a present.' A sudden jolt ran through him.

It was Sunday today. His birthday! The tour Father had promised him round the merchant ship was like a dream from another life. But that didn't matter now. All he wanted was for him to come home.

Jagger rammed the knife down the inside of his boot.

Tom took a step towards him. 'But—'

'To avoid any accidents. You'll get it back before you leave.' Jagger grasped the door bolt with both hands and slid it back. Then, selecting a large rusty key from the ring on his belt, he unlocked the door, pushed it open and stepped aside. 'A visitor for you, Mister Garnett.'

A reek of sour sweat and urine crowded Tom's nostrils. He staggered back, gasping for breath.

Jagger shoved him inside. 'You don't have much time. Use it wisely.' He thrust the lantern at him and slammed the door. A moment later, the key scraped in the lock.

The candle flame sputtered then flared up again, lighting a dirty straw-covered floor and walls smeared with what looked like the tracks of a thousand snails. Tom took a deep breath. 'Father?' His voice sounded small and far away, like he was calling up from the bottom of a well.

Something skittered between his feet. He twisted round just in time to see a grey tail disappearing beneath a mound of filthy rags. He edged towards them, held his breath and prodded them with the toe of his boot. They twitched and buckled. A snaggle of small dark bodies tumbled out and scuttled away into the darkness beyond.

Rats! Tom leapt back, stomach churning. A clink of

chains sounded behind him. He swung the lantern round. The light fell on the figure of a man – but a man like no other he'd seen before. Dressed in nothing but a long tattered shirt, he was slumped on his knees, his grime-covered arms shackled to the wall by two heavy chains.

Tom froze. Could this really be his father? There was only one way to find out. He gritted his teeth and stumbled towards him.

'Father?'

The man jerked his head up then turned away, eyes tight shut, face twisted in anguish.

Tom hesitated, then knelt down before him and touched his clammy shoulder. 'Father? It's me, Tom.'

The man kept his head turned and let out a groan. 'Torment me not, oh Lord, by sending these devils to taunt me!' The voice was ragged and broken, but there was no doubting it.

Tom's eyes pricked. He blinked the tears away. He mustn't cry. Not now. 'Look at me, Father.' He shook him gently. 'I'm no devil.'

The man's eyes flickered open. He peered back at him through a tangle of filthy hair. 'My son? Is it really you?'

Tom's fingers curled into fists as he stared at his father's manacled wrists – the purple bruises and the bloody weals where the irons had pierced his skin. 'Father, what have they done to you?'

His father's eyes widened. 'I have missed you . . . so much.' He gave a rasping cough and writhed in pain.

Tom choked back a sob. 'It's all right. You'll be free soon

and we can go home.'

He pulled back and stared at Tom, a look of confusion in his eyes. 'Home?'

'Yes. Mister Jagger told me. They're going to set you free.'

He dragged down on his chains and groaned again. 'How could he play such a low trick?'

Tom's blood shrivelled inside him. 'What do you mean?'

His father spoke through clenched teeth. 'I was tried yesterday with Father Oliver. They have sentenced us both to death.'

Tom's stomach lurched. It wasn't true. It couldn't be. 'You're wrong! You're getting out of here and then we're going home. Back to Portsmouth. To Mother and Ned.'

His father drew in a juddering breath. 'I'm speaking the truth. We are to be hanged at dawn the day after tomorrow, at Tyburn.'

Tom shook his head and twisted away from him. 'No!'

'Yes. Now listen to me, son. You must have courage. Be strong for your mother. Remember what I said when we parted before.' He coughed again. 'You are the man of the family now.'

Tom slumped forwards, tears spilling from his eyes. 'But I'm not brave, or strong, or any of those things.' *Not like William.*

'Of course you are.'

Guilt knotted itself round his heart, tighter than a noose. 'No! You don't understand. It's my fault you're here.'

'What do you mean?'

He ducked his head down. He couldn't bear to meet his

father's gaze.

'What? Tell me.'

Tom gave a shuddering sigh, then forced himself to look up into his father's grey, pain-scoured face. 'After you left, Constable Skinner and his men came to the house and arrested us. They . . . they threatened to beat Mother if I didn't say anything.' A shiver of ice ran through him.

His father's eyes flashed with anger. 'Those animals!' He clenched his fists and groaned.

'I was scared. I thought they were going to kill her. I . . . I told them you had taken the London road. After that, they took her to gaol.' He hung his head and let the tears burn hot tracks down his cheeks. He thought he'd feel better if he confessed, but he didn't. He felt ten times more a coward instead.

'Look at me.'

Slowly Tom lifted his head. His father's face was a ragged blur. He scrubbed at the tears with his sleeve and steeled himself. He would hear his words like a man at least.

'You are not to blame.'

'What?'

His father shook his head. 'I brought this on myself. You were only doing what I asked – protecting your mother and baby brother.' He gave another rattling cough.

The words were meant to comfort, but the ache in his chest was stronger than ever. 'I could have lied. Told them you'd taken a different road. William . . . he wouldn't have been so stupid.'

'William?' His father frowned. 'Why do you speak of

your brother?'

'Because he was better than me. So God took him and left you with me. And . . . and he was right because I failed you.' Tom bit his lip and looked away.

'Tom, listen.' His father's eyes shone back at him like bright stars in the gloom. 'You must never think that. Your mother and I loved William very much. But we love you and Edward just the same. When Skinner arrested you all, you thought your mother's life was at stake. You didn't have time to think about it.' He shook his head. 'No. If anyone's to blame, it's me.'

'But you were only trying to help him. Father Oliver, I mean.'

'Yes.' His father flicked his tongue over his cracked lips. 'Except the stakes were too high. Though I was doing Our Lord's work, it was wrong of me to put you all in such danger. But tell me – what of your mother and Ned? Where are they now? You say they put your mother in gaol . . . ?'

Tom took a deep breath and told him everything. What happened after he had confessed to Skinner, how his mother had sent him to Cowdray and of what had followed.

'She is free then?'

He nodded. 'That's what the Viscountess told me.'

His father closed his eyes. 'Praise the Lord. Her brother owes her that at least.'

'But why won't they help you too?'

He shifted his knees and grimaced. 'Given all that has happened between us?' He shook his head again.

'What? What happened?'

His father nodded at a pail next to the wall. 'Fetch me some water and I will tell you.'

Tom cupped his hand in the pail and scooped up a mouthful. His father drank deep, ignoring the husks of dead insects and leaves, then gave a deep sigh.

'Your mother's family disowned her many years ago.'

'Why?'

'We met and fell in love, but I wasn't considered a good enough match. We realized the only way we could be together was if she ran away with me. We were married, but although we tried to make our peace with her family, they never forgave her.'

The image of his mother's portrait flitted into Tom's head. Now he knew why she had looked so sad.

'Your mother's father died before his own father – your great-grandfather. So when *he* died, Cowdray passed to your uncle. He was always fond of your mother when they were children. She must have harboured a hope he might take pity on us, which is why she sent you there.' He frowned. 'But Cowdray is a long way from London. What are you doing here?' He coughed. A line of saliva trickled from the corner of his mouth and lodged in his beard.

Tom swallowed hard. He didn't want to lie to him. But he couldn't break his promise to the Falcon. Father's life might still depend on it.

'I . . . er . . . Uncle Montague was coming up to Court. I stowed away on one of his wagons and bribed the turnkey with some coins I stole.'

His father's frown deepened. 'Thieving is a sin, Tom.'

His cheeks flushed.

'And so is lying.' He shot him a knowing look.

Tom stared at his boots.

A key rattled in the lock and the cell door banged open. His heart clenched. They'd run out of time.

The turnkey stood in the doorway. He fiddled with the bunch of keys and gave a gruff cough. 'I'm sorry, Mister Garnett, but you and the boy must say your farewells.'

'Father!' Tom threw himself against his father's bony chest.

'Take care of your mother and baby brother and remember me in your prayers. And know this, son, I love you. I always have and I always will.'

Tom pulled away, blinked back the tears and looked up into his father's face. 'I'm going to save you, I promise.'

Jagger reached for the lantern and hauled him to his feet. 'You and whose army? We must go, sir.' He glanced over at Tom's father. 'The other turnkey will be on duty soon. If we're caught in here, we'll all be for the gallows. Come on now, lad. Leave your father to his prayers.'

'No! Get off me!' He kicked and struggled, but the turnkey's grip was too strong.

'Hush, Tom. You must do as Mister Jagger says. Now, go and God speed.' His father's eyes shone back at him in the last of the lantern-light; then the door slammed shut and he was gone.

Chapter Twenty-nine

'Why didn't you tell me?' Tom rammed his knife back in his belt and glared at the Falcon.

He frowned. 'I only discovered it when we arrived. And I thought it best you hear it from your father first.' He reached for Tom's shoulder.

He jerked away. 'They're taking him to Tyburn the day after tomorrow. They're going to . . .' He dug his nails into his palms. 'They're going to hang him at dawn.'

The Falcon gave a grim nod. 'So I understand.'

'We've got to stop them!'

'We will, Soldier, we will. We strike at Cecil tomorrow night. That gives us time enough to save your father.'

The Falcon sounded confident, but how could he know for sure?

'Come, now. We must make haste. There is still much to do.' With a swish of his cloak, he turned and strode back towards the river stairs.

Tom bolted after him. 'But what if you don't succeed?'

'We will. Unless . . .' The Falcon whipped round, black eyes flashing. 'Did you keep your silence, Master Garnett?'

'Yes . . . I . . . I promised Father I'd save him, but that was all.'

The Falcon grimaced. 'God's teeth! When we are this close.' He pinched his thumb and forefinger together. 'I hope for your sake you have said nothing more.'

'I haven't! I swear it. On my life.' He made the sign of the cross above a pounding heart.

The Falcon clicked his tongue against his teeth and set off at an even faster pace.

Tom glanced after him. The Falcon had risked much to take him to the Clink – to let him see Father. He might be angry with him now, but he was his friend, he was sure of that. So Hunt must be lying. He licked his lips. He had to warn the Falcon and quickly, before the spy found out about the new plan. Otherwise Cat and his men would be captured, and Father would hang for sure.

'Wait! There's something I need to tell you.' He dashed after him.

'Not now, boy. I have more important things to think about.'

'But—'

The Falcon stopped and spun round. 'I said not now!' He fixed him with a fiery stare then turned and marched away.

Tom shivered. He really was angry with him. Better wait until he'd calmed down and they were back at the lodging house. He took a deep breath and tried to imagine himself at home with Father, Mother and baby Ned. But it was no use. All he could see was Father, chained and alone in the dark, with only the rats for company.

They arrived at the lodging house just as the night-watchman called the hour of eleven. The Falcon jerked his head at the door and handed Tom the key. 'Go inside and get some sleep.'

'Where are you going?'

'I have urgent business to attend to before the night is out. I will be back later.' His tone was clipped and impatient. Before Tom could reply, he slipped back into the shadows and was gone.

He hung his head. He'd have to tell him about Hunt when he returned and pray it was soon enough. He turned the key in the lock, pushed the door open and stepped into the passageway. The smell of cooked onions and spices made his mouth water. Guilt jabbed at his chest. He should-n't be thinking of food. Not with Father lying half-starved in prison and waiting to die. But the coney supper seemed like a lifetime ago.

He headed towards the kitchen. The room was in darkness, save for the faint glow of embers in the fireplace. He walked over and peered into the cooking pot. There was still a spoonful or two of stew left. He picked up a bowl from the table. As he dipped the ladle into the pot, something white at the back of the fireplace caught his eye.

He hooked it towards him with the handle of the ladle.

A fragment of paper, badly charred. And some words. His words.

> Dear Mother,
> I wanted . . .
> London . . .
> new friends . . .

A bitter taste flooded his mouth. His message. The Falcon had promised to get it delivered for him. But he'd burnt it instead. A sudden wave of dread rushed through him. What other lies had he told him? He shot a look at the pot of stew and frowned. That extra bowl he'd seen the Falcon help himself to earlier. What if it hadn't been for him but for someone else? Someone under lock and key.

Sliding the remains of the letter inside his jerkin, he reached up and felt for the set of keys. They weren't there. The Falcon must still have them. If he and Browne really had got Cressida shut away somewhere, how was he ever going to rescue her? A memory rippled through him. Something she had said about a boy like him being able to pick a lock. He reached for his knife. Maybe she was right.

A candle stub sat on the fireplace mantel. He grabbed it and dipped the wick in the embers of the fire. The candle caught and flared. He waited for the flame to settle, then crept out of the room and made for the stairs. A few moments later, he was standing on the landing at the bottom of the ladder. He peered up into the blackness and listened. At first, all he could hear was the wild pounding of his own heart.

He listened more closely. Wait. Yes! There it was again. The same moaning noise he'd heard the night before. The wind in the rafters? Or something else? He shivered. Time for some reinforcements. He slunk into the sleeping chamber and fished Jago out of his box.

'Come on, boy. I need your help.' He stroked the mouse's ears, then dropped him inside his waist-pouch, crept back out to the foot of the ladder and began to climb.

The air grew colder the higher he went. A sudden draught caught the candle flame and the walls came alive with twisting black snakes. He reached the top rung and blinked. A shaft of moonlight shone through a hole in the roof above him, throwing a circle of silver on the rough floorboards ahead. Beyond it, half hidden in shadow, was the outline of a wooden door. He hoisted himself up through the hatch and edged towards it.

Another moan.

He froze. Someone or something was definitely in there. But who? Only one way to find out. Gritting his teeth, he counted to three and tiptoed towards the door. He put his ear against the wood. Silence. He waited, the breath hard as ice in his throat. Still nothing. He must have imagined it. He puffed out his cheeks and turned to go.

A sobbing sound made him start. He turned back and pressed his eye to the keyhole. 'Wh–who's there?'

The sobbing stopped and a rustling noise replaced it.

He pulled out his knife and gripped it tight. Time to discover the truth. He thrust the blade into the keyhole and gave it a sharp twist. The lock held fast. He tried again, but it wouldn't budge. He frowned. If only he had a set of spy keys like Hunt. He pulled the blade free then slid it in again and jiggled it up and down. *Come on. Come on.*

With a sudden click the door swung inwards. He held back for a moment, then, thrusting the blade out in front of him, he inched through the gap and into the small room beyond.

'Is anyone there?' He held the candle above his head and peered about him. A pile of blankets lay heaped against the far wall. As he approached, a hand shot out and a splat of something cold and lumpy hit him full in the face.

'Leave me alone, you brute!' A wooden bowl came flying through the air. He ducked. The bowl hit the wall with a clatter, then spun across the floor, rolling to a stop at his feet.

'Stop! It's not who you think.' Tom leapt back, wiping gobbets of rabbit and onion from his cheeks.

The blankets reared up and a white face peered back at him from beneath a tangle of yellow curls. 'Tom? Is that you?'

His stomach lurched. So Hunt was right. She'd been here all along. He groaned and sank to his knees. What was he going to do now?

Chapter Thirty

Cressida pulled free of the blankets and slid over to him. She was dressed in the same blue gown she'd been wearing at Cowdray. Except now it was smeared with mud and stuck with bits of straw.

'I'm sorry. I thought one of those men had come back again.' She crouched next to him and clutched his arm. 'I'm so glad to see you! I thought I was on my own. How did you manage to escape?'

He frowned. 'Escape? What do you mean?'

'Aren't you their prisoner too?'

'No.' The knot in his stomach grew bigger. 'No, I'm not.' He shot a look at the door. If anyone came in now . . . 'Hold this!' He jumped to his feet and shoved the candle at her then darted back to the door and twisted his knife in the lock until it clicked shut.

Cressida's eyes widened. 'I don't understand. Why are

you locking us in?'

Flopping down beside her, he took back the candle and stuck it in a knothole in one of the floorboards. 'It's a long story. What happened to you? I thought you went off to fetch Sergeant Talbot?'

'I did.' She sniffed. 'But I changed my mind. I came back to see if you were all right. Except you weren't there. So I followed the tunnel as far as the outside. And that's when that . . . that great brute jumped out on me.' She closed her eyes and shuddered.

'You mean Browne?'

She snapped her eyes open again. 'I don't know what he's called. He didn't take the trouble to introduce himself. But he has a nasty way with a stick.' She pushed her hair back and pointed at a black mark on her left temple.

He winced. 'Does it hurt?'

'Not so much now. Though I'm sure I look a proper mess.' Her bottom lip quivered. She tugged a twist of matted curls back over the bruise. 'The worst thing was when the vile monster gave me some sort of sleeping potion.' She pulled a face at the memory. 'I wouldn't be surprised if he got the idea from one of Mister Shakespeare's plays.'

Tom's scalp pricked. So the jar of mandrake oil had been to drug her.

'And they've been sneaking it in my food too. I haven't eaten the last two lots and I feel much better. There, I've told you my story. Now it's your turn.' She folded her arms and glared at him. 'Are you with these men or against them?'

He flushed. 'You've got it all wrong.'

'Prove it then!'

He sat back, took a deep breath and told her. About how Skinner had made him betray Father. About the Falcon and his promise of help. And about the meeting with Robin Cat and the plot to kidnap Cecil. From time to time he paused, waiting for her to laugh or call him a fool, but she didn't. She just sat there listening, eyes wide as an owl's. When he got to the bit about seeing his father in gaol, the tears came again and he was forced to look away.

She reached out and squeezed his hand. 'How did you know I was here?'

He blinked and wiped his eyes with his sleeve. 'A man called Hunt, a spy who's pretending to be one of Cat's gang; he told me they'd kidnapped you. That I shouldn't trust them, because they had something bad planned. I didn't believe him at first, but now . . .' His stomach twisted again at the memory.

She raised her eyebrows. 'You mean the plan to capture Cecil?'

He shook his head. 'Worse.'

'What?'

He shrugged. 'I don't know. He wouldn't say. But he told me I had to find you and get away from here as soon as possible.'

She frowned. 'I am sorry for doubting you, cousin.' Her voice was soft; sad-sounding. 'It's not your fault. The constable was threatening your mother. You had no choice. And this man, this Falcon or whatever you call him, has tricked you. He pretended to be your friend when all along he just wanted you to dig his tunnel for him. As for your father ...' Her hand found his again. 'He does not deserve such a fate. He was only doing what any decent person would.' Her blue eyes gleamed back at him in the candle-light. 'You were right. It isn't fair. Why should he and people like him suffer for their faith when others with more money and power like ... like us, can do as we please?'

He stared at her open-mouthed. Was this really the same proud cousin who had lorded it over him at Cowdray? Perhaps that bump on the head had done her some good.

Cressida flushed. 'I know you might think it strange for me to say this after everything that has happened, but I think your father is so brave. He stands up for what he believes in. He and your mother dared to go against the Montagues because they loved each other. Whereas my father ...' She bit her lip and began fiddling with the frayed edges of a bow on the front of her dress. 'He just does what the King tells him.'

He frowned. 'He has a lot to lose.'

She sighed. 'If you mean money and paintings and golden candlesticks, yes.'

'And his family too.'

She gave another sigh. 'No, I don't think so.' She tugged at the bow again then shot him a sidelong look. 'There is more to you than I thought, Tom Garnett.'

His cheeks burned. He glanced at the door. 'Come on, we're wasting time.' He snatched up the candle stub and jumped to his feet.

Her eyes widened. 'Won't they try to stop us?'

He shook his head. 'Not if we're lucky. The Falcon has gone out. That's why I was able to come looking for you.'

He helped her up, released the lock with his knife blade and led her outside. He had his foot on the top rung of the ladder when a door banged somewhere down below.

Cressida clutched his arm. 'What was that?'

'I don't know.' His heart thumped against his chest. What if the Falcon had returned? 'We can't risk it.' He pushed her back towards the attic room.

'But you can't leave me here!' Her grip on him grew tighter.

A stab of guilt spiked him. What else could he do? He uncurled her fingers. 'I'll be back for you soon, I promise. Wait.' He reached inside his waist-pouch and let Jago crawl into his hand. 'Here. Take him. He'll keep you company.'

She wrinkled her nose.

'Go on. He won't bite.'

Reluctantly, she cupped her hands. He dropped the mouse into them. 'Look after him.' He stroked the ends of Jago's whiskers.

She gave a nod, then turned and ducked back through the door.

He pulled it shut behind her, twisted the knife in the lock and crept back down the ladder to the landing. He paused outside the sleeping chamber and held his breath. Voices echoed up from downstairs. The Falcon's, Cat's. Another's too. His head spun with the terrible truth. Cressida was right. These men were his enemies, not his friends. And the Falcon was the worst of all. Pretending to like him, saying he would help him. Taking him to see Father in the Clink when all along he'd just wanted to use him.

Father! He stifled a groan. How was he ever going to save him now? But wait! A wave of hope rushed through him. There was still a chance. If they could escape and find his Uncle Montague . . .

'Master Garnett.' The Falcon's voice called up from below. He sounded impatient.

Tom shivered.

'Where are you, boy?'

'Coming.' He took a deep breath and walked slowly towards the stairs.

Chapter Thirty-one

The Falcon stood grim-faced in a doorway at the foot of the stairs.

A lump formed in Tom's throat. In spite of everything, part of him still couldn't believe this man had only been pretending to be his friend.

'In here.' The Falcon pulled him inside.

The room was lit by candles mounted in sconces on the wall. It was completely bare of furniture save for a table which stood beneath a shuttered window opposite. Two figures dressed in hats and cloaks stood at the far end.

One of them turned as he entered and extended a gloved hand. 'Good evening, Tom. Will you be so kind as to join us?' Robin Cat smiled, but it was a smile which could have turned a puddle to ice.

He swallowed and walked towards him. As he got closer, the other man twisted round and fixed him with a steely glare. He froze. Harry Browne. What was he doing here?

Robin Cat stepped over to Tom and draped an arm round his right shoulder. 'Mister Browne says you had a visitor earlier while my friend, Mister Faw— I mean the Falcon, was with me in Lambeth.'

His heart lurched. So Browne had been spying on them.

'I ... I ... er ...' He glanced at the Falcon but he frowned and looked away.

'Tell the truth, boy,' snarled Browne. 'Or it will go the worse for you.' He shoved his fist under Tom's chin.

'Quiet, Harry. Can't you see you're frightening him?' Robin Cat pushed Browne away. He gave Tom an apologetic smile and pulled him closer.

Tom's nostrils pricked with the smell of pipe smoke mixed with incense.

'Mister Browne says the person who came calling was our new friend Mister Hunt. Is that so, Tom?'

A wave of panic surged through him. The net was closing and he didn't know how to stop it.

'Yes, sir.' He blinked.

'And what did he want?' Robin Cat's grip tightened.

He licked his lips. *Think! Quick!* He glanced at the feather in Robin Cat's hat. A sudden memory stirred of how, once, on a hunting trip with Father and William, they'd used a wooden bird to fool the others into thinking it was safe to land.

A decoy. That was what he needed now. Then with any luck they'd call off the real plot – whatever it was – and let him and Cressida go. He drew in a breath. 'Mister Hunt ...

he threatened me. He said he was one of Robert Cecil's spies. That he knew all about your mission. He wanted me to spy on you and report back to him.'

The Falcon gave a stifled groan.

Robin Cat's eyes narrowed to two green slits. 'And did he give you the details of what he thought our mission was?'

Tom gritted his teeth. If they guessed what he was up to . . . He clenched his fists and forced himself to meet Cat's gaze. 'No. But he knows you plan to kidnap his master, doesn't he?'

Browne went to say something but Cat held up his hand. 'Yes, yes, of course. We have told him as much.'

'Why didn't you tell me about Hunt's visit, Master Garnett?' The Falcon's eyes flashed with orange fire.

Tom looked away. 'I wanted to, but I – I was afraid.' At least that bit was true. He glanced back at his frowning face. The Falcon was a dangerous man – Hunt had made that clear. So why did he feel as if he'd let him down again? He hesitated, then took a deep breath and went on. 'He said if I told anyone, he . . . he would kill me. He's the same man I heard meeting in secret with Mandrake, the Montague's tutor, outside the gates at Cowdray. I recognized the voice.'

'Cowdray, eh?' The Falcon's scar twitched.

Harry Browne glared at Tom. 'You are softer than a bunch of milkmaids if you believe the boy's lies. I'll wager Master Mole here is working for Hunt and has been all along.'

Tom's mouth dropped open. 'No, I—'

The Falcon stepped towards Browne, fists curled. 'What

are you talking about, man? The boy came to London at my invitation. 'Tis nonsense to point a finger at him. And wasn't it you who brought Hunt into our company?'

Browne's hand shot to his belt. 'Are you calling me a spy, sir?'

Robin Cat jumped between them, pushing them apart. 'There will be time to settle any personal scores when our mission is complete.' He spun round and gripped Tom by the chin. 'I hope you are not lying to us, Master Garnett? After all, we have been good to you, have we not? I hear the Falcon even took you to see your father in the Clink.'

Tom blinked nervously. 'No, I mean, yes, I mean . . .'

Cat fixed him with a hard stare, then dropped his hand and sighed. 'What that scoundrel Hunt told the boy rings true with what we suspect, does it not, gentlemen?' He turned and faced the others. 'That we risk being uncovered.'

The Falcon cleared his throat. 'I'll wager Hunt is behind the letters I told you about. The ones sent to warn certain grand people sympathetic to our cause of the blow we intend and how to avoid it. After all, which one of us would be so foolish as to do such a thing and risk Cecil discovering our plans. Unless . . .' He shot a look at Browne.

Browne's face flushed with rage. 'Another insult!' He glanced at Cat then pulled a kerchief from his sleeve and wiped the beads of sweat from his forehead. 'I will do as Robin says for now, but when all this is over . . .' He threw the Falcon a hate-filled look.

The Falcon snorted. 'It matters not who sent the letters now. The big mistake was in trusting one of Cecil's spies.'

Robin Cat held up a hand. 'Enough! From what you told me, the letters do not give the detail of our plans. And we have been careful to keep them secret from our friend, Mister Hunt, which means he cannot yet know for sure the exact time and place or our method. So' – he glanced from the Falcon to Browne and back again – 'we will carry things through tomorrow night as agreed. And our brave and loyal young comrade shall be with us all the way, eh, boy?' He grabbed Tom by the shoulders and hugged him close.

Tom forced his lips into a smile. Except smiling was the last thing he felt like doing. The decoy hadn't worked. A bolt of fear shot through him. Unless he could find a way to escape, he'd have no choice but to go along with whatever Cat and his gang had planned.

Chapter Thirty-two

The men talked into the night. The sound of their voices drifted up the stairs and wound in to where Tom sat huddled under his blanket in the sleeping chamber. He strained to hear what they were saying, but it was no use; he couldn't make out their words. He sank his head between his shoulders. He still didn't have a clue what their true plan was. And in just over a day's time Father would go to the gallows. He shivered and closed his eyes.

An image of a young woman flickered in front of him, her pale face framed by wisps of blonde hair. It was the girl in the portrait at Cowdray. Except now her blue eyes brimmed with tears. As he watched, the tears spilled over her lashes and trickled down her cheeks, dissolving them into mist.

Mother? He reached out but she was gone.

He flicked open his eyes and listened. The men were still

talking down below. There'd be no chance of rescuing Cressida while they were here. He wrapped himself in the blanket and closed his eyes again.

This time, sleep came quickly.

Monday 4 November

A pale grey light shone in through the window. He blinked and rolled over. The space where the Falcon slept was empty. He leapt to his feet, tiptoed across to the door and pressed his ear to it.

Silence. Had they gone? If they had, now was his chance. Snatch Cressida, then leave, find his uncle and raise the alarm. But he had to be sure. He was about to lift the latch when a pair of footsteps started up the stairs. He shrank back and held his breath.

The footsteps came to a stop outside. The latch rattled and the door swung open. A shadow slanted across the floorboards.

'Where are you, Master Mole?' Harry Browne's voice rang out icy cold.

A shiver rippled down Tom's spine. He slid into the gap between the door and the wall. *Don't let him spot me, please.*

Browne stepped into the room and looked about him, then marched over to the mattress. He kicked at the blanket and threw a glance up at the window.

Seizing his chance, Tom dashed for the door.

'No you don't.' A hand yanked him back by the belt, swung him round and shoved him face down on the mattress.

'Leave me alone.' He made to roll away, but Browne's boot pinned him to the spot.

'My comrade should've cut your throat when he first clapped eyes on you. Snooping about in that tunnel and poking your nose into our business when it didn't concern you.' The boot pressed harder. 'But instead, the fool let sentiment get the better of him and now we have a spy in our midst.'

'But I'm not a spy!' He tried to wriggle free.

Browne jerked him back down. 'You may have survived my slip with the shovel yesterday, Master Mole, but this time, I fear, you won't be so lucky.'

A bead of sweat trickled down the side of Tom's face. 'Wh–what are you going to do?'

Browne seized a thick wooden club from beneath his cloak. He traced a gloved finger over its pitted surface. 'You will find out soon enough. But first I'm going to put you to sleep again.' He curled his lips into an unpleasant smile, jerked back the club and brought it down with a crack.

A bolt of pain shot through Tom's head. Then a tide of blackness flooded in and swallowed him whole.

He woke with a start and winced. His head was pounding fit to burst and his mouth had been filled with what tasted like a plug of wet sawdust. He made to scoop it out, but his hands were tied fast behind his back. He jiggled his feet. His ankles were bound together too. A bolt of panic shot through him. He flared his nostrils and sucked in a breath.

Stay calm. There's a way. There has to be.

He wriggled his wrists. The rope burned his skin. The more he tried to free himself, the tighter it dug. He shrugged off the blanket that covered him, rocked himself into a sitting position and jabbed his tongue against the plug. Not sawdust; cloth. He gagged, pursed his lips and coughed. Once. Twice. Three times. At the fourth try, the cloth sprang free. He spat it out and gulped in a mouthful of air. There was a strange taste in his mouth. From the cloth or something else? His arms and legs felt strangely heavy too. Had Browne given him some of the mandrake oil to keep him quiet?

He took more deep breaths, trying to clear his head. His nose filled with the smell of damp earth. He peered about him. Faint shafts of grey-blue light shone through a row of slits in the wall opposite. He glanced up at the vaulted ceiling. It looked like some kind of cellar. The one next door to Cecil's palace? But why would Browne take him there? And how long had he been unconscious for? He shivered. He'd find out soon enough.

A series of low groans echoed around him. He froze. What was that? Had Browne locked him up with some kind of wild animal? He jerked up his knees and got ready to kick. 'Come near me and—'

Something clammy clutched at his wrist.

'Get off me!' He yanked free, heart pounding.

A pair of eyes gleamed back at him. Human eyes. 'Hmmph. Hmmph.'

'Cressida?' He peered into the shadows. She was lying on

her side, half wrapped in a dirty blanket, hands tied behind her, a kerchief knotted across her mouth. 'Hold still.' He crawled alongside her. Then, sitting with his back to her, he positioned his hands in front of her mouth and tugged at the kerchief until it came free.

She licked her lips and let out another groan.

'Are you all right?'

'Yes. Apart from being tied up like a common criminal.' She struggled up and glanced round. 'Where are we?'

'I don't know. Some kind of cellar, I think.'

'How did we get here?'

'Browne. He must have brought us in the cart. I'm sorry.' Tom pulled a face. 'I was going to come back for you, but they stayed up talking most of the night. Then Browne hit me with a stick and knocked me out.'

Cressida grimaced. 'He's good at that.'

'Did he hurt you again?' He glanced at her forehead.

'No. Not this time. Just fed me more of that disgusting potion. Wait until my father finds out.' Her eyes filled with blue sparks, like his mother's when she was angry. 'Anyway, never mind about him.' She tossed her curls. 'Did you find out what the Falcon and Cat have planned?'

He shook his head. 'No, but whatever it is, they're going to act tonight. Cat said so.' He hesitated. 'Talking of cats, I . . . I suppose you don't know where Jago is?'

A smile flickered across her lips. 'Don't worry. Your furry white friend is safe.'

A surge of relief rushed through him. 'Where?'

'In here.' She jerked her head at her left sleeve. 'Though I think he might be asleep.'

His eyes widened.

'These fancy dresses have their uses, you know.' Her smile broadened then shrank to a sudden frown. 'Will the brute come back for us?'

He shrugged. 'I don't know. But I don't plan on being here if he does.'

'We won't get very far like this.' She nodded at the rope tied round her wrists and ankles.

He sighed. She was right. A sudden thought flashed through his head. He twisted round. 'Is my knife still in my belt?'

'I don't know. Wait . . . Yes!'

'Can you reach it?'

She shuffled round so they were sitting back to back. 'I think so.' She tugged at his waist. 'Keep still, will you?'

'Have you got it?'

'Nearly . . .' She gave another sharp tug. 'Yes! Here.'

His fingers brushed against the cold, hard surface of the blade. 'Good. Now I'll guide it to the rope . . . like this . . . and you start cutting.'

'But what if it slips?' She sounded scared.

'It won't if you grip it firmly.' His words were sure, but his chest was tight as a drum. He clenched his jaw. It was their only chance. He laced his fingers tight and pulled his wrists as far apart as he could. The rope juddered as the knife bit into it.

At last, after an age of cutting and sawing, his hands

sprang free. He rubbed his wrists, grabbed the knife and cut Cressida loose, then sliced through the rope at his ankles.

He jumped up. 'Now, quickly, let's get out of here.'

Chapter Thirty-three

Thin fingers of moonlight slanted through the window slits and across the stone floor. Tom peered about him looking for a door. He spotted an archway to their left and dashed over to it.

A patter of footsteps sounded behind him. 'What have you found?' Cressida pulled up beside him.

He glanced beneath it. A bunch of barrels had been stacked inside and bundles of wooden faggots propped against them. 'Some sort of storeroom, I think. Come on. Let's keep looking. There must be a way out of here somewhere.'

'Wait.' She wrinkled her nose and sniffed. 'What's that smell?'

She was right. He could smell it too. Rotten eggs mixed with charcoal. It was coming from a single barrel a few steps in front of them. He darted over to it. Someone had left the lid off. He swished his knife blade through a pile of what sounded like gritty sand. The smell grew stronger. A memory flitted into his head of a trip he and Father had made down to the harbour once to watch a man-o'-war being loaded with guns and cannonballs.

He reached inside and let a fistful of the black powder trickle through his fingers. 'Gunpowder!'

Cressida gazed at the barrels open-mouthed. As her eyes flicked back to him, his heart jolted. They were thinking the same thing.

'So it wasn't my father's wine they were smuggling after all...'

He shook his head slowly, then frowned. 'The Falcon told me he worked for your father once. He must have thought the tunnel was a safe place to hide it. Until they needed it.'

'Needed it for what?'

Tom stared at the woodpile, then back at the barrels. A shiver of fear ran through him. There was enough gunpowder here to blow a whole army to smithereens. Except it wasn't an army above them. He staggered back from the barrels, eyes bulging.

Cressida clutched his arm. 'Tom? What's wrong?'

'They're not going to kidnap Cecil. They're going to blow him up. Him, his palace and everyone inside it.'

'What?' Her grip tightened.

He clenched his jaw. There was no doubting it. These new friends of his, they were murderers, every one of them!

Cressida started. 'What was that?' She spun round and

peered back into the main room.

Tom held his breath. A scrape of boots followed by a rattle of metal and a creak of wood. Someone was coming.

'Quick!' He dragged her down behind the nearest stack of barrels.

A door banged open and a pair of footsteps echoed towards them. Browne. It must be. Come to finish them off. But wait. A second set of footsteps. If it *was* him, he wasn't alone. Keeping low, Tom edged along behind the barrels until he found a gap. He pressed his right eye to it and peered out. Two figures stood in the middle of the cellar, their faces masked in shadow.

'Is all in order?' The voice, low and silky-smooth, was Robin Cat's.

The other man cleared his throat, then, spurs chinking, he turned and strode towards the barrel store. Tom yanked Cressida back against the wall.

'Yes.' There was the thud of a fist or boot against one of the barrels. 'There's enough powder here to blow them all sky high.'

The Falcon. Tom froze.

''Twill be the most explosive opening the Parliament has ever seen.'

The words sliced through Tom like a blade. He rammed his fist against his mouth. He'd been wrong. They weren't next to Cecil's palace. They were beneath the building where the Parliament was going to meet. And it wasn't just Cecil Robin Cat and his men were planning to kill. It was the King and his ministers too. And worst of all . . . His stomach twisted. Worst of all, he, Tom Garnett, had been helping them.

'Rest assured, Robin, we may fling the scorched bodies of the King and his ministers heavenward tomorrow morning, but their miserable souls will be lodged in Hell for all eternity.'

As the men's laughter bounced against his ears, the last flicker of doubt fizzled inside Tom and died. There was no denying it. Hunt was right. The Falcon was a ruthless killer who had lied to him all along. How could he ever have trusted him? He slumped down, head in his hands. *Stupid! Stupid!*

The Falcon made a hawking noise and spat. 'James Stuart and his cronies have visited much pain and suffering on us and our fellow Catholics. It is time for them now to pay.' His boots chinked back out into the main room. 'When do you set off to raise the revolt?'

Cressida let out a gasp. Tom shook his head and put a finger to his lips. He crouched forwards and put his eye to the gap again.

'As soon as I leave here.' Cat slapped his gloves against his left palm. 'The others are ready and waiting. When they get the news that the King and most of his family are dead, they will ride to Coombe Abbey and take the Princess Elizabeth as planned. She is still very young and will need some education in our ways, but I am sure, in time, she will make a most excellent and sympathetic Queen.'

Tom's eyes widened. So that was their plan. Kill the King and put his young daughter – Elizabeth Stuart – on the throne as their puppet.

'What of the Montague children? Browne says he stowed the boy up in the attic with the girl this morning, but we can't keep them there for ever.'

So Harry Browne had lied to them.

Robin Cat stroked his beard and frowned. 'In all truth, they are something of an inconvenience.'

'No need to harm them.' The Falcon's voice was gruff. 'They are only children.'

Tom swallowed a sigh. The Falcon might have deceived him and kept Cressida locked up in the attic; but at least he didn't want them dead. Not like Browne, who clearly intended for them to be blown up along with Parliament and the King.

'Well, my friend, you should have thought of that before you brought them to London.'

'I didn't have any choice with the girl. Browne had already taken her. As for the boy . . .' The Falcon paused and cleared his throat. 'I like him. He reminds me of how I used to be when I was a lad. It's hard to lose your father when you're young. I know that from bitter experience. And Master Garnett's father is a brave man, wrongfully imprisoned by the tyrant's lackeys.'

Robin Cat laughed. 'I didn't think a soldier capable of such sentiment. Well, if you succeed here, you may do with them as you will. The boy seems much taken with you and I'm sure with a little gentle persuasion, you can make him do your bidding.'

'I'd like to think so. And as you know, I harbour a hope

of reuniting him and his father.'

'I'm sure our new Queen will oblige you on that score. Meanwhile, the Montague girl has not seen your face, I think?'

''Tis true. I disguised myself when I took her her food.'

'So, why not "rescue" her when all this is done and collect your reward from Lord Montague? If he and the other Catholic lords have any sense, they will heed the mysterious letters they have been sent warning them to keep away from the Parliament tomorrow.'

'Maybe . . .' The Falcon frowned.

'Now.' Robin Cat grasped the Falcon's right hand and shook it hard. 'Night comes on. I must find myself a wherry from the river stairs nearby and get back to Lambeth to collect my mount.' He fished an object from beneath his cloak and handed it to the other man. 'Here is a pocket watch so you may mark down the hours.'

The Falcon nodded. 'I will return around midnight as planned and prepare the barrels for firing.' He turned and glanced over at the storeroom entrance.

Tom shrank back from the gap and held his breath.

'God speed, my friend. And when the deed is done, deal quickly with your affairs here for you must to Flanders and tell the Spanish King how things lie. We'll need his support to tame any resistance and secure the safety of the country.'

The two men turned and strode back across the stone floor. A few moments later, the door banged shut and Tom and Cressida were alone again.

Tom sat there in a daze, grappling to make sense of what

he'd heard.

'So that spy of yours was right.'

He jerked his head up. Cressida's eyes shone back at him in the gloom. He nodded and licked his lips.

'Well.' She tossed her head in the direction of the door. 'I doubt that other brute will be back anyway. He must have hoped we'd die along with the King.'

The mention of the King jabbed Tom into action. He leapt to his feet. 'We've got to warn him, while there's still time.'

Cressida frowned. 'But how?'

'We must go and see him, tell him to his face.'

She laughed. 'Are you mad, cousin?'

'What do you mean?'

She jumped up and faced him. 'First, we've got no idea which palace the King is staying in.'

'You mean he's got more than one?'

She rolled her eyes. 'Of course. He's the King! And second, even if we find out where he is, do you really think his guards are going to let us in?'

Tom slammed his boot against the nearest barrel. 'But it's a matter of life and death.'

She let out a sigh. 'All right, supposing we did get inside. Third, do you think the King would believe us? I mean – look at us.' She stared down at her grimy skirts and tattered sleeves. 'Even the greatest actor in London couldn't convince anyone they were of noble blood dressed like this.'

Tom clenched his jaw. She was right. But they couldn't stand by and let these men murder the King and all those innocent people. 'What about your father? The King would believe him, wouldn't he?'

'Maybe, but we'd have to get to his house in Southwark first.'

'So?'

'The quickest way is by boat. But we need money to pay the wherryman. So unless you've got a secret stash of coins …?'

He shook his head then balled his fingers into fists. 'We can't give up now. We'll have to stop them ourselves!'

She put her hands on her hips. 'And just how do you propose we do that?'

Chapter Thirty-four

Monday 4 November — Night

Tom stared at the barrels of gunpowder. There must be thirty of them at least. And they were heavy. Too heavy for him and Cressida to shift. He ran over to the door, scrambled up the steps in front of it, then lifted the latch and peered out.

It was dark outside. Clouds scudded like sailboats across the face of the moon. A gust of wind blew the dank, chill smell of the river towards him. A nearby clock began to chime the hour. Others joined it. *Seven. Eight. Nine.* Three hours to go before the Falcon returned.

He glanced across the wide paved courtyard in front of him. A brick gatehouse stood in the opposite corner. Through its arch he caught sight of a street beyond. If they couldn't get across the river to his uncle's house, maybe they could try and find a watchman or a constable instead. Except they might not believe them either. Or, worse still, accuse them of being mixed up in the plot.

Think, Tom Garnett! Think! He dashed back inside and scanned about him. A set of three pails stowed by the wall next to the storeroom arch caught his eye. Robin Cat had said they were near to some river stairs. He ran over and snatched up the pails.

'Here.' He kept two of them and threw the other one to Cressida.

She pulled a face. 'What am I meant to do with this?'

'Come with me. I've got an idea.' He ran back to the door.

Reluctantly she followed. 'Where are we going?'

'You'll see.' He climbed back up the steps.

She hesitated.

'Hurry. You heard what he said. He'll be back soon.' Darting outside, he raced across the courtyard and poked his head through the gatehouse arch. To his left stood a row of crooked houses. To his right the walls of a great stone hall soared into the night sky. It was the same building he'd seen from the lodging house yard.

Cressida pulled up alongside him and peered over his shoulder. 'That's Westminster Hall. And the House of Lords where the Parliament meets is above the cellar.' She tapped him on the arm and pointed back at the building they'd just come from. 'I saw them once before when I came up to London with Mother to visit Father and we went to one of Mister Shakespeare's plays. A tragedy. It was so sad.'

She gave a loud sigh. 'I kept the playbill as a souvenir.'

He rolled his eyes. There she went again talking about Mister Shakespeare and plays and stuff when they had more important things to think about. Like saving the King from certain death. He glanced back at the building's arched windows and shuddered. There wasn't a moment to lose.

'Which way to the river?'

'This way I think.' She led him out through the arch and on to the street and signalled at a narrow alley to their left. A distant sloshing sound echoed along the walls of the mean-looking houses that lined it.

'Come on then.' He tugged her arm but she dug her heels in and refused to move.

'Do you want to save the King, or not?'

'Of course I do. But I don't see how going down a slimy alleyway that leads nowhere is going to help. We don't have the money for a wherry. You said so yourself.'

'No. But river water is free.'

Cressida's eyes widened in horror. 'Surely you're not expecting me to *swim* across?'

He sighed. The potion Browne had given her had turned her soft in the head. He lifted up the pails he was carrying and slammed them together. 'Wetted gunpowder doesn't light.'

She wrinkled her nose. 'If you think I'm going to haul great pail-loads of water up and down this . . . this open sewer.'

'Suit yourself.' He ripped the pail from her hand. Why had he ever thought she would help? He turned and slithered down the alley without a backward glance.

The damp air wound around him and slid down the back of his neck. His teeth began to chatter. He tightened his grip on the pails and followed the smell of the river until he came to a dark-shuttered tavern. The slap-slap of water drew him down a flight of steep steps next to it. When he reached the bottom one, he squatted and peered into the swirling current below him. A shiver rippled through him as he remembered the Falcon's words about dead men's bones.

A rumble of thunder filled the air. He jerked his head up and stared at the opposite bank. The lights of houses and taverns winked back at him in the darkness. Father was out there somewhere, all alone in that stinking cell. His heart clenched. He'd promised to save him, but what were his chances of doing that now?

A splash of cold water hit his forehead and ran down the side of his cheek. He blinked and shook himself. If he didn't fill the pails and get them back to the cellar fast, he'd be a traitor twice over. Setting two of them down, he gripped the third and dipped it into the inky-black depths. He'd nearly filled it when a sudden surge of water yanked at the rope handle, tugging it from his grasp. As he made a swipe for it, his boots slipped from under him. He tumbled forwards, arms flailing and . . .

SPLASH!

He hit the surface and went under. A torrent of ice-cold water flooded his nose and mouth forcing the breath from his lungs. He hung there for a moment like a piece of seaweed, twisting and turning in the murky current. Then a jolt in his chest jerked him up.

WHOOSH! His head broke the surface again. He gulped in a mouthful of frost-filled air and blinked.

Once . . .

Twice . . .

Three times . . .

Out of the darkness, a glint of something metal.

A ring. An iron ring dangling from the wall to his right. He snatched. His fingers brushed against it. He snatched again but before he could get a grip, the current spun him round and swung him away.

Icy hands clutched at his legs and arms, dragging him down.

Down

and down

to the dead men.

He kicked against them.

They were strong.

Too strong . . .

He closed his eyes and let himself drift.

'*Swim, Tom!* You've got to *swim*!'

The words shocked him awake. A torrent of cold river water gushed down his nose and throat. He choked it out, thrust his head back and sucked in another mouthful of air. A sudden memory of playing at being fish in the sea with William shot through him. With a kick of his legs, he turned and struck out for the bank.

He was halfway there when a giant snake came twisting

through the air and splashed down next to him.

'Quick! Grab the rope, before it's too late!'

He swiped for it and missed, then swiped again.

This time his fingers closed tight round the rope's tarry surface.

'Now *pull*!'

Taking a deep breath, he kicked and hauled himself through the whirling black current. As he reached the stairs, the dead men snatched at him one last time, trying to pull him under.

But Cressida's grip was stronger. 'Got you!' Puffing and panting, she heaved him clear of the current.

A surge of muddy river water flooded up his throat. He spat it out and fell back against the cold stone ridge of the steps.

'That was close. Are you all right?'

He blinked and looked up into a pair of worried blue eyes.

'Th–th–the pail. I lost it.'

'We have the others.' She swung the remaining two pails in front of him.

He nodded. She was right. They could still do this. He drew a deep breath, then dragged his legs up out of the water and clambered shivering to his feet.

'It will be easier to fill them here, where the water is quieter.' Cressida pointed to a place where the water lapped gently between the stairs and the tavern wall.

Tom coughed and hugged his arms to his chest. 'Why didn't I spot that before?'

'Well, if you will go off in a huff.' She flashed him a smile then handed him one of the pails. 'Come on, Tom Garnett. We've got some gunpowder to ruin.'

They lugged pail after pail back up the alleyway, across the courtyard and into the cellar. Tom used his knife to prise the lid off each barrel before they sloshed two loads of the cold, stinking river water over the gunpowder.

Halfway through, Cressida glanced up at him. 'Will it be enough?'

He gnawed his bottom lip. 'It'll have to be. We haven't got time for more.' As he spoke, distant chimes struck the hour. Eleven o'clock. One hour before the Falcon returned. 'We've got to speed up.' Grabbing the empty pail, he dashed back outside.

Not long after, it started to rain. They staggered up and down the alleyway, hauling yet more pail-loads between them.

'Only five barrels left.'

Cressida groaned and clutched at her sides.

'Are you all right to go on?'

She wiped the rainwater from her eyes and thrust her head in the air. 'I'm a Montague, aren't I? And Montagues never give up.'

'You're right. We don't.' He gave a grim smile then picked up his pail and headed for the cellar door.

When they had soaked the final barrel-load of powder, he threw the pail to the floor and heaved a sigh. 'We've done it. Come on, let's get out of here.' He draped one of the blankets over her shoulders and tied the other one round his neck.

'Aren't you forgetting something?'

He frowned. 'What?'

Cressida darted behind the woodpile and lifted up an old lantern. The shadow of a mouse sat hunched behind the horn-covered door.

'I stowed him in here earlier. I thought he'd be safer.'

Tom bit his lip. Poor Jago. What kind of a friend had he been to him? Dragging him all the way to London, keeping him locked up in a small poky box, forgetting to feed him. And if it hadn't been for Cressida, he would have left him behind now too. He took the lantern from her and pressed his fingers against the cover.

'Sorry, boy. As soon as we're safe, I'll find you some food and—' The words froze in his throat. Footsteps. 'Quick!' He yanked Cressida down behind the barrels. The pair of them held their breath and waited.

The door creaked open. A beam of yellow light danced across the walls.

The Falcon. It had to be.

As the footsteps chinked closer, Jago let out a squeak.

'Shhh, boy.' Tom hugged the lantern to him, trying to muffle the sound.

Eek . . . eek.

'Pesky rodents.' The beam of light swung towards them. Tom ducked, but not fast enough.

A gloved hand shot out and hauled him from his hiding place. 'God's teeth! What are *you* doing here?'

Chapter Thirty-five

Tom shoved a hand in front of his eyes to shield them from the light. 'I . . . er . . .'

There was a rustle of silk behind him. 'Leave him alone, you great bully!'

The Falcon drew a sharp breath. 'The girl too. But Browne said you were both locked up in the attic. Why, the pox-ridden—' He clenched his fist.

'Yes. And thanks to him we know everything.' Cressida tossed her head in the direction of the barrels of gunpowder.

The Falcon's eyes narrowed to two black chips. 'And pray what do you mean by that, Mistress Montague?' He set his lantern down carefully on top of the nearest barrel.

Tom gave her a swift kick in the shins. But it was no use; she was like a river in full flood.

'That you and your gang aim to blow up King James and

his ministers when they come to the Parliament tomorrow. Which, in case you didn't know it, is treason.' Her eyes sparked blue and gold.

The Falcon slammed his fist against the barrel lid and muttered a curse. He glanced back at them, then sighed and pulled off his gloves.

'You may have lived a sheltered life, Mistress Montague, but there are plenty of honest Catholics who have suffered dearly since the man you call your King took the English throne. He made promises before he was crowned, that things would go better for us. But' – forehead furrowing, he shook his head – 'the words he spoke were honeyed lies. Instead, he has chosen to follow the same path as his predecessor, the tyrant Elizabeth Tudor. Fining good Catholic families, imprisoning those who attend Masses and executing holy priests who dare to preach the words of the one true religion. Truly, I do the Lord's work in ridding the country of him.' He turned to Tom. 'You should understand that more than most, boy. With your father locked up and about to die for an act of kindness to a priest.'

A flare of anger shot through Tom. He thrust Jago's lantern at Cressida and sprang forward, fists raised, 'It's you that's the liar! You said you were going to get Cecil out of the way so the King would listen to you. But you were planning to kill them both all along. Father will hang tomorrow. And now it's too late to save him!' His eyes smarted. He bit his lip and turned away.

The Falcon gripped his shoulders and swung him round. 'It isn't. Don't you see? The Scotchman and that fox, Cecil, will be dead in a few hours. Then we will set the young Princess Elizabeth on the throne. And she will have no choice but to do our bidding and free your father and all those other wretched souls that have been wrongfully condemned.'

Tom widened his eyes in disbelief. Did the Falcon really think what he was doing was right? He wrenched free and glared back at him. 'Murder is wrong. It says so in the Bible.'

The Falcon frowned. He glanced at the ring on his finger and twisted it round. The bird's diamond eye gleamed in the lantern light, dancing strange patterns across his face. 'You speak truly.' He sighed. 'But sometimes a man is forced to commit a necessary evil for a greater good.' He shot him a look. 'Have you not done so yourself, Master Garnett?'

Tom's stomach twisted at the sudden memory of Mother's tear-stained face and Skinner's threats. But no. He shook his head. It wasn't the same. He'd never wanted to betray Father and he'd tried so hard afterwards to make it right. Except now . . . now he never would. He blinked back the tears.

'You don't agree? Well, whatever you and young Mistress Montague here might think, I am not a scoundrel like Browne.' The Falcon grasped his shoulder again. 'I do not actively seek the death of innocents. At least, not if it can be helped.'

'But what have the King and the others done to you?'

The Falcon's eyes glittered black in the lantern light. 'I have already told you why they must die. Now, stay true to me, Soldier, and I promise I will keep you and your cousin safe. 'Tis just a few short hours before I must light the fuse; though God knows I wish it were sooner. After the deed is done, we will run from here together and I will take you to your uncle's house across the river. He is a good Catholic. When he and his friends see the way things lie, they will be swift to support our cause.'

'Excuse me.' Cressida pushed in front of Tom. 'Aren't you forgetting something?'

'And what might that be, little mistress?' The Falcon gave her an amused smile.

'The lord my father will be at the opening of the Parliament with the King.'

He shook his head. 'Not if he has taken heed of certain letters written to the Catholic lords to tell them to keep away. So' – he threw Tom a glance – 'what do you say, Soldier? Are you with me? Remember, if we succeed, your father goes free.'

Tom's heart jolted. He wanted to rescue Father more than anything. But not if it meant blowing up the King. He glanced at the barrels. They'd done their best to ruin the gunpowder. If they could get out of here and raise the alarm, there might still be a way to save him from the hangman's noose. But how were they going to escape? He licked his lips. He needed a plan and quickly.

'Come, Soldier? Are we not friends?'

He frowned. Friends? They had been once. But wait. An idea flashed into his head. He threw back his shoulders and jutted out his chin. 'No! I won't do it! I won't be a traitor.

I'd rather die. So either let me go … or … or silence me now.'

'What?' The Falcon's eyes blazed with a sudden orange fire.

Fingers trembling, Tom drew his knife from his belt and held it out.

Cressida gasped. 'No, Tom!' She leapt between them.

'Get out of my way, cousin.' He shoved her aside and thrust the knife hilt-first at the Falcon again. 'If it's a choice between being blown up and this . . .' He gestured to the knife and fixed him with a level gaze.

The Falcon grimaced. 'I am no child-slayer. You should know that, boy.'

'Then let us go.' Tom gritted his teeth, willing him to take the bait.

The Falcon's eyes narrowed. 'What, and have you running off to that traitor Hunt – or whatever his real name is – to tell him what we intend?' He shook his head. 'No, sorry. If you won't join me, then you leave me no choice but to bind you both fast and keep you close until my work here is done.' He made a grab for Tom.

A cry rang out behind them. 'Take that, you fiend!'

A pail shot past Tom's right ear and smacked into the Falcon's forehead. He groaned and staggered backwards, clutching his head with both hands. Before he had time to right himself, a second pail came flying through the air. It thudded into his chest, winding him, forcing him to his knees.

'Run!' Cressida snatched Tom by the arm and yanked him towards the door.

He rammed the knife in his belt and stumbled after her, then jerked to a stop. 'Wait! Jago!' He twisted round and darted back past the Falcon into the storeroom. Scanning desperately about him, he spotted the lantern on top of one of the barrels. He grabbed the handle and spun round just as the Falcon lurched to his feet.

'Quick, cousin! Before it's too late!'

Tom took a deep breath, put his head down and barrelled past him. The Falcon clutched at his makeshift cloak, but he ripped free and kept on running.

'Wait! Come back!' The Falcon's voice echoed after him.

Heart racing, Tom dashed up the stairs and out through the door to where Cressida was waiting.

'Come on!' She lifted up her skirts and ran.

A pair of spurred footsteps rang out behind them. They careered through the gatehouse arch, out on to the street.

Tom seized her by the hand. 'This way.' He dipped down the alleyway that led to the river, then realized his mistake. In a few moments more, they'd be at the river steps and the Falcon would have them cornered like a pair of rats. He scoured about for a place to hide. The footsteps drew closer. A dark figure appeared at the top of the alleyway.

'There! Look!' Cressida pointed to a narrow gap between two tumbledown houses. They darted across to it and edged inside, pressing their backs against the wall. The footsteps echoed down the cobbles then came to a sudden stop. Tom clasped Jago's lantern to him, held his breath and peered back into the alley. The Falcon stood almost level with their hiding place. He cast around him, eyes piercing the darkness.

'I know you and your cousin are close, Master Garnett. Come; stay with me and I promise, once the deed is done, I will go back to the Clink and free your father myself.'

Tom's chest tightened. The Falcon had been good to him. Saved his life on the road and taken him to see Father at great risk to himself. But what kind of a person could think that blowing up the King and all those innocent people was right? He clenched his knuckles and stood firm.

The Falcon waited a moment longer then let out a sigh. ''Tis a pity, Soldier. We could do with more men like you. Still, in spite of our differences, I will do my best for your father once the day is ours. Now, I must return to my post, bolt myself in and make my preparations.' He raised a hand in salute, then turned on his heels and marched back the way he had come.

Chapter Thirty-six

Tuesday 5 November — the early hours

Tom waited until the Falcon's footsteps had died away then squeezed out from their hiding place and looked back up the alleyway. There was no sign of him. Heaving a sigh, he held up Jago's lantern and peered at the small shadow behind the door.

'All right, boy. He's gone.'

A finger jabbed him in the back. 'What were you think-ing of, Tom Garnett?'

'What?' He spun round.

Cressida stood there, hands on her hips, eyes flashing. 'Giving that man your knife. What if he'd used it?'

He flushed. 'I knew he wouldn't.'

'Oh, really? Why?'

He puffed out his chest. 'You heard what he said to Cat.

He likes me.'

She raised her eyebrows. 'Well, he has a strange way of showing it.'

He pulled a face. But she was right. Things hadn't quite worked out the way he'd planned. He shot her a grim smile. 'Thanks. If it wasn't for you, we'd be his prisoners now.'

'Yes, and if he finds out what we did to his precious powder and comes after us . . .'

Tom frowned. Had they done enough to ruin the gunpowder? He hoped so. But what about Father? He glanced down the alleyway towards the river.

A hand yanked his sleeve. 'Tom?'

He shook free. 'We've got to get to your father's house before he sets off for Parliament. Tell him what's happened and get him to beg the King for Father's life.'

'But the problem still remains.'

'What?'

'We need money to get across the river.'

A sudden thought flashed into his head. 'Wait.' He fumbled inside his waist-pouch and pulled out the tinderbox. 'Would a wherryman accept this?'

Cressida's eyes widened in surprise.

'Mother gave it to me.'

She took it and weighed it in her palm. 'Silver. It's worth trying.' She handed it back to him.

'Come on!' He grabbed her by the hand and set off down the alleyway. At the top of the river stairs he stopped and scanned the glittering black current. Where had all the wherries gone? His heart sank. If they had to go overland

and cross the bridge, it would take too long. He was about to give up hope when a light bobbed towards them. He raised both arms and swung them above his head.

'Over here!'

A voice rasped back at him above the lap of the waves. 'I've finished for the night.' There was a creak of oars and the light moved off downriver.

Cressida cupped her hands to her mouth. 'We will make it worth your while.'

Silence, then a creak and a sudden swoosh. The light swung round. Tom held his breath as a small boat cut through the water towards them, the figure of a man hunched at its oars. As the boat reached the stairs, the man's whiskery face leered up at them.

'And why should I believe a pair of good-fer-nothin's like you?'

'Because we'll pay you well.' Tom flashed the tinderbox at him.

'Let me see.' The wherryman lifted up from his seat.

Reluctantly Tom dropped the tinderbox into the man's grimy palm. 'It's solid silver.'

The wherryman held it up to his lantern, peered at it with milky eyes then bit the lid with the stump of a rotten tooth. He shot them another look, then shoved the tinderbox inside his patched jerkin. 'All right. Where you goin' then?'

Tom stifled a groan. If Mother found out he'd given her precious gift away . . . But he couldn't help that now. They had to get across the river and quickly.

An elbow jabbed him in the ribs. 'Come on, cousin!' Cressida hoisted up her skirts and jumped into the boat. 'The nearest stairs to Montague House, Southwark. And hurry! We are on the King's business.'

The wherryman raised a bristly eyebrow. 'The King's business, eh? Well, p'raps I should charge you double then?'

Tom glared at Cressida. Why did she have to go and say that? 'She's only joking, sir.' He scrambled in after her and sat down before the wherryman could change his mind.

'Funny sort of joke.' The man scowled, then dipped the oars into the current and began to row.

The crossing was rougher than the night before. Twice Tom was forced to stick his head over the side of the boat and retch.

Cressida pulled a face. 'I thought you'd be used to boats, living down by the sea?'

He wiped his mouth on his sleeve and frowned. 'I am. I just haven't found my sea legs yet.'

'Oh, I see. Well, I hope they come running soon.' She giggled.

He was about to tell her to shut up when another large wave slapped against the side. He groaned and hung his head back over the water.

As they neared the opposite bank, a church tower loomed above them. It was the same place he and the Falcon had landed at last night. He had shown him a great kindness then. Tom shivered. How could one man be such a tangle of things? The boat banged against the step. He pulled the blanket tight around him and jumped out on to dry land.

'Give me Jago.' He held out his hand.

Cressida passed him the lantern. 'This way.' She clambered out of the boat and led him up the steps in the direction of the church.

He stopped in front of the entrance and stared along the murky alleyway next to it. Father was down there somewhere, just a street or two away . . . His shoulders slumped. He might as well be in the New World.

A clock chimed out above him. He waited for it to carry on striking. But it didn't. One o'clock already. Only five hours, six at most, before Father met the hangman. A jet of sour liquid shot up his throat. His knees buckled and he staggered sideways banging the lantern against his thigh.

Jago let out a squeak of fear.

Cressida spun round. 'Tom? Are you all right?' She ran back to him and propped him up with her shoulder.

He closed his eyes and swallowed. 'Still a bit seasick . . .'

'Come on. It's not far now. I'll fetch you something to drink when we get there.' Taking the lantern from him, she led him down the side of the church, beneath an archway and into a small square.

A grand-looking brick house stood in front of them. Tom glanced up at the windows tightly shuttered against the night. He hugged his arms to him. What if no one was there?

A set of stone steps led up to the door. Leaving him with the lantern, Cressida dashed up them, raised the iron door knocker and struck it hard against the wood.

Silence.

He bit his lip. *Please let there be someone. Please.*

She was about to knock again when the sound of hurrying footsteps echoed from somewhere inside.

He murmured a quick prayer of thanks then held his breath and waited. The footsteps came to a sudden stop. There was a rattle of keys and the door swung slowly open. The silhouette of a man stood before them, the edges of his long gown lit by a faint glow of candlelight.

'It is me, Mistress Cressida. Let us in.'

The man stepped back into the shadows and let them pass.

A waft of must pricked Tom's nostrils. He frowned. That smell. He knew it from somewhere . . .

Cressida patted her curls and smoothed the front of her gown. 'Where is the lord my father? We must see him at once! It is a matter of life and death.'

The door banged shut behind them. 'I'm afraid that won't be possible.' The man swooped past them and snatched up a lighted candle from a table next to the wall. He turned and thrust the flame under Cressida's chin. 'You see, sadly for him, he is about to be unavoidably detained.'

Chapter Thirty-seven

A knot formed in Tom's throat. Mandrake! What was he doing here? He gripped a tight hold of the lantern and took a step backwards.

The tutor lifted the candle above his head. 'Ah! Master Garnett. Welcome! When I last saw you, you were grubbing around for water at the bottom of a chalk pit.'

His eyes widened. So he'd been right. There *had* been someone following them on the road to London.

Mandrake gave a yellow-toothed grin. 'Oh, yes. I was on your tail all the way. I had my orders not to let that traitor out of my sight. What d'you call him? The Falcon, isn't it?' He narrowed his eyes and traced a pale, worm-like finger down the candle's waxy side.

'Orders from who?'

The tutor tapped his bony nose. 'It matters not, boy. Suffice it to say I work for a higher authority than Lord

Montague, as you shall shortly discover.' He shook his head and let out a sigh. 'It is a sad fact that your association with that scoundrel is likely to cost you dear.' He shifted his snake-eyed gaze to Cressida. 'As it will your father, Mistress Cressida. But no! Let us cease this charade and call you by your proper name, *Mistress Maria*.'

Cressida flushed. 'How dare you! When the lord my father finds out about your insolence, he will have you thrown into the deepest dungeon in the land.'

Mandrake's tongue darted across his lips. 'Oh, but I fear you have it all wrong. It is not me who is going to gaol.' He placed the candle-holder back on the table.

She stamped her foot. 'What do you mean?'

'Lord Montague has made some – how shall I put it? – unwise alliances.' The tutor hooked a strand of oily black hair behind his ear and reached inside his gown. 'Take this letter for example, which came into my hands just a few hours ago.' He pulled out a folded piece of parchment and waved it in the air. 'It warns him to stay away from the opening of the Parliament if he values his life. The author is unknown, but 'twill be proof enough of your father's association with those assassins and their plot to murder our beloved King.'

'No!' Cressida's hand flew up to her mouth. She stumbled against Tom.

He steadied her then glanced at the letter and gritted his teeth. They had to get it off Mandrake and destroy it before he showed it to the King.

The tutor gave a high-pitched laugh. 'Oh, but there is

more. Including the time Master Garnett's friend, the Falcon – or Guy Fawkes as he is really called – spent in your father's employment.'

Tom's heart missed a beat. Guy Fawkes. So that was his real name . . .

Mandrake shot him a knowing look. 'Your friend is a man of many identities. But wait!' He switched his gaze from Tom back to Cressida. 'We mustn't forget the barrels of gunpowder he kept stored underground in Lord Montague's secret tunnel and which he has brought to London by stealth with your own cousin's help. My master and I could not be sure exactly what mischief he and the others intended with them. Now, thanks to this letter, I think I can make a fair guess. But wait! Perhaps Master Garnett would like to confess all?'

Tom clamped his mouth tight shut. If Mandrake thought he could trap him that easily . . .

'No? Well, let me tell you then. The barrels your friend had stashed beneath Cowdray are piled high in Westminster, waiting to blow the King and his lords to kingdom come. And now the plot is uncovered, Mister Fawkes, your uncle, and you too, Master Garnett, unless the King shows you mercy, will all die.'

Cressida leapt forwards. 'You're wrong! My father loves the King. He would never hurt him. And as for Tom—'

Mandrake put up a hand. 'Enough! If a man knows of a threatened harm and does not lift a finger to stop it, it is still treason. And this letter is proof of your father's guilt.' He waved the parchment above his head.

An icy voice rang out behind them. 'What is this talk of treason under my roof?'

Tom twisted round and watched in amazement as a tall, thin figure dressed in a black and gold nightgown started down the stairs.

'Granny!' Cressida ran towards her.

The old lady jerked to a stop and clutched her fingers to her throat. 'Where have you been, child? Your father has been sick with worry. And as for you, Master Garnett . . .' She fixed him with a granite stare.

He glared back at her. What did she care about him?

'Oh, Granny!' Cressida buried her face in the Viscountess's gold-threaded skirts. 'Mister Mandrake says the lord my father is to be arrested on suspicion of being part of a plot to murder King James.'

'I heard him.' The old woman turned her gaze on the tutor and thrust out a bony hand. 'Give me the letter.'

Mandrake slid it inside the sleeve of his gown. 'Forgive me, Lady Magdalen' – he gave a sly smile – 'but I must keep it safe for my master. He will be here directly. Once he has read it himself, I am sure he will be only too happy to reveal its contents to you.'

The old lady banged her ebony cane on the flagstones. 'Ungrateful wretch! After everything my grandson has done for you.'

Mandrake's eyes flashed gold in the candlelight. 'It was the least he could do when your own husband did my father such a terrible wrong!'

'What are you talking about, man?'

'Having trouble remembering, eh?' Mandrake shook his head and sighed. 'That is just like you privileged folk. Well, let me remind you, My Lady. 'Twas the winter of eighty-two. The crops had failed again and my father could not pay the rent he owed. Your husband threw him from the land he farmed, even though he had a wife and five children to feed.'

The Viscountess pursed her lips and frowned. 'I don't remember the case. But my husband was not a cruel man. I am sure he would have given your father more than one chance to make good his debt. And when all is said and done, a man must pay his dues.'

'Indeed.' The tutor stabbed a finger at her. 'And now it is your turn.'

Rat-tat-a-tat.

Tom spun round knocking Jago's lantern against his leg.

Mandrake gave a whining chuckle. 'That will be my master, come to collect the evidence.' Reaching inside the sleeve of his gown, he darted to the door.

'Stop him!' cried Cressida.

Tom leapt towards Mandrake and snatched at the back of his gown. The tutor swung round and shoved him aside, then turned and flung the door open. The candle flame flickered in the draught. A figure dressed all in black stepped quickly inside.

'Welcome, master. You have come at just the right time. I have uncovered a whole den-full of traitors for you.'

The newcomer's pale eyes shone out from the gap between the brim of his hat and the muffler which covered his nose and mouth.

'What is the meaning of this?' There was a swish of velvet and the click of a stick on stone.

'My Lady.' The man pushed past Mandrake. He lifted his hat, slid the muffler from his face and gave a stiff bow.

Hunt. Tom gasped. So it *was* him Mandrake had met in secret outside Cowdray's walls.

The Viscountess jerked up her head and fixed Tom with a sharp stare. 'Do you know this man?'

'Yes . . . I . . . er . . .'

'The name is Solomon Wiseman, My Lady. Although' – the man glanced back at him – 'the boy knows me by a different name. I—'

'Silence!' The Viscountess turned to Tom. 'Let Master Garnett tell me in his own words.'

He hesitated.

'Go on, boy.' Her voice had a softer edge to it now.

He gripped the lantern handle and sucked in a breath. 'He . . . he said his name was George Hunt. At first I thought he was part of the plot the Falcon' – he bit his lips – 'I mean Fawkes and the others had planned. The one to kidnap Cecil.'

'You mean Robert Cecil?' The Viscountess's forehead creased into a hundred tiny furrows.

'Yes. But then this man – Mister Hunt – he told me Fawkes had captured Cressida and they were planning something much worse.'

'Worse?' The old lady widened her eyes. 'What do you mean?'

Wiseman cleared his throat. 'A plot to kill the King, My Lady.'

Mandrake scurried forwards. 'Yes, and thanks to some new evidence, I know what they are planning, sir. I—'

'Enough, knave!' The Viscountess fixed him with a steely grey stare.

Wiseman gave Mandrake a brisk nod. The tutor hissed and took a step back.

'I am glad Master Garnett here took my advice, rescued his cousin and got away while he could. If he hadn't, it would have been the worse for him.'

The Viscountess's frown deepened. She turned back to Tom. 'Explain yourself, boy. How did you come to be mixed up in all of this?'

He chewed on his lip. Wiseman and Mandrake might know about the stash of gunpowder in the tunnel at Cowdray, but they had to prove for certain it belonged to Fawkes. As long as he didn't tell them that's where he'd first met him and he could work out a way of getting hold of the letter, his uncle – and Father – still had a chance. He glanced at Mandrake. His long, pale fingers hovered close to his sleeve. Any moment now, he'd pull the letter out and—

The sharp rap of the Viscountess's cane on the flagstones made him jump. 'I am waiting . . .'

He had to think of something and quickly. He licked his lips. 'Well . . . er . . . after you locked me in my room—'

The Viscountess's mouth pinched into a hard line. 'A punishment well deserved!'

'Yes . . . well, after that I decided to run away. So I climbed down the drainpipe and sneaked out through the front gate. I was on my way back to Portsmouth when I bumped into Fawkes outside a tavern.'

He flashed a glance at the Viscountess and Wiseman. From the look on their faces, they believed him so far. He took another breath and carried on. 'Fawkes offered to take me to London and introduce me to his friends. He and Mister Cat said if I helped them dig a tunnel under Cecil's palace so they could capture him, they would make sure the King granted Father a pardon.' His chest tightened. 'I thought he was my friend. But . . . but he lied.' He bit his lip and stared down at the lantern. Jago's shadow flickered behind it like a tiny grey ghost.

There was a rustle of silk as Cressida joined him. She laced her fingers through his then turned to face the Viscountess. 'And they kept me prisoner in a filthy attic, Granny, and gave me some foul-tasting potion to drink to keep me quiet. But then Tom found me and we were going to escape except that bully Browne . . .'

'Enough!' The Viscountess raised her cane. She narrowed her eyes and turned back to Wiseman. 'And to what do we owe the honour of your visit at such a late hour, sir?'

Wiseman smoothed a stray wisp of yellow hair back from his forehead and frowned. 'As my man here may have told you, I have reason to believe, My Lady, that Lord Montague is complicit in this plot, or at least has some knowledge of it.'

The Viscountess fixed Wiseman with an iron-hard stare. 'We Montagues are the King's most loyal servants. Surely you do not believe the words of this . . . this snake-in-the-grass.' She jabbed the end of her cane at the tutor.

Mandrake cleared his throat. 'I'm afraid I have proof to the contrary, sir.' He slid between her and Wiseman and wormed his fingers inside the sleeve of his gown.

'No!' Cressida let out a scream.

Tom's stomach shrivelled inside him. He had to act now, or it would be too late.

Chapter Thirty-eight

The lantern jiggled against Tom's fingers.

Jago! It was as if the little mouse was signalling to him. Suddenly he knew what to do. He flipped the lantern door open and scooped him up.

You can do it, boy!

He gave Jago's head a quick stroke and set him running across the floor. The mouse scurried towards Mandrake's slippered feet. He paused for a moment when he reached them and sniffed the air, then darted up the side of the tutor's gown.

'Here it is, sir.' Mandrake pulled the letter free with a final flourish. 'Arrghh!' He staggered backwards, fingers clawing at the folds of his gown. 'What witchery is this?' A flash of white fur shot across his chest, jumped on to his shoulder and scooted up a strand of his greasy black hair. 'Get it off me! Get it off me!' He batted his hands about his head as if trying to swat a giant fly. The square of parchment fell from his grasp and spun through the air.

Tom dropped the lantern, leapt forwards and snatched it up. 'Quick, get the candle!'

Cressida whirled round and tore it from the holder.

He grabbed it from her and shoved the letter into the heart of the flame.

'Sir! The evidence!' Mandrake lunged towards him.

'No you don't!' Cressida hung on to the tutor's sleeve.

'Why, you—' Ripping free of her grasp, Mandrake dashed at Tom. He didn't spot Jago's lantern until it was too late. He tripped and spun backwards, colliding with Wiseman, then thudded to the floor with a groan.

Wiseman stumbled but managed to right himself. He clenched his jaw and glared at Tom. 'Give it to me, boy.'

Tom glanced at the parchment. It was already half burnt. He backed away, shaking his head.

'Don't be a fool! This isn't a game.' Wiseman swiped at the burning letter, but Tom was quicker. He twisted away and bolted for the stairs.

The spy made to follow, but the Viscountess blocked him. 'You have come far enough!' She rammed the knob of her cane against his chest. 'Unless, that is, you would knock an old lady down?'

Wiseman's jaw twitched. He clenched his fists and looked up the stairs to where Tom now stood, holding the parchment over the banisters.

He let the flames lick across its surface destroying all trace of the writing, then released his grip. The remains of the parchment spiralled down like a black and orange moth, landing at Wiseman's feet.

For a moment everyone was silent. Then a loud squeak pierced the air. A pink nose and a pair of ruby red eyes peered out from beneath Mandrake's left ear.

Tom jumped to attention. 'I'm coming, Jago!' He hurtled down the stairs and sprinted over to where the unconscious tutor lay. Bending down, he stretched out his palm and let the mouse crawl on to it. 'Well done, little friend!' He lifted him up and pressed his nose against Jago's. 'I don't know what I'd do without you.' He brushed a finger against his whiskers then stowed him safely inside his waist-pouch.

A tight smile flashed across Wiseman's thin, chapped lips. 'You are blessed with a pair of clever grandchildren, My Lady.' He picked up his hat and dusted it off with the back of his sleeve.

Viscountess Montague shot a glance at Tom and Cressida and jutted out her chin. 'Why would you doubt it? They have Montague blood flowing in their veins.'

'That's as may be.' Wiseman's expression changed. 'But I am afraid their cleverness will not be enough to prevent me from arresting Lord Montague. During the time of my man's employment at your grandson's country house, he has gathered enough other evidence to incriminate him. Of course it is a pity you have destroyed the absolute proof, Master Garnett.' He flashed him a look. 'But as soon as I bring Mister Mandrake round, I have no doubt he will make clear the true nature of the plot against the King, and

Lord Montague's part in it.'

'No!' Tom jumped between Wiseman and the Viscountess. 'You've got it all wrong. My uncle has nothing to do with it. And anyway, we've stopped them!'

Wiseman raised a pale eyebrow. 'What? How?'

'The gunpowder. They put it in a cellar below where the King and Parliament are going to meet.'

The spy gripped his shoulder. 'Go on, boy!'

'Fawkes is going to set a match to it, but it won't work because we soaked it with river water.' Tom bit his lip. Perhaps he should have kept quiet about the Falcon. After all, if the water had done its job, he and the gunpowder were both harmless now.

Wiseman's eyes widened.

'It's true.' Cressida leapt to Tom's side. 'I tried to tell you earlier. That bully Harry Browne knocked us out and took us to a cellar below the House of Lords. It was stacked full of gunpowder barrels. He left us there to die, but Tom found some pails and we went down to the river, and he nearly drowned, but I saved him and—'

'Well, well.' Wiseman's eyes flicked shut. He murmured something under his breath then snapped them open again. 'And now, you and your cousin are going to show me where your Falcon is perched so we may stop him from making his strike.'

'But I told you, the gunpowder's ruined.'

'That doesn't matter. If we catch him in the act, it will be more than enough to hang him and all his traitor friends.' Wiseman's eyes narrowed to two silver slits. 'And if the King finds out what part you both played in thwarting the plot, it may just be enough to save Lord Montague – and Master Garnett's father too.'

Tom's heart jolted. Save Father? Did the spy really mean it?

'Now, if My Lady will excuse me, we have some unfinished business across the river.' Before the Viscountess could reply, Wiseman pulled on his hat, tugged his muffler back over his face and steered Tom and Cressida towards the door.

As they stepped outside into the chill night air, he raised his hand. A pair of guards sprang from the shadows. 'Take them to the river. And be quick about it.'

The guards nodded. They marched them out through the courtyard, then back past the church and down to the river stairs. Two wherries bobbed against the bottom step.

Heart pounding, Tom peered across the water to the opposite bank. What if the Falcon had already discovered the gunpowder was ruined and gone to warn the others? And if the gang got away, would Wiseman still ask the King to free Father? Or would the hanging go ahead?

A clock chimed the hour. *One . . . two . . .*

His stomach clenched. In three hours, Father would be on his way to Tyburn. There was no time to lose. He broke free of the guard holding him, raced down the steps and jumped into the nearest wherry.

'Steady, Mister Garnett, or you'll sink us before we've begun.' Wiseman stepped on board and hunkered down next to him. He waited until the guards had climbed into the second wherry with Cressida, then waved a gloved hand at the wherryman. 'Now, take us to the stairs by Westminster. We have a traitor to catch.'

Chapter Thirty-nine

Tom closed his eyes and willed the wherryman to row faster. At last, with a grinding and splashing of oars, they reached the opposite bank. He scrambled out on to the steps where they'd filled the pails earlier.

Wiseman signalled to the guards to bring Cressida then gripped Tom by the shoulder. 'Which way now?'

He tipped his head in the direction of the main street. 'Up there, then right.'

As they made their way over the slippery cobbles, he remembered what the Falcon had said about locking himself in. He glanced at the guards. They looked strong enough to break down any door. He shivered. What would they do if they found him?

They reached the top of the alley and turned on to the street. It was deserted, save for the shadowy figure of a fox which skittered away as they approached.

'In here.' Cressida pointed at the gatehouse.

The guards shoved them through the arch and into the moonlit courtyard.

Tom jerked to a stop. 'It's . . . it's over there.' He nodded at the cellar door.

'All right. Wait here.' The spy's voice was ice cold.

'But—'

Wiseman's jaw hardened. 'It's best you don't come in with us.'

'Why? What are you going to do to him?'

'Nothing – unless he resists us. But if he does, my men are instructed to use whatever force they need.'

The knot in Tom's stomach tightened. He clutched at the spy's cloak. 'You . . . you won't kill him?'

Wiseman yanked it free and fixed him with a hard-eyed stare. 'The man is an assassin and a traitor. Surely you don't approve of what he and his friends are doing?'

'No, but—'

'Good. Because if you did, I would be forced to arrest you too. Now stand aside and make sure you and your cousin keep out of our way.' He waved a hand at the guards. They dragged the pair of them back beneath the gatehouse arch.

'Follow me, men.' Wiseman strode across the courtyard. When he reached the cellar door, he stood aside and gave a quick nod. One of the guards marched up to it, tried the latch then pounded against it with his fist.

Silence.

Tom's breath caught in his throat. He slid back out into

the courtyard with Cressida close on his heels.

Wiseman stepped up to the door and rattled the latch. 'Open up, in the name of the King!'

It stayed shut.

'Kick it down.'

The guards raised their boots and slammed them into the wood – but the door held fast.

'Wait!' Wiseman pushed in next to them. 'After my count. One . . . two . . . *three*!'

All three turned their shoulders to the door and heaved. There was a splintering sound.

'Again!'

This time when their shoulders struck, the wood gave an ear-splitting crack.

Cressida grabbed Tom by the arm. 'They're through!'

His chest tightened. He took a few paces forward.

The guards kicked the door panels out with their boots.

'Give yourself up, or it will go the worse for you!' Motioning the guards behind him, Wiseman pulled a dagger from beneath his cloak and stepped over the threshold. The two men drew their swords and followed him in.

Tom curled his fingers and held his breath.

Silence. Then shouting, the sound of scuffling and a wave of stomach-churning groans.

He flinched. It was three against one. Surely they'd overpowered the Falcon by now? He bit his lip and stared down at his boots.

A few moments later, a set of footsteps rang out on the steps.

Cressida shook him. 'They're coming back out.'

Wiseman appeared at the cellar entrance then strode across the courtyard towards them. The guards followed, the limp body of a man slumped between them.

Tom's heart lurched. He didn't need to see the man's battered, bloody face to know it was the Falcon. As they approached, Cressida tugged him back into the shadows of the gatehouse arch.

The spy paused before it and gave the guards a stiff nod. 'We have our bird, boys. The Master will be pleased with us.' He stood back and let them pass.

Tom shivered as the guards drew level with them. He didn't want to look but he knew he must. He sucked in a breath and raised his eyes.

The Falcon's head hung down between his shoulders. His arms flopped at his sides.

He gasped. What had they done to him?

The Falcon's head jerked up at the sound. He blinked and peered into the darkness. 'Soldier?' His eyes widened. 'Is that you?' He coughed, then gave a hoarse laugh. 'I fear our friendship has been the undoing of me.' He stumbled and coughed again. A splash of blood landed on the cobbles at Tom's feet.

'Shut up, you flea-infested cur!' The guard nearest them struck him hard across the face.

'Yes, quiet, Fawkes, or we will be forced to silence you some other way.' Wiseman's eyes gleamed silver in the shadows. 'Now, to the Tower with him and let's see what a good racking will do to loosen his tongue.'

'No, please!' Tom leapt in front of them. 'I told you. We ruined the powder. He couldn't have blown up the King if he'd tried.'

The Falcon drew in a ratchety breath. 'I always knew you were a clever one, Soldier. Resourceful too.' He clenched his jaw. 'The boy speaks the truth. The powder is soaked through. Every last barrel of it.'

'Enough, traitor!' Wiseman drew his dagger and jabbed it at the Falcon's chest then signalled to the guards. 'Take him away.'

As they yanked him out on to the street, he lurched to one side and gave another groan.

Tom's throat tightened. He dashed after them and blocked their way again. 'I'm sorry. I—'

The Falcon sucked in another breath then lifted his head up high. 'It's all right. I understand. Now listen.' He fixed him with his coal-black eyes. 'I go to meet my Maker willingly. My life in this world is done. But yours is just beginning. Make courage your watchword, Soldier. It will serve you well when all else fails.' The ghost of a smile stole across his bruised lips.

The guard struck him again. He cried out in pain then his head fell forwards and he was silent.

Tom reached out a hand, but the guards shoved him aside and marched on.

Wiseman seized him by the collar. 'Did you not understand me before, boy? Now get out of our way. Unless you want to join your father on the gallows?' He pushed him back against the wall.

The knot in Tom's throat squeezed tighter still. 'But . . . but you said you'd try to save my father!'

The spy waved a hand above his head. 'Don't pester me with that now. I have a nest of traitors to uncover.'

Hot tears sprang to his eyes. 'Please! You've got to help—'

Ignoring him, Wiseman reached beneath his cloak and pulled out a coin. He thrust it at Cressida. 'Here. Now take the other wherry and get back to your father's house before the nightwatchman arrests you both for vagrancy.' He swished his cloak about him and strode after the guards.

Tom watched as they disappeared down the street that led to the river stairs. 'They'll hang him, won't they?'

Cressida nodded. 'Draw and quarter him too. That's what happens to traitors.' She glanced at him then looked away again quickly.

Tom groaned and sank to the ground. The Falcon was going to die – and so was Father. Instead of saving him, he'd let him down all over again. What was he going to do now? 'Father . . .' He gave a shuddering sigh and let the tears spill thick and fast.

Cressida knelt down beside him. Her warm fingers circled his wrist. 'Cousin . . . I'm sorry.'

He stared at the damp stones between his feet until they wobbled and blurred into one.

'There must be something we can do.'

'There isn't.' He slid his knees up, pressed his forehead against them and closed his eyes. The Falcon's last words echoed in his ears.

Make courage your watchword.

A fluttering started up in his chest. He might not be able to save Father, but he could still go to him. Explain what had happened. Tell him he'd tried his best to save him and beg his forgiveness.

He leapt to his feet.

'Tom?' Cressida jumped up beside him.

'Father! I've got to see him one last time, before . . . before . . .' His eyes filled with fresh tears. He dashed them away with the back of his hand.

'I'll come with you.'

'No. Go back to Granny. She'll be worried about you.'

'But you can't go on your own.'

He gritted his teeth. 'I must. Besides, I've got Jago for company.' He patted his waist-pouch and forced a smile.

Cressida paused for a moment. Then, eyes shining, she darted forwards and gave him a quick hug. 'Take care, Tom Garnett. I will see you back at my father's house.'

He nodded, took a deep breath and set off down the dark, gloomy street ahead.

Chapter Forty

The journey to Tyburn took longer than Tom expected. Partly because he lost his bearings, partly because his feet were like ice blocks and his stomach was cramping from lack of food.

He had to ask the way more than once and ducked out of sight whenever a nightwatchman approached. As the church bells tolled the start of the new day, shadowy figures began to appear on the street around him, all of them heading in the same direction. At a place where the road crossed another, the crowd thickened and spilled out into the open field beyond.

'There 'tis. The old Tyburn Tree,' a man in front of him boomed. He swung the small boy at his side on to his shoulders and pointed up ahead of him. 'It won't be long now before 'tis growing papist fruit.'

Tom jerked to a stop and stared up at the three-sided

scaffold silhouetted against the fading stars. His blood turned to powder inside him. So this was it. This was where they were bringing Father. The crowd surged around him, bumping and jostling against him. He clenched his fingers. If he was going to stand a chance of seeing him, he had to get closer. He pushed his way through the mass of sour-smelling bodies until he was as close to the front as he could get.

He glanced up. The sky was beginning to lighten. He felt inside his waist-pouch. Jago's tiny heart bumped against his fingers. Tom trembled and closed his eyes. Their games in Portsmouth seemed a lifetime ago.

An elbow jabbed him in the ribs. 'Oysters! Lovely oysters!'

He snapped his eyes open. A woman stood in front of him holding out a tray stacked high with crinkled grey shells. ''Ere, lad. You look a likely fellow.' She chucked him under the chin with a pock-marked finger. ''Ow about one of these tasties to breakfast on while you watch those Catholic devils swing?' She thrust one of the slime-covered shells at him. The fishy stink made him gag. He backed away.

'No? Well, I 'ope your belly 'olds out for the 'anging.' She leered at him then disappeared back into the crowd.

Tom closed his eyes again. His head drooped and he toppled forwards. He started and blinked himself awake. How could he let himself fall asleep when in an hour or two, Father would be brought here to die? He shook his arms and legs and gulped in a lungful of cold, damp air.

The sun rose, pale and milky, like a half-dead thing. The crowd grew restless. They began to boo and jeer.

'Trust a papist! Can't even be on time for their own 'anging,' the man next to him yelled. He clamped a hand on Tom's shoulder and gave him a stump-toothed grin.

Tom twisted free, jutted out his chin and looked straight ahead.

'Not one of 'em, are you?' The man seized his arm again, eyes glittering with a sudden menace.

He backed away. 'I . . . er . . .'

A shout went up behind them. 'Here they come!'

The man let go and turned with the rest of the crowd to face the road. Tom stood on tiptoe and followed their gaze. A knot of soldiers marched past, the blades of their halberds glinting in the dawn light. They were followed by a sharp-faced man dressed in black velvet and a pair of mealy-mouthed attendants, trotting at his heels. And finally, some way behind them, a cart, pulled by a tired-looking horse, its sides lined with a row of sharp sticks.

Tom groaned and hung his head. He couldn't do it.

The wheels of the cart rumbled closer.

His chest spiked. He had to. For Father's sake. He steeled himself and looked up again. Behind the barricade of sticks stood two ragged men, their hands tied behind their backs. The one in front had his head bowed and was praying, but the other one – his stomach twisted – the one with his eyes fixed straight ahead, was Father.

Yells of 'Traitors!' and 'Papist swine!' rang out around Tom. He closed his ears to them and made to push through.

But it was no use; he was pinned fast. Heart pounding, stomach churning, he watched as the cart trundled up the hill to the scaffold then lurched to a stop.

It was then he saw the two nooses dangling from the cross beam.

'String 'em up and let's see 'em dance!' screeched a woman in front of him.

A black hooded figure peeled out from under the scaffold, dragging a ladder behind him.

The hangman! Tom's head began to spin. He had to get closer, before it was too late. He hunched his shoulders, took a deep breath and shoved his way forwards. He was almost through to the front when a row of broad straight backs pulled him up short. Soldiers. How would he ever get past them? He scanned the line looking for a break. He'd nearly given up hope when the soldier in front of him bent his head to talk to his comrade. Seizing his chance, Tom stood on his toes and forced his head and shoulders through the gap.

The hangman had climbed up the ladder on to the cart and was busy fitting one of the nooses round the neck of the first prisoner. As the man lifted his head, Tom recognized the sunken cheeks and pinched lips of the priest.

He shivered and glanced at his father. His eyes were closed too now and he was murmuring a prayer. Tom wriggled his arms free and thrust them in front of him.

'Father! Father!' But the noise of the crowd drowned the words.

The hangman stepped back from the priest, then turned

to face Tom's father. He slipped the second noose over his head and yanked it tight.

Tom shuddered. 'Father, please!' He clawed at the soldiers' shoulders, trying to prise them apart.

The soldier on his left swung round. 'Get away!' He knocked him backwards with his elbow.

Tom staggered, then righted himself and barrelled forwards again.

The hangman climbed back down the ladder. He tossed it to the ground then plodded towards the front of the cart and grabbed hold of the horse's reins.

'No!' Tom took a step back, ducked his head down and made one last charge.

'Oof!' The soldier in front of him lurched and fell sideways.

Seizing his chance, Tom darted through the gap and hurtled towards the back of the cart.

'Father! It's me!' He snatched hold of one of the sticks and clung to it with all his might.

'Tom?' His father twisted round, but the rope jerked him back.

'I'm sorry. I tried to save you but—' He gulped and sucked in a breath but the words were like stones wedged in his throat.

There was a sudden creak of wheels.

'No, please!' He yanked on the stick and rammed his heels hard into the mud.

But it was no use. He wasn't strong enough.

The cart juddered forwards, knocking him to the ground.

His father's feet slipped out from under him. He gave a strangled cry, then he and the priest spun away, heels kicking against the air.

A stab of pain shot through Tom, sharper than the sharpest knife. He leapt up and dashed towards him, tears streaming down his face. 'Father! I love you!'

A gloved hand shot out and seized him by the collar. 'Make way! Make way!'

He bucked against it.

The hand gripped tighter.

A thud of boots and a clang of metal filled his ears. The crowd roared, the sky went black and Tom knew nothing more.

Chapter Forty-one

Three months later . . .

Friday 31 January 1606

The wind whistled down the chimney, sending up puffs of ash at Tom's feet. He walked over to the kitchen window and stared into the courtyard. It had started to rain. He shivered and glanced around the room. The shelves and table were bare, the pots and pans already packed away and sent down to the harbour. It wasn't home any more; but he wasn't sure how he felt about leaving it behind.

The hammering of a fist on wood echoed down the passageway outside.

'Go and see who that is, please, while I change your brother,' his mother called from upstairs. 'And then we must away to the harbour.'

He ran into the passageway. A short, thickset man stood in the open doorway, his woollen cloak spattered with mud. 'Message for Master Garnett.' He thrust a small leather pouch at him.

'Who's it from?'

The man shrugged. 'I'm just the messenger.' He puffed out his cheeks and clapped his arms across his chest. 'And a soaked-through one at that. The man who gave it me in London told me I had to deliver it by today or it would be too late. Now I've done my duty, I'm off to the nearest tavern to get warm.' He tipped his hat and stepped back out into the cold, grey January day.

Tom frowned. The messenger had said London. Who would write to him from there? He was about to open the strings of the pouch when light footsteps sounded on the stairs behind him.

A warm hand touched his arm. 'Who was that?'

He shoved the pouch inside his jerkin. He'd tell her about the message later, when he'd had a chance to read it. 'Just a traveller. He was looking for a tavern.'

His mother peered out at the rainswept street. 'Well, and who can blame him? It is not good weather for making a journey. But, for us there is no choice.' She sighed and bent to kiss his cheek. 'Now go and fetch your things. I am almost done here and the tide will not wait for us.'

The rain had stopped by the time they boarded the merchant ship. Tom hung over its side and looked back at the bustling harbourside. Merchants inspected barrels of freshly delivered wine or supervised the loading of bales of sheep's wool. Old sea dogs wove paths round the sacks of grain stacked on the cobbles as they headed to the nearest alehouse. And women, carrying baskets piled with onions, cockles and turnips, cried their wares and scared the gulls away with their aprons.

He glanced about him. He was alone. Now would be a good time to read the message. He reached inside his jerkin for the pouch.

'Tom!' The figure of a girl in a blue velvet cape appeared at the bottom of the ship's gangplank. She waved at him, then threw back her hood to reveal a mass of fair curls.

Cressida! Tom snatched up Jago's new wooden cage from the deck and dashed back down the gangplank, narrowly avoiding a collision with a sailor who cursed at him before lumbering on with his load.

'What are you doing here?' He took her hand and led her to a low wall to sit down.

Cressida's mouth curved into a smile, but her eyes were sad. 'Granny told me you and your family were leaving. I persuaded her to lend me one of the servants so I could come and see you off.' She pointed behind her to where a grey-haired man stood holding a pair of horses by the reins. Her forehead furrowed. 'You've heard about the plotters?'

He shook his head. 'Only rumours. It takes months for news to reach us here.'

'They've all been captured or killed. Their leader Robert Catesby – the one who called himself Robin Cat. And

Harry Browne, whose real name was Thomas Percy. Would you believe he was a distant kinsman of the Duke of Northumberland? The pair of them were shot dead by the same bullet. Just imagine!' She shivered. 'Even Mister Shakespeare couldn't have come up with a better ending for them than that.'

Tom's chest tightened. 'What of the Falc— I mean, Fawkes?'

'He is to hang today at one o'clock in the Old Palace Yard at Westminster, opposite the scene of his attempted crime.'

A feeling of dizziness swept over Tom. He gripped the handle of Jago's cage and took a deep breath.

Cressida put a hand on his arm. 'I'm sorry, cousin! It must remind you . . .' Her blue eyes flashed with concern.

He raised his shoulders and lifted up his chin. 'It's all right.'

'Do you have to go?'

He nodded. 'It'll be better for us in France. Mother says the French King is a Catholic and people like us can live more freely there.' He frowned. 'What about your father? Mother told me he'd been arrested.'

'Yes.' She bit her lip. 'And imprisoned in the Tower. That snake Mandrake must have made up some other evidence. But Granny says if my father pays a large enough fine, the King will forgive him.'

'Do you miss him?'

She shrugged. 'I . . . I don't know. I never saw him much. I don't think he approves of me really.'

'Why?'

'Because . . .' She looked down and fiddled with the ribbons on her cloak. 'Because I told him I wanted to go to London to be an actor.'

He puffed out his cheeks. So that explained why she was always going on about acting.

She glanced back up at him. 'It's why I call myself Cressida.'

'What do you mean?'

'She's the heroine of one of Mister Shakespeare's plays. *Troilus and Cressida*. Remember how I told you I'd been to the playhouse in London? Well, that's what we saw. It's a great tragedy. Although' – she twisted a blonde curl round her finger – 'in truth Cressida is often quite badly behaved.'

'But I thought girls weren't allowed to act.'

She frowned. 'Not now. But one day they might.' Her eyes sparked with a blue-gold fire.

Tom shook his head. She was a strange one, this cousin of his.

She poked a finger through the wooden bars of Jago's cage and stroked his whiskers. 'I hope your mouse has better sea legs than you.'

'We'll find out soon enough. Won't we, boy?'

She smiled. 'I wondered if . . . if we might write to each other?' She shot him a look. 'I could let you know what mischief Granny gets up to next – although I'd have to use some of that orange-juice ink of hers for the secret stuff – and you could tell me all about the strange customs and manners they have in France.'

'I'd like that.' He smiled back at her.

Cressida's cheeks flushed. She glanced over her shoulder. 'I had better go. I promised Granny I'd be back by nightfall. Thank you, cousin. It's been an adventure.' She leant forwards and brushed her lips against his cheek. And now it was Tom's turn to blush.

The sea beyond the harbour wall rose and fell in a grey swell. Tom hoped it wouldn't be too rough a crossing. A wherry on the river had been enough for him. He held up Jago's cage and peered at the pile of quivering straw in the corner.

'Are you feeling all right, boy?'

The mouse poked his nose out, sniffed the air then burrowed back inside.

'I didn't think so. I'll take you back down below and find you some cheese before we set sail.'

But first he had to read the message. He put the cage down on the deck and wedged it firmly in a coil of rope. Slipping his hand inside his jerkin, he reached for the pouch, untied the drawstring and pulled out a stiff square of parchment. He slid his forefinger under the blob of red sealing wax and opened it. The handwriting was thin and spidery, as if the writer had been reluctant to put quill to paper. He held it up to the light and began to read.

Dear Master Garnett,

I write to you in confidence with a message from a man who pretended to you once he was your friend. As you now know, he took the wrong path and, as punishment, his life on this earth is soon set to end. He has been judged and found guilty in the King's court. But before he is sent to his Maker for the last and final judgement, and cast down into the fires of Hell, he has asked for one last favour.

You will find in the pouch that accompanies this letter a ring. The man in question wanted me to give it to you. Was most insistent, in fact. He proved a traitor to the end, refusing to admit the treachery of what he and his friends had planned. Indeed, he only agreed to sign his confession in exchange for a particular favour which he asked for on your behalf . . . But do not feel gratitude to him. Instead, let this ring be a warning to you never to put your trust in such a man again.

I wish you and your family safe passage.

S.W.
PLEASE DESTROY THIS LETTER WHEN YOU HAVE READ IT.

Wiseman. Tom folded the parchment and felt inside the pouch for the ring. He pulled it out and stared at it. The bird's head gleamed back at him, its diamond eye glinting like a tiny solitary star. So the Falcon must have kept his word after all. A strange ache started up in his chest and the bird's head began to blur. He scrubbed at his eyes with his sleeve and gritted his teeth. The Falcon might want him to have the ring, but it was a gift he couldn't keep. He leant forwards, held it out over the water and closed his eyes.

Footsteps sounded on the deck behind him. He snapped

his eyes open again, curled the ring up in his fist and dropped his hand back to his side.

A figure came towards him. For a moment Tom thought it was a trick of the sea light.

And then he knew . . .

A wave of happiness surged through him. 'Father!' Heart pounding, he dashed forwards and flung his arms around him.

'Tom! Tom! My son.' His father grasped him with strong, warm hands.

Tom pressed his face against his father's doublet and breathed in deep. He smelt of wool and leather, like he used to. Tears sprang and flowed hot and fast down his cheeks.

'Come, lad.' His father pulled him away then looked at him with worried grey eyes. 'Or are you not glad to see me?'

Tom gulped and blinked the tears away. 'No – I mean yes – I mean, I thought they weren't going to release you for another month?'

'They weren't, but I think someone in Cecil's pay must have taken pity on me and let me go early.' His father coughed. 'And besides, three whole months in gaol is three months too many. Although, alas' – his eyes darkened – 'others have paid a far higher price.' He put a hand to the cloth which covered his throat.

Tom clenched his jaw. He knew all too well what he meant. Although the King's men had cut Father down from the scaffold, Father Oliver had not been so lucky. He bent his head, crossed himself and said a quick prayer for the Jesuit's soul, then glanced up again. His father's hair was flecked with grey and there were dark shadows under his eyes. His own eyes filled with more tears.

His father hugged him to him. 'Come. You saved me, didn't you?'

Tom's heart fluttered against his chest. 'But it wasn't me, it was—'

'Hush, son. If it hadn't been for you and your cousin's bravery and quick-thinking, neither I nor our King would be alive today. We both have a lot to thank you for.'

Tom bit his lip. It was the truth, but only part of it: it was the Falcon who had really saved Father's life. That was the favour he'd bargained for with Wiseman in return for his confession. He fingered the ring. He wanted to tell everyone – to make them understand how, although he was a traitor, Fawkes had been a brave man too . . . but for his family's sake, perhaps it was best to leave it unsaid. They stood together in silence looking out across the water. After a few moments, his father cleared his throat and scanned the ship's deck.

'This is not quite the same as the birthday trip I had planned for you back in November.'

Tom lifted his shoulders and smiled. 'It doesn't matter. Have you seen Mother? Did she tell you the news about Uncle Montague?'

His father sighed. 'Yes, but I understand the King values his friendship; so let us hope his confinement will not be a long one. Although' – the shadow of a smile played over his lips – 'I believe that the gaol cells of noble prisoners are more comfortable than mine was . . . Still, we will make time to pray for him on our crossing to France.' He held the battered prayer book up. 'Your mother gave this to me. I understand it's been on quite a journey?'

Tom flushed. 'Yes.'

'You must tell me about it once we have set sail. What have you got there?' He pointed at Tom's fist.

Reluctantly Tom uncurled his fingers.

His father raised an eyebrow. 'How did you come by that?'

Tom traced a fingernail over the bird's diamond eye. 'A soldier gave it to me.'

'I see.' His father frowned. 'And was he an honourable man?'

The ache started up in Tom's chest again. He shrugged. 'I don't know. He did bad things, but some good ones too.'

His father's frown melted into a smile. He ruffled his hair. 'Then he is human, like the rest of us.' He pressed his fingers back over the ring. 'Keep it, son. In memory of the good.'

Tom nodded. He opened the pouch and dropped the ring inside.

Somewhere back on land, a church bell tolled the hour. One o'clock. He shivered. A shadow passed across the deck. He glanced up. A black shape arrowed through the sky above them.

'What's that?'

His father shaded his eyes. 'A falcon, I think. Although I've never seen one so close before.'

They watched for a moment as the bird tumbled

through the air then swooped up again on the sea breeze. Tom felt his father's hand warm on his shoulder.

'France lies just across the water.' He pointed to the horizon beyond the harbour walls. 'A new start for us all, Tom.'

Tom glanced at his father quickly, then looked away. 'Won't you miss William?'

'What do you mean?'

'Being so far from where he is buried.'

His father's eyes clouded, as if remembering. He gave a deep sigh and shook his head. 'William is always close to me. I carry him here.' He placed his right hand over his heart. 'Along with you and your little brother.' He smiled.

A gurgling sound rang out behind them. Tom turned. His mother approached carrying Edward in her arms. His stubby fingers clutched the model of the merchant ship Tom had carved for him with Father's knife.

'Here, look after your baby brother for a bit.' She handed Edward to him. 'Your father and I have much to talk about.' She linked arms with his father and tugged him away.

Edward chortled and buried his face into Tom's chest.

'Look, Ned. A falcon.' He lifted him up and pointed, but the sky was empty.

The bird had gone.

About the Book

Black Powder is a story. But like all stories, it contains truths as well as fiction.

The Gunpowder Plot was a serious attempt by a band of desperate men to blow up King James I of England, members of the royal family, the King's ministers and his bishops and Parliament too. If they had succeeded, they would have changed the course of Britain's history.

The idea for the story was first sparked by a visit I made to the ruins of Cowdray Park, a Tudor palace on the edge of the town of Midhurst, in West Sussex. During my visit, I discovered that a certain Mr Guy Fawkes had worked there as a footman, when a young man.

I was intrigued. And it didn't take long for a whole bunch of 'What ifs?' to start buzzing around inside my head. What if, years later, Guy Fawkes returns from his time as a soldier abroad and stashes a secret supply of gunpowder at Cowdray? What if, when he comes down from London to collect it for use in the plot he and his friends have planned to blow up the King and Parliament, he has a chance encounter with a young boy who has arrived at Cowdray on a desperate mission of his own? And then, what if he agrees to take the boy to London with him?

I knew very little about the Gunpowder Plot, except the brief outline of the story I had learnt years ago at school. But the more I researched it, the more I realized it had all the elements of a brilliant adventure story – some of which you really couldn't make up if you tried!

To tell the whole story – or what is known of it – would need a different kind of book. But here are some of the more interesting facts about the people, places and events featured in *Black Powder* and one or two confessions about what I have invented in order to tell my tale of Tom and the Falcon.

People

The Plotters

There were thirteen plotters in total, but, to avoid things becoming confusing, I've featured only the key ones in my story.

Guy Fawkes (1570–1606) was born in York into a family of mixed faith. He was baptized a Protestant, but converted to Roman Catholicism as a young man. His family crest included a falcon and it was this that inspired me to give him a gold falcon-headed ring and to have him encourage Tom to call him 'the Falcon'. He was a man of many identities in real life too.

After serving for a short time in the Montague household as a gentleman servant, he became a soldier and learnt how to light a 'slow train' of gunpowder – a skill which earned him his crucial role in the Gunpowder Plot. Although at first Tom is afraid of the Falcon and not sure he can trust him, as events unfold and he learns more about him, he comes to admire him for his bravery. The real Guy Fawkes earned just such a name among the men who fought alongside him. Even King James was impressed by his strength and self-control at his interrogation. Guy Fawkes had a reputation for being strongly committed to his faith and was convinced that killing the Protestant King was best for both his fellow Catholics and the whole country too. He was fanatical and misguided, but it is hard to deny his courage. In my story, he confesses after a few hours of torture in return for the guarantee of Tom's father's life. But in reality he held out for several days.

Guy Fawkes was recruited into the gang of plotters by their leader, the charismatic **Robert Catesby** (circa 1572–1605), known as Robin by his friends. Catesby had been involved in earlier plots and it was he, not Guy Fawkes, who was the mastermind behind the Gunpowder Plot. He used religious arguments to justify his actions, and refused to put a stop to the plot when another of the plotters told him that their plans had been discovered. His foolhardiness contributed to the plot's failure.

Thomas Percy (circa 1560–1605), who goes by the false name of 'Harry Browne' in my story, was a poor relation of the Earl of Northumberland. Another convert to Catholicism, he was energetic and clever but also ambitious and regarded by some at the time as 'a dangerous knave', having killed a man in his youth during a skirmish. 'Harry Browne' is the enemy of the Falcon in my story, although there is no basis for this in real life.

Lords and ladies

The Montagues were a wealthy, influential Catholic family who, in spite of their religious beliefs, managed to keep in favour with both the Protestant Queen Elizabeth I and her successor, King James.

Their country seat was at Cowdray but they also owned Montague House in Southwark, London. Cressida is my own invention, but both Tom's 'Uncle Montague' and 'Great-Granny', **Magdalen, Viscountess Montague** (1538–1608), really did exist.

Although **Robert Cecil, 1st Earl of Salisbury** (1563–1612), is a shadowy figure in the story, he is as crucial to the events in it as he was to the solving of the Gunpowder Plot in real life. Cecil was chief minister and spymaster to both Queen Elizabeth and then King James. He was known to his enemies by a number of nicknames, including 'the hunchback' and 'the fox', but in truth, he was a brilliant and clever statesman who was prepared to go to sometimes extreme lengths to create political stability in England. One of the tools that helped him was the network of spies and informers he controlled. He posted men like Solomon Wiseman and Mister Mandrake (although they are my inventions!) across the country and abroad to gather evidence of intrigues, plots and assassination attempts on the King.

It has been suggested that the Gunpowder Plot itself was devised by Cecil to flush out Catholic troublemakers and to put an end to Catholic chances of gaining equality and toleration. But this has never been proved, and it's not something that happens in my story.

King James I of England and VI of Scotland (1566–1625) was intelligent and politically very clever, but his own behaviour definitely fanned the flames of the plot. Before he came to the English throne, he appears to have made certain promises – including to Thomas Percy ('Harry Browne' in my story), who eventually became one of the plotters – that he would show toleration to the English Catholics. Some Catholics even thought mistakenly that James was about to convert to Catholicism. James worried about his own safety, and for good reason. Within the first year of his reign in England, two plots against the new King – one led by Catholic priests seeking greater religious toleration – had been uncovered. When new anti-Catholic laws were introduced by the King's Parliament in 1604, it convinced the plotters, led by Robert Catesby ('Robin Cat' in my story), of the need to act.

Priests

Catholic priests, and in particular the Jesuits, had been outlawed during the reign of Elizabeth I. They were accused of working with the Pope and the Catholic King of Spain to prepare the way for a Spanish invasion of England, and put a Catholic replacement on the throne. If captured they were put to death as enemies of the state. Although King James made peace with the Spanish in 1604, Catholic priests were still seen as a source of unrest and were again outlawed. Robert Cecil, who disliked the Jesuits, built a case against them that they were behind the 'Powder Treason' and several of them were tried and executed as a result.

Places

The settings in the story are, in the main, based on real locations. In one or two instances, I have made things up to suit the story – for example the street layouts in Tom's home town of **Portsmouth** on the south coast of England. And although Tom and the Falcon travel over two nights and days to London from Cowdray, it would in all likelihood have taken even longer. Travel by horse and cart in those days, on badly rutted roads, was very slow.

Cowdray House was once one of the greatest mansions in England, visited by King Henry VIII and his daughter, Elizabeth I. Sadly, in 1793, it was destroyed by fire and is now a ruin, although thanks to a recent renovation project, you can visit it. You can still cross the causeway as Tom did and see the gatehouse and ruins of the Buck Hall; but the tunnel used for smuggling the Catholic townsfolk to the chapel and where the Falcon stores the gunpowder is my invention.

London was by far the most important city in England and a dangerous one too. **The Clink** in **Southwark** was a notorious gaol where Catholic prisoners, including priests, were held. So it would have been highly likely that both Tom's father and Father Oliver would have ended up there once captured.

London Bridge was the only bridge across the River Thames in those days. Like Tom, in the story, everyone had to pass beneath the mouldering heads of so-called traitors, stuck up on the south gate as a warning to those thinking of committing treason; the heads of Guy Fawkes and some of his fellow plotters ended up on spikes there after their execution. The only other way to cross the river was by ferries or smaller boats called wherries which zigzagged across its murky depths between different sets of stairs on each bank – the equivalent of stops on the London Underground today.

The **tunnel** which Robin Cat asks Tom to help excavate remains one of the many mysteries linked with the true story of the Gunpowder Plot. There is no clear evidence it existed. However, in my version of the tale, I have suggested it did and that the plotters, many of whom were tall men, needed a boy's help in digging it.

Tunnel or no tunnel, the final place the gunpowder was brought to was a storeroom belonging to a house (John Whynniard's house) located in the heart of Westminster, beneath the **House of Lords** where the King was due to open Parliament on Tuesday 5 November.

Finally, **Tyburn**, near present-day Marble Arch in London, was the site of public executions from the late twelfth until the late eighteenth century. There is a memorial to the Catholic martyrs who died at Tyburn in nearby Tyburn Convent.

The Gunpowder Plot

The events in my story happen much quicker than they did in real life, occurring over a few days rather than over the many months of the real-life plot.

I have tried to follow the history of what is known about the plot as much as possible, but there are a number of things I have made up for the sake of the story. For example, it is believed that the gunpowder was brought by river to its final location from wherever the plotters sourced it, and not by road. The real stash of gunpowder was also found to be damp when the plot was discovered, most likely due to poor storage conditions, although historians say it would probably still have exploded if Guy Fawkes had ever managed to light the fuse. Of course, in my story, Tom and Cressida soak the gunpowder with river water. And it is because Solomon Wiseman forces the children to lead him to the cellar that Guy Fawkes is captured. Whereas in real life, he was taken prisoner after the King's men spotted a tall stranger lurking near some piles of wood and barrels in a cellar under the House of Lords around midnight on 4 November.

A mysterious letter, possibly written by one of the plotters, was sent to at least one Catholic lord – Lord Monteagle – warning him to stay away from the opening of Parliament on 5 November. It supposedly played a big part in helping to alert the authorities about the plot – although some historians believe Cecil may already have known about it and had the letter written himself as 'evidence'. However, in my story, it is Lord Montague who is the recipient of a letter which Tom then manages to destroy.

In late January 1606, Guy Fawkes and the surviving plotters were found guilty and sentenced to be hanged, drawn and quartered – a grisly but common end for all traitors.

Afterwards
The 'Powder Treason' backfired in more ways than one. As a result of it, English Catholics suffered great persecution and hardships for centuries to come.

And starting from the day the plot was uncovered, people burnt bonfires on 5 November to celebrate its failure and the saving of the King's life. They have done so ever since, often burning effigies of Guy Fawkes on top of the flames.

Every year, on the night before the state opening of Parliament by the British monarch, the cellars beneath the Palace of Westminster are searched by members of the Yeoman of the Guard ('Beefeaters') in a ceremony marking the thwarting of the plot which, had it succeeded, would have changed the face of the country for ever.

And the events are also commemorated in the famous rhyme: *'Remember, remember, the fifth of November, Gunpowder Treason and Plot.'*

Were the plotters wholly bad men? Tom puzzles on this himself when he thinks about his friendship with the Falcon. To help you make up your own mind, here are some suggestions for more reading and possible visits you can make to find out more about the Gunpowder Plot and the people caught up in it.

More Information

Read

• *Guy Fawkes and the Gunpowder Plot* by Peter Brimacombe (Pitkin Publishing 2009)

• www.bbc.co.uk/history/the_gunpowder_plot – BBC web pages on the Gunpowder Plot

• www.gunpowder-plot.org/ – website of The Gunpowder Plot Society

For adults

Antonia Fraser's book *The Gunpowder Plot: Terror and Faith in 1605* is an excellent historical account which is also a page-turning read and one I am much indebted to for the facts which lie behind my own story.

Visit

• Cowdray House, Midhurst, West Sussex – home of the Montagues. www.cowdray.co.uk/historic-cowdray/

• The Tower of London – where Guy Fawkes was tortured and imprisoned after he was captured. www.hrp.org.uk/tower-of-london/

• The Clink Prison Museum – built on the original site of one of London's most notorious prisons. The Clink is where Tom's father is taken after his arrest. www.clink.co.uk/

There are also a number of National Trust properties with links to the Gunpowder Plotters including Coughton Court, Baddesley Clinton and Lyveden New Bield. www.nationaltrust.org.uk/

Acknowledgements

If an author is very lucky, the seed for a story may blow in their direction and plant itself in their head. But it requires the care, nurturing and hard work of a whole bunch of other people for it to take root and grow into a published book.

Black Powder has been very lucky to have so many loving and green-fingered gardeners to help it thrive and bloom. Without further ado, my sincere and heartfelt thank you to:

My parents, George and Beryl Burt, and my sister, Elisabeth, for providing the essential compost of bedtime stories and make-believe games in the garden, all bound together by a huge dose of unconditional love and support.

The many wise teachers and tutors who have, over the years, raked the soil and provided the fertilizer of inspiration, wise words and sound advice including: Mrs Branson, Mrs Laub, Judith Heneghan and Vanessa Harbour. And Lady Antonia Fraser for her excellent book on the Gunpowder Plot which was my bible and guide on what happened and when in the real plot – all historical inaccuracies and inventions are my own . . .

My many dear friends – you know who you are! – and fellow writers and early readers – Cath, Jill, Lizzie, Sharon, Barbara, Patty and Shelley – who kept the soil moist and aerated with a generous watering of interest, encouragement and critical feedback.

My wonderful publishers at Chicken House and in particular Barry Cunningham for spotting the first green shoots of something he thought might be promising; Rachel Leyshon, Kesia Lupo, Esther Waller, Sue Cook and the rest of the editorial and production team for their nimble-fingered weeding, training of the tendrils and pruning of wayward stalks and stems; and Rachel Hickman, Jazz Bartlett, Laura Smythe and Elinor Bagenal for planting *Black Powder* out in the sunshine and giving it the chance to bloom.

And not forgetting the fantastic Society of Children's Book Writers and Illustrators who helped set my story on the path to discovery and Rachel H., artist Alexis Snell and designer Steve Wells for the gorgeous cover – my story in a powder keg!

Lastly, and most important of all, my deepest love and gratitude to my very own special gardener and lovely husband, Steve, who has given me boundless supplies of light, oxygen and the all-important space in which to grow and to reach for the sky.

Finally, my wish for you, dear reader, is that my story brings you as much pleasure to read as it has brought me to write.